LADY VIOLET SAYS I DO

THE LADY VIOLET MYSTERIES—BOOK EIGHT

GRACE BURROWES

DEDICATION

This series is dedicated to my nephew Jackson

CHAPTER ONE

Violet

I had become a mother, to my most glorious delight, and I was married again, another development to be celebrated at least in some regards. Nonetheless, I had yet to embark in a meaningful sense upon the duties of a peer's wife.

To the world, I had become the Marchioness of Dunkeld late in the previous year. In my heart, I was still Lady Violet Belmaine, only daughter of the Earl of Derwent and widow to the late Frederick Belmaine.

Sebastian, Marquess of Dunkeld, had been the dearest companion of my youth. We'd become estranged when he'd gone for a soldier, and our rapprochement over the previous two years had been gradual and halting, culminating with Sebastian's gallant offer of marriage. After the birth of my daughter, he'd deposited me at his family seat and promptly dashed off.

His motivations for leaving, like much of the man, were a mystery to me and a constant source of vexation. He was not Maeve's father in truth, but as far as the world was concerned, he'd agreed to play the part.

Would he play the part of husband or be my husband in truth?

"More tea, Violet?" Aunt Hibernia asked, brandishing a porcelain teapot adorned with fat, pink thistles and hungry-looking eagles.

"No, thank you. I am for the nursery."

"Take the child to the parapets," Aunt Maighread said, peering at her needlework—more thistles. "The fresh air will put roses in your cheeks."

In England, a lady avoided the sun, rubbed her skin with raw potatoes, and resorted to cosmetics to ensure her cheeks were fashionably pale. I was in Perthshire, Scotland, and had not seen my homeland for months.

"High summer is a fine time to travel," Aunt Bernie observed to nobody in particular. She perched on the sofa, the picture of a benevolent dowager, save for the two black long-haired cats who kept vigil along the sofa back. The feline familiars told the real story.

The aunties always meant well, but they never ignored an opportunity to meddle. Would I age into the same tendency, here in my husbandless Highland stronghold?

"I refuse to go south without a summons from Sebastian," I said, rising. "He knows the baby is a good traveler and that I have weathered many a mile on Britain's roads."

"We know our nephew," Aunt Maighread said. "He is likely sitting in that cesspit referred to as London, waiting for any sign that you'd welcome him home. He is pretending to busy himself with the great affairs of the realm, but nobody worth the bother is in Town this time of year."

"He's sulking," Aunt Bernie observed, scratching one of her beasts on the chin. She could tell them apart, I could not. "Brooding, to use the manly term. You must be gracious in victory, Violet, and show him some mercy."

"I wasn't aware that Sebastian and I had engaged in hostilities." I snatched a piece of shortbread from the tray. "Besides, he's not in

London. He's biding at Ashmore, bringing the property up to standards."

Ashmore was a pretty manor house on the border of Kent and Sussex. That put it a half day's ride from my father's family seat, Derwent Hall, and an enormous distance from Perthshire.

Sebastian and I had been married at Ashmore in a quiet ceremony by special license. My father, my two married brothers, and their wives had been in attendance. Sebastian's small family had been unrepresented, but Hugh St. Sevier and his wife, Ann, had been on hand. I'd hoped their presence had been meant as a show of support for Sebastian as well as for me.

Throughout the ceremony, I'd been dyspeptic and thus had not lingered among our guests. When a bride is far gone with child, allowances must be made.

"Sebastian keeps you apprised of his movement?" Aunt Bernie asked.

"He does." Short notes, inquiring after my health and my daughter's wellbeing. Sometimes Sebastian reported his activities—*called upon your father, who was fortunately not in residence at the time*—and so forth, but his missives were dispatches rather than a new husband's epistles to his bride.

Mine to him were even worse. I said little about the baby, other than to assure him of her great good spirits. I did not know the neighborhood gossip well enough to relay much of that. Which left... elegantly penned weather reports.

And me, missing the husband who was doubtless not missing me.

And Sebastian, kilting about the Home Counties and probably wondering what he'd got himself into.

As I made my way up a winding stone staircase to the nursery, I realized why marital bewilderment felt so familiar. I'd barely left the schoolroom when I'd married Freddie Belmaine, scion of a respected and prosperous gentry family. Freddie had had many fine qualities— I could say that now with very little rancor. He'd been charming, financially generous to me, an attentive escort, and, at bottom, probably well intended, but he'd been merry, self-centered hell as a husband.

We had not been in love, of course, and by the time of his death five years into the marriage, I had given up hoping for more than a cordial friendship. I'd been handed widowhood instead, an occasion for profound sadness, which had blossomed into vexation and then—a fascinating discovery for a lady to make well into adulthood—a temper.

I came to the nursery, an airy suite of rooms on the topmost floor of the "new" part of the castle. Two hundred years ago, some MacHeath ancestress had tired of communal meals in the great hall, and had grafted a country house onto the family citadel. The modernization had been carefully done, such that the castle still made a grand first impression on the main approach.

Visitors emerged from a bend in the wooded road to behold a grand fountain, crenelated parapets, a stout drawbridge, and a central turret topped by a flapping pennant silhouetted against the brilliant blue of the Scottish sky. A fairy-tale edifice that I'd liked on sight.

Sebastian deserved such a home, though his feelings about the place had been conflicted even before he'd abandoned me here. My feelings about my daughter were not conflicted. I heard Maeve's laughter as I opened the nursery door, and all woes and misgivings fled my heart.

"Baa!" Maeve waved a chubby fist in my direction and offered me a gummy smile over her nursery maid's shoulder.

"We are in a good mood this afternoon," Bevins said, jostling the baby gently. "All full of ourselves."

I took the child from Bevins, delighting as always in the solid feel of a healthy infant—*my* healthy infant. I'd suffered two miscarriages in my first marriage and been worried half out of my mind while carrying Maeve. She was to me the embodiment of rejoicing. After her birth, I had waited for that giddy excess of maternal sentiment to fade, but it had only deepened and strengthened.

She gurgled against my shoulder and kicked at my middle.

"Milady is in high spirits," Bevins said, pushing a lock of red hair behind her ear. "Proud of them new teeth and more on the way."

Bevins was barely twenty years old, but I trusted her implicitly. She'd been on nursery duty since the age of ten and was the oldest daughter in a brood of eleven. What Bevins did not know about babies was likely unknown to God Himself.

"I'll take herself up on the walk for some fresh air," I said. "You may nip down to the kitchen for a cuppa while Maeve and I will sort out all the troubles of the world."

"No troubles for that one," Bevins said, passing me a shawl. "She was born under a lucky star."

She'd been born on Saint Valentine's Day—a bit of irony, that. "She's had lunch?"

"Both lunches. You'd think mashed peas were Christmas pudding to watch that child at her tucker. That's the Scot in her."

Not a drop of Scottish blood flowed in Maeve's veins, alas. I waved Bevins on her way, swaddled Maeve in the shawl, and prepared to soothe myself with two of my favorite tonics: my daughter's company and the view from the parapets.

The castle heights were not even breezy for a change, but bathed in peaceful sunshine and fresh air. I settled with Maeve on a bench of ancient provenance and looked out over the fields and piney mountainsides of my husband's holdings.

The vista I beheld met a need in my soul for beauty balanced with wildness. England offered no such landscapes, and the first time Sebastian had shown me the prospect I now admired, I'd gained a whole new appreciation for how homesick he must have been as a boy.

The previous marquess had banished his heir to England at a young age to acquire English airs and graces. Sebastian had been entrusted to distant relatives on the estate next to Derwent Hall, and thus he and I had become acquainted. We'd both been lonely, both outcasts in a sense, and a friendship had sprung up.

Did we still have a friendship? I'd hoped so, but two months after

Maeve's birth, Sebastian had escorted me north to Perthshire and then taken himself back south to "see to matters at Ashmore."

I had had two days' notice of his departure and regular dispatches since, but no clue why he'd left or if he'd return.

Those dispatches, which had been weekly at first, were less and less frequent.

"What is his lordship getting up to?" I asked my daughter. She smacked my chin and tried to grab my lip. "He was my best friend in the world once, and I have always esteemed him greatly."

Maeve caught my nose in a surprisingly strong grip.

"His eyes are as blue as yours," I said, which was nonsense, but what a joy, to be *entitled* to spout a mother's nonsense to my offspring. "The marquess named you."

Lady Maeve Fleur Caledonia MacHeath. Fleur was a nod to me —Violet, the family flower, as my brother Mitchell had once put it— and Maeve had been Sebastian's grandmother's name. Nothing about the name was English, and I liked that.

And in some quirk of celestial humor, my daughter had flaming-red hair. My nondescript brown hair had reddish highlights in strong sun, but by no aberration of aesthetic truth would I have called myself a redhead. Her father, however, had luxurious chestnut locks and brown eyes.

The summer sun was strong, so I was careful to keep Maeve in the shade. My own complexion was of less concern to me. I had never been a diamond or anything approaching an incomparable. I was of medium height with regular features, brown hair, and blue eyes. Despite my middling attributes, I had always expected to make a good match because I was an earl's well-dowered daughter.

I *had* made a good match—a good, miserable match. I hoped my second attempt at matrimony would improve on the first.

I did not for one moment believe Sebastian was brooding away in the south, waiting for me to wave some wifely white flag. Sebastian and I were not at odds, and I was, in fact, beholden to him. He had married me to give Maeve legitimacy, and for that, I would always be grateful.

Hugh St. Sevier—whom I also esteemed greatly—was Maeve's father in a biological sense. Complicated circumstances in the person of Hugh's presumed-dead wife had arisen after Hugh and I had become engaged, and as Hugh and Ann had embarked on a reconciliation, I had realized I was with child.

Sebastian had stepped in to offer matrimony. Had he been plain, untitled, and barely solvent, his proposal would still have been the act of a kind and generous man. In fact, Sebastian's dark good looks had doubtless provoked many a swoon in Mayfair. His title was lofty and his wealth significant.

He'd assured me that he was offering as much out of self-interest as gallantry, but perhaps the reality of our union had taken Sebastian unawares. Had Maeve been a boy, despite her irregular antecedents, she would have been heir to Sebastian's title and the marquessate's holdings. She was a girl, though, a delightful, bouncy, robust miracle of a girl, and that meant Sebastian still needed an heir.

A part of me dreaded his return, because he and I would have to negotiate the specifics of our circumstances. Sebastian needed sons—the more the better—and yet, we had not married with a view toward anything but solving my need for a husband.

"It's complicated," I whispered against my daughter's copper curls.

"Baa!"

"That is your answer to everything, my lady."

Did Sebastian think of me as Lady Violet? Lady Dunkeld? That woman wafting awkwardly about his castle?

I pondered those bleak questions while strolling the walkway that ran the length of the parapets and circled around the perimeter of the whole castle. I had never seen the view in winter, but I longed to know it in all seasons.

Maeve had become a drowsy bundle against my shoulder when I caught a movement from the tail of my eye. Far below, a rider on a large, dark horse emerged from the trees and plodded on toward the castle.

I knew that horse. Hannibal was the last mount Sebastian had ridden on campaign in Spain, a sizable, elegant gelding well suited to his... While my mind took in the dust on the horse's coat and the sweat matting his neck and flanks, my heart gave a sidewise leap.

Sebastian had come home.

Though one part of me had misgivings about the terrain he and I would have to navigate, another part of me faced a difficult truth: I had spent much of my adult life missing Sebastian MacHeath, and in the past few months, I had missed him more than ever.

~

I did not bother returning Maeve to the nursery, but instead took myself down to the medieval great hall that served as the castle's receiving area.

The great hall had taken some time for my English soul to appreciate. A vast array of weapons decorated soaring white-washed walls, and dozens of targes and shields hung from blackened crossbeams. Two suits of armor—the largest I'd ever beheld—guarded a fireplace twenty feet across and eight feet high.

The martial effect was not in the least softened by the fact that swords, firearms, crossbows, and arrows were arranged in fans, wheels, and other artistic patterns. Pots of blood-red geraniums adorned the three-foot-deep windowsills, and when I'd suggested some pink blooms might create a softer contrast, the aunties had reacted with dismay.

Blood-red was the point, of course.

I waited before the enormous fireplace in which many an ox had doubtless been roasted. The original laird's chamber sat atop the chimney space, meaning a heated bedroom floor had been among the amenities the castle owner had enjoyed in former times.

While I, despite the mild summer day, was abruptly chilly.

Should I go to the courtyard? Wait outside the door as a one-woman welcoming committee? Summon the butler to admit the lord of the manor while I pretended to gracious detachment?

Maeve squirmed in my arms, and I was reminded that I was a mother, and mamas were not flighty creatures. I had crossed the room, intent on ducking through the pass door onto the castle's front terrace, when Sebastian opened the door from the other side.

He came through, a squeeze for a man of his height and muscle, and straightened.

"Greetings, my lady." His smile was tired and subdued. "My ladies, rather. Were you thinking to take some air on the courtyard?"

He spoke as if he'd been out for a pleasant hack, not gone for months with no explanation.

"I saw you from the parapets—we saw you. Welcome home." My greeting felt both presumptuous and inadequate. The castle was not my home, though I lived here, and in some regard, it wasn't Sebastian's home either. He owned the property, managed its complicated finances, and his father had been born here, but some quality I associated with a true home was lacking in his regard for the castle.

"You look well, Violet," Sebastian said, brushing the back of a finger over Maeve's cheek. "Thriving, the pair of you."

I'd missed even the sound of his voice. "You look road-weary," I replied, "and you are doubtless in need of a decent meal. Shall I have a bath drawn for you?"

"Please," he said, making no move to touch me. "And if you'd join me for that meal, I'd appreciate it. I bring letters for you, from Katie, Lady Ellersby, and Ann St. Sevier. While I soak off the dust, you can catch up with your correspondents. Your father and brothers send greetings."

I wanted to *catch up* with my husband. "I can read the letters later. Was there a reason you didn't warn me you were coming north, my lord?"

He scrubbed a hand over his face. "We are in our own home, with nobody present save our daughter. Might you call me Sebastian?"

Our daughter.

From the moment of Maeve's birth, Sebastian had treated her with as much affection, protectiveness, and paternal pride as if she'd been his own progeny. If I had no other reason to respect my husband —and I had many—I'd have respected him for that.

"Sebastian," I said. "I am glad you are home, but if I'd had some warning, I could have had your rooms aired." And braced myself mentally for the reunion.

"I'll open a window." He bent to remove his spurs, bracing himself on the heavy table that sat along an interior wall. "I did write to you, Violet."

Was that a truculent note in his voice? Resentful? "I received your letters. I hope mine found you?"

He straightened, spurs in hand. "Aye. We apparently have a cheerful baby."

"Maeve is eating peas." I felt equal parts foolish and proud to report this accomplishment. "Bevins says thin porridge isn't far off."

"And if porridge is on the menu, then our girl will soon be having a wee dram." He lifted Maeve from my arms and nuzzled her cheek. She dimpled and grabbed his chin, and the two of them beamed at each other.

My heart ached at the sight, though with joy or regret, I could not have said, nor what I'd be regretting. I did not regret Maeve—never, ever that.

"Come along," I said, starting for the door. "The staff will be all a-swither now that you are home, and MacRae will change the pennant before Hannibal's saddle is off his back. The invitations will start arriving before nightfall."

Sebastian trailed me, Maeve cooing at him as he strode along. "Tell MacRae not to hoist the laird's pennant just yet. I want a few days with my family before the barbarians storm the gate."

"You'd best tell him yourself. MacRae's hearing isn't what it used to be, at least when I suggest something to him."

"Violet, the man's not forty years old."

"Maybe my accent is too hard to understand." I started up the grand staircase that split on the first landing. To the right lay the family wing, to the left the historic parts of the castle as well as the gallery and ballroom. "I'll take Maeve back to the nursery."

"I'll carry her, my lady."

Maeve appeared delighted to be in Sebastian's arms, and provoking a tiff over who carried the baby would have been petty of me.

But would it have been asking too much for Sebastian to have bowed over my hand? Bussed my cheek? Offered a hug in greeting? He'd been an affectionate youth and very solicitous of my condition as a new husband.

Though I also knew that Sebastian was shy at heart. He could play the boisterous Scot when the occasion required him to, but as a boy, he'd been happiest reading for hours on a blanket by the side of a stream.

"The older I get," Sebastian said as we reached the first floor, "the more stairs this castle acquires. Have the aunties been treating you decently?"

"They have been all that is friendly, and they will be delighted to see you." My words lacked warmth, so I tried again. "*I* am delighted to see you." A grudging admission, when I'd meant my words as a gesture of wifely goodwill. They also happened to be true.

"You missed me?" Sebastian asked, shifting Maeve to the opposite hip.

"I did, and I worried about you. Travel can be hazardous."

"Said the woman who racketed the length and breadth of the realm."

I'd done my racketing with St. Sevier's escort for the most part, and the only time I'd come to harm had been on my father's property.

"I'm a mother now, not an anchorite. I hope my racketing days are not entirely behind me." *Next time you leave, take me with you. Take us with you.* Had it not been for Maeve and some neighbors with whom I'd had a prior acquaintance, I would have expired of boredom in Dunkeld's fairy castle.

I'd had enough of boredom in my first marriage, and mourning had rendered boredom my sworn foe.

I opened the door to the nursery, finding that Bevins had returned to her duties. She sat by the window, embroidering one of Maeve's dresses, and sprang to her feet when she realized the marquess himself was on hand.

"My lord." She curtseyed prettily. "Good to see you home, sir. Shall I take the baby?"

Sebastian passed Maeve over and said something in Gaelic that had Bevins blushing as only a redhead could blush. My efforts to learn the language proceeded at a glacial pace, in part because the aunties could not agree on any point of vocabulary, grammar, or pronunciation.

And in part because Sebastian's native tongue was diabolically complicated, at least compared to French.

"See me to my apartment," Sebastian said when we quit the nursery. "Tell me how you've been going on."

I paused long enough to inform a grinning footman that his lordship required a bath and a tray in the laird's suite. The fellow—another MacRae—moved off at double-time march. Word was doubtless spreading throughout the castle, if not the shire, that Lord Dunkeld had come home.

"I have been going on well enough," I said. "Maeve is usually up only once a night lately, though she does seem to rise with the sun." Of course, summer nights in Perthshire meant about six hours of not-quite-full darkness.

"Is she napping?"

"Morning and afternoon."

"Are *you* napping?"

What business was that of...? Except it was Sebastian's business. He was my husband. "Occasionally." I preceded him into the laird's suite, which had its own balcony looking out on the majestic firs on the opposite hillside and the silver ribbon of the River Tay below.

The apartment was dusted and aired regularly—which I would not admit to Sebastian—and like the nursery, the exposure maximized the sunlight streaming through the windows.

"I always expect to see my uncle when I walk into these rooms," Sebastian said. "He'd insist on a blazing fire in high summer and clad himself head to toe in tartan wool all year round. I'm relieved when I don't find him here."

"Your memories of the castle are unhappy." Much like my memories of Derwent Hall. The Hall had been my home in childhood, also the place where I'd lost my mother, failed to live up to her memory, and always been the odd sibling out with my four brothers.

Sebastian continued into the bedroom. My own apartment abutted this one, and a connecting door joined the dressing closets.

"I did not care for my uncle," he said, opening the French doors, "and he bitterly resented me, a mere nephew where a son should have been. Then he sent me south—my parents were powerless to gainsay that decree—and the resentment became mutual."

I wandered into his bedroom, though it was a space I'd avoided. "Would you rather dwell in England?"

He braced a shoulder on the jamb of the French door and surveyed the view I found so lovely. "I am constantly discontent," he said. "When I am in the south, I miss my Perthshire hills, and when I'm here, I'm restless."

I wanted to go to him and slip my arm around his waist, to rest my head on his shoulder and ask if he'd missed his wife.

My impulse was stifled by the arrival of the footmen rolling an enormous copper tub into the sitting room. A parade of maids and underfootmen followed, each toting a pair of steaming buckets. The last maid carried a tray laden with sandwiches, fruit, cheese, and tea cakes, and a teapot swaddled in plaid toweling.

They would dither about, pouring the water into the tub, arranging soap and scrub brushes, until Domesday. They wanted a peek at Sebastian, or a peek at the lord and lady of the manor making an awkward business of a reunion.

"Thank you," I said, while Sebastian remained out of sight by the French doors in the bedroom. "That will be all."

They trooped out, smiles snuffed by my dismissal. The last to go pulled the door closed in his wake rather harder than necessary.

"Will you have something to eat?" I called, inspecting the offerings on the tray. "The kitchen sent up enough to feed a regiment."

Sebastian padded from the bedroom and helped himself to a sandwich. "Upjohn should be here with the luggage by sunset," he said. "If you could scare me up some togs, I'd appreciate it. The aunties will expect me in all my kilted splendor at supper."

This much wifely assistance I was capable of. While Sebastian poured a cup of tea and did justice to the tray, I busied myself at the wardrobe in the bedroom. Highland attire, I had learned, could be casual, dress, or formal. I assembled a kit suitable for a family dinner and chose a plain leather sporran such as Sebastian preferred.

I thought to ask him if he'd rather wear something more dashing— the badger-pelt sporran, which I personally detested, for example— and had taken four whole steps into the parlor before I realized that my husband had begun his bath.

Sebastian filled the tub, his knees forming islands in sudsy water and his bare chest already wet enough to shape the hair into dark whorls.

"How I do adore a hot bath," he said, sniffing the hard-milled French soap bought for his particular use. "Help yourself to a sandwich, Violet, and—"

"Excuse me," I said, barreling for the door. "Cook will want to discuss tonight's menu, and I mustn't keep her waiting."

CHAPTER TWO

Sebastian

As I soaked in a tub that wasn't half large enough for a man of my proportions, I heard my uncle's voice in my head. *Well, laddie, ye bungled that splendidly.*

Uncle had ever pointed out my failings with a combination of glee and disgust. As a boy, I had taken to cataloging his shortcomings with equal enthusiasm in my letters to the aunties. They had replied with chatty dispatches about a neighbor's mare having twins or the first frost coming early.

I had treasured those letters and still had some of them. Now they struck me as... empty gestures, as my letters to my wife had been. I managed the awkward business of pouring rinse water over my hair and general person, stepped from the tub, and considered Violet's hasty departure.

She and I were married for all the wrong reasons and—I hoped—a few of the right ones. She had seen me in the altogether in my youth, though I had yet to catch her in anything more scandalous than a nightgown, robe, and slippers.

As her pregnancy had progressed, she had become blunt—even for Violet—about the bodily repercussions of gestation. She had tolerated my escort with unusual docility, her balance having been among the casualties of impending motherhood, particularly in the last month or so.

Because Violet had had two miscarriages during her marriage to the worthless wastrel, I had been cautioned by no less medical authority than Hugh St. Sevier not to consummate our vows until well after the birth.

In my imagination, a dour and dodgy place, St. Sevier's name never came up without me wanting to append *physician without compare*. He was, in fact, a damned fine doctor. He'd also been Violet's friend, lover, and fiancé, about which my feelings were complicated.

And St. Sevier was Maeve's biological progenitor. We were all muddling on as best we could with that. St. Sevier's wife, Ann, had insisted we do so as friends. Madame was a native of my own Perthshire and formidable in a quiet way.

The truth was, I had not been *invited* to consummate any nuptial vows with Violet, and as I donned my shirt and pinned my kilt, I wondered if that invitation would ever be issued.

Was I supposed to do the inviting? I hoped not, because the thought of Violet tolerating my advances out of wifely long-suffering turned my stomach. She'd suffered enough as the wife and widow of the handsome hound.

A tap on the door interrupted my attempts to put a *trone d'amour* knot in my cravat.

"You're through bathing already?" Violet asked, peeking around the door. "I'd thought to rinse your hair for you." She was blushing, and Violet wasn't the blushing sort.

"The tub is too small to lounge in properly," I said, mentally kicking myself for abandoning my ablutions. "Is Cook threatening us with haggis, neeps, and tatties?" Traditional Scottish fare actually appealed to me, though I didn't expect Violet to subsist on turnips, potatoes, and a glorified sort of baked tripe hash.

"Cook?" She studied my neckcloth, then marched across the room to scowl mightily at my chin. "My lord, this will not do."

She undid the knot I'd so carefully tied and slipped the linen from my person.

"You propose to *dress me*, my lady?"

"Upjohn does." She opened and closed the drawers of my clothes press, one after the other. "The whole castle is in alt over news of your arrival. You will be inspected by every underfootman, chambermaid, and porter before you lay your head on a pillow tonight. I will not have my-husband-the-marquess failing a sartorial examination. Hold still."

She'd produced another length of starched linen and, by virtue of leaning close to me, draped it around my neck. Violet's scent had always fascinated me. Millefleurs, or something equally sweet and complex. She still wore it, though her fragrance also had a softer herbal note anchoring all the florals.

"Stand up straight," she said, measuring the ends of the linen against each other. "The *trone d'amour* is too austere for the prodigal's first family dinner upon returning home. The mathematical is more relaxed and better suited to summer temperatures."

"Was that Belmaine's opinion?" I knew the question was ill-advised even as the words were leaving my mouth, and yet, I plowed onward. "He was quite the dandy, wasn't he?"

"Quite, and Freddie had opinions about every knot, color of cravat, style of gloves, design of walking stick... Did you know that the preferred hue for the mathematical by day is *couleur de la cuisse d'une nymphe emue*? One can only wear white for evening, but..."

She whipped the linen this way, tugged it that way, and stepped back. "I'm sorry. I did not mean to speak French."

Because St. Sevier was French. He lurked like a shade between us, and yet, that wasn't a fair characterization. I had occasion to know that St. Sevier and his wife were in charity with each other. More to the point, no mortal of marriageable age sprang from the head of Zeus without a past, without family, or without regrets.

"Speak all the French you like, Violet, though I fail to see what the color of a sentimental nymph's thighs have to do with anything."

Violet began tidying up the riding attire I'd discarded on the sofa. She batted at my shirt and coat vigorously enough to send dust motes wafting on the afternoon sunbeams.

"Freddie and I were never at a loss for conversation if he was in a fashionable mood. I paid attention to his pronouncements because I thought that's what a wife was supposed to do." She retrieved a pair of sleeve buttons from the vanity in the bedroom—little silver thistles that were the devil to fasten onto a cuff.

"Did Belmaine listen to you?" I asked as she dropped the jewelry into my open palm.

"What could I possibly have had to say that was worth listening to?" She watched me struggle with my blighted sleeve buttons. "Let me do that. The aunties believe in sewing buttonholes on a scale that would suit an elf."

Violet dealt with my cuffs while again managing not to touch me, and I wrestled with the urge—both old and new—to plant the late Freddie Belmaine a facer.

"Belmaine did not deserve you," I said as Violet resumed fussing with my dusty clothes. "And in a completely different sense, you did nothing to deserve him." I knew that now. As a young man, I'd been allowed to draw all manner of wrongheaded conclusions about how and why Violet had married somebody other than me.

"Freddie and I did not suit," she said, giving my riding breeches a few hard shakes. "In my logical mind, I know that. We were young, we had different expectations of the institution of marriage, and eventually, we would probably have become fond friends, but I had nobody to tell me that." She made a stack on the sofa of my dirty clothes, draping stockings and wrinkled cravat atop shirt, waistcoat, breeches, and jacket. "Where are your boots? They'll need attention."

To the nearest bog with my rubbishing boots. "Upjohn will see to them. Are we still friends, Violet?"

She ceased her tidying and gave me an owlish look. "What prompted that query?"

Not a yes. "I want us to be friends. We were boon companions once upon a youthful time, and I had hoped that we might be again." We had made significant progress from the estrangement that had taken hold during my soldiering years, but then the whole business with Ann St. Sevier's return and Maeve's impending arrival had sprung up.

And then Maeve had graced the earthly sphere with her presence, and I no longer trusted my assumptions where Violet was concerned.

The owlish look shifted to a scowl that put me in mind of a younger Violet, one vexed past all bearing with the adolescent pigheadedness of her brothers, and sometimes with me.

"Do friends hare off to the south with no notice and bide there for weeks, my lord? Do friends reappear again virtually without notice? Do friends limit their letters to dispatches from the English front?"

She picked up the stack of clothing and carried it into the bedroom at a brisk march. My wife had regained her balance, apparently.

"Friends," I said, following her and trying to ignore the swish of her skirts, "don't hang about underfoot when a woman is barely getting any sleep. Friends don't drone on and on about weather and crops when a lady has a new baby to occupy her. Friends don't..."

She took the clothing into my dressing closet and set the lot of it on a wicker hamper. "Yes?"

Violet crossed her arms, which had the effect of reminding me that her proportions had changed. She had always been what my uncle Archie called a pleasant armful. Neither slender nor plump, but nicely curved and tidily proportioned.

She considered her looks passable—dark brown hair, blue eyes, adequate figure—while I had spent years measuring every other female against her standard. Not for beauty—what did beauty matter thirty years on or when a sick child needed comforting?—but for honesty, for common sense, for determination. Violet had a ferocity about her that she'd learned to disguise behind manners and decorum. The occasional glint in her eye reassured me that she had not fashioned all of her swords into parasols.

"I did not want to impose," I said, "as you and Maeve were getting acquainted. You needed to rest and to focus for a time on the child." True enough.

"I will focus on that child whether you are galumphing through the castle's galleries or kicking your heels in Kent, my lord. If you left for my sake—which proposition I take leave to doubt—why did you come back?"

I missed you. Missing was too tame a label for the emotions Violet inspired in me. She had always been able to pique my pride as well as my affection as well as my purely masculine interest.

"Do I need a reason to return to Perthshire, Violet Marie? This is my home. My family is here. I was banished from this castle as a boy, and I count it among my greatest pleasures to return at my whim and pleasure."

At this pronouncement, the old marquess in my head went off into wheezy whoops.

Violet's expression became unreadable, which was better than that scowl. "I've moved dinner up," she said. "We'll dine at six, despite the sun lingering in the sky until all hours. You might want to look in on Annis before supper. She'll doubtless learn of your return and fret until she sees you with her own eyes."

Along with my horse Hannibal and a quantity of luggage, I'd brought a girl child back with me from Spain. Annis had been one of countless war orphans begging in the streets, smaller and more delicate than most. I'd had myself declared her father—a biological impossibility, given her age and the distance between Spain and Britain—and set her up as the only denizen of the castle nursery.

"How is my wee Annis?" I asked, trying not to sound as if I dreaded the answer.

"She's subdued," Violet said. "Maeve's arrival has upended many routines, and your absence did not help. Annis has fixated on you as the lodestar of all her security, and then you disappear and reappear *at your whim and pleasure*... She cried herself to sleep for a week, Sebastian."

Not well done of you lingered unspoken in the air.

"I will take myself directly to the schoolroom to make my apologies." I'd brought Annis a stuffed horse the same shade as Hannibal, to whom she was inordinately attached. I'd thoughtlessly stashed the gift with the trunks on the baggage coach.

I'd have to make amends for my absence without the fortification of a bribe.

"I'll see you at dinner," Violet said. "I'd accompany you to the schoolroom, except I'm sure Annis would rather have you to herself. She was upset at your departure, Sebastian, and I did not know what to do for her. She resents me, Maeve, the aunties' cats, and Mrs. Yancy's every direction. Lucy seems to get on well with her, but I'm not about to surrender my lady's maid to the nursery staff, nor would Lucy willingly accept the demotion. Annis hoards your letters as if they've been handed down to her directly from the celestial realm."

If anybody would sympathize with a girl child at odds with the greater household, Violet would, though *she* apparently did not treasure my letters.

"I'm off to greet Annis this instant, but the child will have to learn that adults have concerns outside the nursery, and the tail doesn't wag the dog."

Violet looked like she might say more. When we'd been younger, we'd been appallingly honest with each other. I learned all manner of arcana from Violet—about female biology, what girls really meant when they said they had a megrim, and that gender was no bar to curiosity regarding strong spirits.

Then Violet had been sent off to some select academy for bothersome hoydens, and her honesty had become tempered with feminine reserve. She'd still seen fit to practice her kissing on me for one precious, perilous summer, though she'd declared me utterly gormless as a dashing swain.

As a husband, my prospects appeared equally dismal.

I took myself up to the schoolroom, prepared to be greeted with a hug from at least one female, though when I arrived, Annis was nowhere to be seen.

"Run off again?" I asked the governess, a patient, sturdy individual of about thirty years. Mrs. Yancy had followed the drum in Spain and been left in parlous circumstances upon the demise of her officer husband. More to the point, she was competent in Spanish, the only language Annis had spoken upon arriving at the castle.

"My lord." Mrs. Yancy curtseyed. "Welcome home. You have the right of it. I do apologize. Miss Annis was supposed to be napping, but she is most willful and apparently doesn't need much rest. She can't have gone far. I was about to alert the staff."

I thought of Violet's reproaches and the hurt in her eyes when she'd mentioned Annis crying herself to sleep.

"No need for a general alarum," I said. "I'll find her. If I've not brought her back to the schoolroom in two hours, you may alert the staff then."

Mrs. Yancy was accustomed to following orders, though she clearly did not approve of this one. She bobbed another curtsey that somehow conveyed her reservations.

"Very well, my lord." She consulted a watch pinned to her bodice. "Two hours. Not a moment more."

~

I had forbidden Mrs. Yancy to raise the hue and cry in part because I did not want the rest of the castle knowing of Annis's reaction to my return. The child was troubled—understandable, given her past—but she also had a knack for *creating* trouble.

The first time I'd made an extended trip south, Annis had turned hiding in the castle into a high art. I'd sent Mrs. Yancy a list of all the best hiding places and consulted my sister, Lady Clementine, for her list as well. Uncle Archie and the aunties had added a few suggestions, as had our butler, MacRae.

Annis had soon tired of the game.

She could be silent for days, though in the midst of one of those campaigns, I'd overheard her chatting amiably with her stuffed animals. She tried speaking only in Spanish for a time. I'd suggested the staff reciprocate by addressing her only in Gaelic. She'd been so fascinated with my native language that she'd given up that game as well, and she was turning into something of a polyglot with no apparent effort.

I did not understand her, but neither did I regret bringing her home with me. The castle had rallied around her to some extent, and I was yet hopeful that Annis would eventually settle in.

As I made my way to the stable, I was struck by an uncomfortable thought: The Earl of Derwent, Violet's father, had not known what to do with his daughter. He'd had no sisters and hadn't even claimed a direct relation to any aunties. A daughter arriving after four sons had not been in his lordship's plans.

Then his countess had died well before Violet's come out, and Derwent's awkward attempts to parent Violet had devolved into outright bungling. Violet's marriage to Freddie Belmaine was Derwent's fault—something to do with a water meadow Derwent had coveted. Derwent hadn't made any better showing as a father when Violet had been bereaved.

Was I bungling just as badly, with not only Violet, but also with Annis?

"Where is my favorite wee besom?" I yelled as I entered the stable. A dozen equines eyed me with lazy curiosity over open half doors. A groom—one of the endless MacRaes in service at the castle—tugged at his cap, winked, and pointed to Hannibal's loose box.

"I travel the length of the realm," I went on, striding past stalls, "push poor Hannibal to the limit of his powers, and I find nobody waiting to greet me in the schoolroom. Is this how my loyal hench-woman welcomes her laird?"

I opened Hannibal's stall, and he, predictably, was nose-down in a pile of fragrant hay. Sitting at the edge of the pile was a dark-haired, dark-eyed sprite whose braid was coming undone. Annis might have passed for Black Irish or one of the petite Pictish throwbacks popu-lating the Western Isles, except that her complexion was Mediter-ranean rather than Celtic.

"You greet Hannibal," I said, sidling into the loose box and closing the door behind me, "but you don't greet me. What of High-land hospitality, Annis MacHeath?"

She continued braiding Hannibal's forelock, which—doubtless because it interfered with his meal not at all—he tolerated graciously.

"I am not your vassal," she said in Spanish.

I mentally opened a rather dusty linguistic cupboard and replied in the same language. "A henchwoman is not a vassal. Her service is given out of respect, while a vassal is bound by a legal obligation." The distinction was more subtle, something a native Scot grasped intuitively.

Annis ignored me, undid the braid in Hannibal's forelock, and stroked his nose.

"Annis MacHeath?" Having gone to the trouble to dress in a deal of wool, I wasn't about to settle beside the child in the hay and straw.

"I'm not a MacHeath," she said in Gaelic, "not truly."

Who had told her that? "I have taken legal responsibility for you." I again replied in the language she'd chosen. "That makes you family, and as I am a MacHeath, so are you."

She stood and shook out her short dress and pinafore. "Yancy says that's not how it works. You told the army I was your daughter, but I'm not."

She had grown in just the few months I'd been gone, and I grasped, as I hadn't grasped before, that she would be a beautiful woman. This was not entirely a good thing—for her, or for me as her guardian. I did not know how old Annis was. Poverty stunted growth, and she'd known the harshest deprivation in her earliest years.

I avoided lying to the child at all costs. "The law provides no means whereby I can become your legal father, but I assumed the role anyway. I told my commanding officer that you were mine, I attested to it in an affidavit, and I have given you my family name."

"If I am your family, why do you go away so much? You go away from the aunties and from Violet. You sent Uncle Archie away to Aunt Clemmie. You even went away from *Maeve*."

She was alluding to some concern, some quirk of childish logic that I could not quite see. That last observation—that I would decamp from the baby—was somehow the most telling.

"Archie always looks in on Aunt Clemmie in the summer." He looked in on Aunt Clemmie's trout and salmon streams too. "I will always come back, Annis. I had business in the south."

"You have *a lot* of business in the south." No native-born Scot could have referred to England with more contempt.

"And I always will," I said, holding out a hand. "England has its charms. I have friends there and properties."

Annis gave me a peevish look.

"Hannibal's sire came from England." A snorty little Iberian stud with a very fine opinion of himself. The Clydesdale mare he'd been put to hadn't been all that impressed with him. "Will you go for a hack with me tomorrow morning? Hannibal shouldn't stand about after a day of travel. He'll need to work out the kinks, and so will I."

"Yancy says I'm getting too big to ride up before you."

In this, Mrs. Yancy was probably correct, from a social standpoint if not strictly with regard to Annis's diminutive size. "Then you will ride Hannibal on the lead line, and I will ride Finnegan."

What diplomacy and paternal authority could not accomplish, mention of a lead line debut on Hannibal did. Annis threw her arms around me and squeezed hard. I was reminded of the previous summer, when St. Sevier's older daughter, Fiona, had been allowed to sit on her mother's mare at the walk. St. Sevier and I had provided a few pointers, Violet and Ann had watched from the rail, and for a time, all the complications and undercurrents had not mattered to any of us.

"I can ride Hannibal?" Annis said. "Truly? On my own?"

"Provided he's on a stout lead line, in case he has any frisky ideas." I threw caution to the wind and hoisted Annis to my hip. She was more substantial, no longer the wraith she'd been. "You'll want your trousers, and one of these days, we'll have to find you a sidesaddle."

"Lady Violet says she will sew me a habit, but first we must pick out fabric and trimmings. I will need shiny boots, too, and a hat that sits just so. If I ride Hannibal, my skirts can be very long and still not touch the ground."

She babbled on, a happy little girl whom I still did not comprehend. Perhaps a letter to Lord Derwent was in order—an astonishing notion.

"Let's inspect the foals," I suggested, carrying Annis into the sunshine. "Have you given them names?"

"Lady Violet said I could, though you will give them official names for when you sell them. Like you are Sebastian to the aunties but Lord Dunkeld to MacRae. Violet calls you 'my husband' or 'that man,' and Uncle Archie always calls you 'the lad.' Put me down. I can walk."

I put her down and was ordinately gratified when she took my hand. "You call the marchioness Lady Violet?"

"Everybody does, or just Violet. She said I could call her Violet, but nobody calls her Lady Dunkeld or the marchioness."

Why the hell not? "She mentioned that I'd upset you when I traveled south," I said as we ambled down the bridle path that led to the mares' pasture.

"I *hate it* when you leave, and you leave *a lot*." Annis was speaking English now, and I hadn't noticed when she'd shifted from the Erse.

"I will always come home too, Annis. Depend upon it."

She gave me a look much like one of Violet's—owlish, skeptical, as if an off odor had wafted in on the breeze.

"We are family." I wasn't sure why convincing her of this point had become so important to me. "Someday, Annis, you will leave the castle and leave me. You will take your place in the world, and I will miss you, but you shall visit. You will write. I will come see you."

She dropped my hand and skipped ahead to climb the fence rails. "Will you cry if I leave?"

I'd get drunk, which was possibly the manly version of weeping. "I will be happy for you, if you're moving on to a life that pleases you." I sounded completely in possession of my faculties, but the notion of this dear little person taking on the world... unthinkable.

Unfathomable, and of no appeal whatsoever.

A mare noticed Annis perched on the fence and wandered in our direction.

"Lady Violet cried when you left," Annis said, stretching a hand in the direction of the horse. "I heard her sniffling. My bedroom is next to the nursery, and she'd cuddle Maeve in the rocking chair after we read our story and she'd tucked me in. She told Maeve you'd come back. Maeve is too little to understand, but she told her anyway. Over and over. 'He'll come back.'"

If I'd had a flask on my person, I would have drained it before replying.

"And here I am. Did you name Bathsheba's filly?" The mare was a leggy, glossy chestnut and the filly her mirror image in miniature.

"Mac the Groom says she'll be the first to go to the sale, she's so pretty. I don't want to give her a name. It must be awful to be a horse."

I was still reeling from the news that Violet had wept at my departure and could barely follow Annis's chattering.

"What's so bad about being a horse? You spend most of your days eating grass, swishing at flies, or napping, especially if you're a filly."

Violet had wept. I'd gone south mostly to give her and Maeve time to get acquainted and settle in without me—what term had she used? —*galumphing* about the galleries.

"I would not want to be a horse," Annis said, climbing down from the fence and ripping up a handful of grass to feed the mare, "because the prettier you are, the stronger you are, the better behaved you are, the sooner you are sold away from all of your friends, your home, and your family."

The mare daintily lipped the offering from Annis's palm, gave me a placid inspection, and then returned to her grazing.

"I need to get back to the castle," Annis said. "Yancy thinks I'm napping, and she'll be in a flutter if I'm not in bed when she comes to wake me for my pianoforte practice. Lady Violet used to sneak out at naptime. She told me so herself."

"Lady Violet was prodigiously talented at sneaking out, and I hope you do not seek to emulate her." Half the time, at least when Violet had grown older, she'd been sneaking out to meet me.

While I had been reduced to sneaking off to university, war, and lately to England, to anywhere to avoid her, the lady whom I loved with my whole heart.

CHAPTER THREE

Violet

I had rarely participated in family dinners at the castle, and even less frequently when Sebastian, in all his lairdly splendor, occupied the head of the table.

I was not relying on a wet nurse, which meant my schedule for the past six months had been driven by Maeve's demands. Thus I'd missed more evening meals, breakfasts, and lunches that I might have shared with my husband. When Maeve napped, I often napped, because my sleep at night was invariably interrupted.

My decision regarding a wet nurse had drawn criticism from both aunties, Mrs. Yancy, and Mrs. Baird, the housekeeper.

Both Ann St. Sevier, who came from a long line of professional midwives, and Hugh St. Sevier, had advised against a wet nurse, as had my own instincts. Maeve was *my* daughter, and if I nursed her myself, I'd be that much better attuned to her welfare simply by virtue of my increased presence in the nursery.

Sebastian had respected my decision, and Maeve was thriving.

Conversation at dinner had also been robust, with the aunties regaling their favorite nephew with all the neighborhood gossip, the latest news, and proposed plans to drag him about on various local calls. I was to be spared those outings, *what with the child and all.*

By the time the fruit and cheese had been on the table for a quarter hour, Sebastian was eyeing me down the length of the table with an air of veiled masculine impatience. Inspiration hit, along with the recollection of how fatiguing travel could be.

"Aunties," I said, "we shall not stand on ceremony. Rather than leave his lordship to commune in lonely splendor with his wee dram, I propose to have him all to myself in my private parlor for a few minutes before shooing him to an early bedtime. I have not yet had a chance to catch up with Dunkeld regarding our mutual acquaintances in the south, and I'm sure that conversation would bore you."

Hibernia and Maighread exchanged glances, a swift, silent consultation on strategy.

"Of course, dear." Aunt Bernie finished her wine at one go. "We would not think to intrude. Mags and I will have a quiet game of chess before the fire, and we can organize the schedule of social calls with Sebastian over breakfast. Come along, lad, and escort a pair of dowagers to their parlor."

She infused that last command with stoic good cheer and pointedly did not bid her hostess good night. Aunt Bernie was issuing a friendly warning that snatching Sebastian away would not be tolerated in future. I had learned in my first marriage that a husband went where he pleased, and a wife's entreaties for more of his time were meaningless.

If the aunties wanted to parade Sebastian about the shire, they would hear no argument from me.

"My lady, I'll meet you in the library," Sebastian said as he held Aunt Maighread's chair. "And I will pay no calls until I and my horse are well and truly rested and my wife and daughters and I have had time to enjoy one another's company. I am already committed to taking Annis out for a hack in the morning, so don't think to spoil my breakfast with more wheedling."

I took a sizeable bite of my berry tart, the better to stifle a cheer.

Maighread, who could stride the parapets by the hour, leaned heavily on Sebastian's arm. "You mustn't blame us for wanting to show you off, my boy. Bernie and I grow restless and lonely if we can't socialize, and to keep you all to ourselves would be unneighborly."

As the aunts left the dining room with Sebastian's escort, Bernie launched into a chorus of additional reasons why Sebastian had to cram his schedule with outings—tradition, the laird's duty, a cousin's new baby—while I finished my berry tart and admitted to considerable fatigue.

Ann St. Sevier had warned me that motherhood was tiring, a race the mama embarked on from many yards behind the starting line. Gestation, childbirth, and readjustments to every other relationship made new motherhood a battle with exhaustion. Once the baby arrived, needing nigh incessant attention, the battle became a war.

She'd assured me that time helped, as did good staff in the nursery and a jealous regard for any opportunity to rest. I had excellent support in Bevins and her assistants, and Maeve was a wonderfully healthy baby. I could manage the occasional social call now, though I—again—had been left out of those plans.

I made my way alone to the library, bringing with me four more berry tarts wrapped in a linen table napkin. They were small and delicious, and I was constantly hungry—another effect of lactation. We mothers—from broodmare to barn cat to marchioness—needed our sustenance.

Sebastian was some time joining me in the library, and when he arrived, he stalked into the room with a less than genial air.

Fatigue did that, or so I told myself. "Would you rather have enjoyed your wee dram in lonely splendor?"

He tossed a square of peat on the fire and stood staring at the flames. "God, no. I've had a bellyful of lonely splendor in recent weeks. Are those two getting worse, or am I imagining things?"

I offered him a berry tart. "They are getting worse. My arrival has upset their plans, and they refuse to give ground without making me fight for it. For all that, they mean no real harm."

Sebastian popped the tart into his mouth. "That is part of the reason I sent you word of my impending return, Violet, so you could prevent that pair from launching this campaign to flaunt me before the neighbors. I specifically told you I did not want the laird's pennant raised upon my return, because I knew they would try something like this."

I was being scolded, and that did not comport with *my* plans. "Told me when? I haven't heard from you for nearly a month, and before then, most of your epistles were little better than descriptions of your location and the last book you'd read. I told MacRae not to raise the pennant as soon as I left you at your bath, but I was too late."

"I wrote to you..." Sebastian peered past my left shoulder. "Letters sometimes go astray."

I let that dubious theory pass rather than point out that the British mail system had long been the envy of its Continental counterparts.

"Speaking of letters," I said, "you have great piles of correspondence. I did not open anything, but I did ask the house steward to sort them into business and personal. He said doing so would require reading the contents, and he was unwilling to intrude on your privacy to that degree. You have a chore ahead of you, I'm afraid, but you can use the task to keep the aunties at bay for a few days."

Nobody hid emotions as effectively as Sebastian. I'd seen him bluff at the card table and walk away with considerable winnings. His humor could be so subtle as to elude notice by any who did not know him very well, and his ire was even harder to detect.

His expression when he swung his gaze to me was unreadable—ominously so. "Does anybody in this castle do as you ask them to, Violet?"

"Bevins, Lucy Hewitt, some of the younger undermaids. Annis and I get on fairly well. Mrs. Baird is never overtly rude, and Cook is generally courteous to my face."

"You're saying our people are *disrespectful* to ye?"

The previous spring, I had traveled to Perthshire—with Hugh St. Sevier, of course—and for the first time encountered Sebastian on his native turf. His burr was more in evidence here, but his speech had remained public-school-perfect in every other regard.

That he'd drop a *ye* into the conversation suggested a momentary lapse of the self-control he wore like one of those gleaming suits of armor in the great hall.

And that lapse inspired me to drop some of my own reserve. "Why should the staff indulge me when my own husband treats me like so much wrinkled linen, to be dropped at the laundress's and forgotten until he's short of clean cravats?"

Sebastian's brows rose, and I hoped he might serve me a brisk retort, an accusation, another attempt at a scold—anything but indifference. We'd had some grand donnybrooks in our youth, and Sebastian could give as good as he got. When I'd become too opinionated as a girl, which had happened nigh daily, my middle brothers would retreat into quoting Fordyce's sermons, my oldest brother would simply leave the room, and my youngest brother would try to change the subject.

Papa had descended into muttering about impertinence and what-would-your-mother-say, but Sebastian had never ceded the field.

"I do not treat you like wrinkled linen." His t's were as sharp as the dirk sheathed at his knee, and his jaw had taken on a geologically fixed quality.

I advanced on him, and he merely watched me with his signature glacial detachment.

"You haul me up here," I began, "stay with me only long enough to ensure that Maeve and I have weathered the journey with no ill effects, then trot off right back to Ashmore, as good as flying a pennant over the castle informing the world that you'd like England —my homeland—to yourself. Wife and children had best keep to their places here in bucolic obscurity."

I took to pacing before the hearth rather than distract myself cataloging Sebastian's features.

"Then," I went on, "you decide the English summer heat does not agree with you, and here you are again. You might well have sent a letter warning me of your return, but I did not receive it, so I am left looking like a complete gudgeon, or perhaps marriage to me simply slipped your mind."

Sebastian folded his arms over a broad and muscular chest. "Do go on, my lady."

As if he could stop me. "Is it any wonder that the steward leaves your correspondence to pile up when I ask him to sort it by address? Your aunts go calling without me and expect you to do the same. The housekeeper pretends to forget her English when I point out the great hall needs dusting. Cook avers that anything I say must have slipped her memory. With MacRae, his hearing is intermittently unreliable."

Sebastian stalked off to try to open one of the tall windows that made the library such a light-filled space by the day. The hinge shrieked at his efforts.

"Before you start telling me how to manage my own household, my lord, I did ask MacRae to oil the hinges in here as the weather moderated. He must not have heard me on any of the three occasions I put my request to him."

Sebastian stared for a moment at the view out the window—the back gardens were in high summer glory—then scrubbed a hand over his face.

"Let me guess," he said, taking a seat on the window bench. "If the aunties mention to the cats that a tea tray would be lovely, the tray appears in less than five minutes, with all the trimmings." He patted the place beside him, and I accepted that olive branch.

"Precisely. I have children to see to, Sebastian. I am not interested in besieging this castle in the grand Scottish feuding tradition. My energies are yet limited, and the aunties have been running this household for years. The staff is loyal to them, and—they are betting —so are you."

"I owe the aunties," Sebastian said, no heat in his tone. "I do owe them, but I've also looked after them generously. I can say the same about Archie. He deserted you?"

"Uncle Archie's loyalty is to the trout." And to his flask.

Sebastian had been an affectionate young fellow, far more willing to pat my shoulder, take my hand, or loop an arm around my waist than my brothers had been. Sitting next to him was comforting, and because his proportions made the window seat a snug fit, I also enjoyed his physical warmth.

"They would not let you finish a sentence at supper," he said, straightening the folds of his kilt. "They talked over you, unless you were strictly within your role of lady of the house."

"Imagine three meals a day like that, and you can see why I sometimes share breakfast with Annis in the nursery."

"I told MacRae to take down the damned pennant and leave it down until I order otherwise. I truly am tired, Violet."

I rose because my understanding of fatigue had become woefully thorough over the past year. "I won't keep you up. I am glad to see you, Sebastian, but the situation here has been trying."

He took me by the wrist and prevented me from making a grand exit on that dignified understatement.

"I could send the aunts to Clemmie."

I sat back down, and Sebastian let go of my wrist. "They would blame me, and Clemmie would wonder." I liked Lady Clementine—she was brusque and good-humored, and in her very lack of sentimentality, she revealed a kind heart. She was unimpressed by her brother's many honors—his title, his status as war hero, his political acumen—and she'd told me all of his favorite dishes and a few of his boyhood secrets. He'd paid for an express to forbid her from running away when Uncle had banished him to the south, for example.

Brother and sister were loyal and loving toward each other, and Clemmie alone had expressed genuine joy that Sebastian and I were wed.

Sebastian draped an arm across my shoulders. "Why didn't you tell me you were dealing with an insurrection, Violet? Annis says the staff also disdains to address you by your married title."

I yielded to the pleasure of resting my head on his shoulder. "In the first place, I suspect Hibernia tampers with the mail. She has spies at the posting inn, and apparently at least one of your letters went astray. If I'd whined to you, she might well have read the letter and stopped it from reaching you."

"I dislike this." Sebastian had muttered those words in his native tongue, and I—rejoice, my heart—could translate them.

"I would not have relayed the situation here to you in any case. If you want the aunties to continue managing this household, I have no authority to gainsay you. I have no authority to order the steward to sort your mail. No authority to pension MacRae now that his hearing is so unreliable."

I yawned behind my hand before continuing. "I have pin money, and no means of spending it, and two girl children whose welfare takes precedence over the MacHeath family dramas. Sort the aunties out if you please to, and the battle will resume the next time you canter off to England. They will keep their powder dry and then resume firing with renewed intensity the moment you decamp. I had the same problem with Freddie's staff for the first two years. I know exactly how this business works."

Then I'd conceived, and lost the baby, and Freddie had not acquitted himself at all gallantly. The staff's loyalties had undergone a subtle shift.

Sebastian was quiet for a moment, and I was reminded that one of the first qualities I'd learned to appreciate about him was his capacity for silence. He was a thinking man, a shrewd man, one who chose his words carefully.

"Do I conclude that my marchioness knows exactly how this marriage business works?" he asked.

"I have more experience of marriage than you do," I retorted, sitting up.

Sebastian rose and stretched, a great beast of a man in his prime. I barely resisted the urge to run my hand down his back to delight in the feel of his muscles bunching and rippling.

"We are both tired," he said, assisting me to rise. "Do you look in on the children before retiring? I'll light you up, if so, and then I'm for bed myself."

"We haven't resolved matters, Sebastian."

He kissed my knuckles. "We have the rest of our lives to resolve matters, and we'll make a much better job of it if we've had some sleep."

I agreed with his logic, but I badly wanted to argue nonetheless. As we climbed the steps and took the various turnings that led to the nursery, I realized that much of what my father had labeled contrariness in me had been something else entirely.

I had needed to be seen, to be heard, to be an *acknowledged* member of the Deerfield family. My brilliant adolescent arguments and shocking opinions had done the opposite, shoving me further to the family's margins. Perhaps that experience was why I'd not taken on the aunties and why I'd made such a bad job of taking on my husband—my *first* husband.

"You're quiet," Sebastian said as we approached the nursery arm in arm. "Would you like to ride out with me and Annis in the morning? I've offered to put her on Hannibal on a lead line. Mrs. Yancy has declared that Annis is too big to sit up before me."

Annis was by no means too big to ride up before Sebastian, especially not on a mount as substantial as Hannibal.

"Mrs. Yancy is an accomplished horsewoman now, to make such decisions for our daughter?"

He sighed and stepped back. "Valid point. We'll see how Annis does on her own, though Hannibal won't put a hoof wrong if he knows what's good for him. Will you join us?"

I wanted to—this, too, was an olive branch—though I had no idea if my habit still fit, and my first obligation upon rising was to visit Maeve.

"I would like to ride out with you, Sebastian, but for tomorrow, let Annis have you to herself. A daughter needs time with her papa."

"Another time, then." He kissed my forehead. "Good night, Violet, and thank you." He strolled away, all languid, kilted grace, and I was left in the corridor staring into the shadows.

He'd been smiling a mischievous, sweet, boyish grin that I hadn't seen in ages, and the sight of it had me leaning heavily on the oak door. What on earth was he thanking me for, and what had that smile been *about?*

~

I was penning a reply to my youngest brother Felix's wife, Katie. She had attended my lying-in and had faithfully sent best wishes for my wellbeing and Maeve's ever since. Sebastian and I were godparents to Felix and Katie's firstborn son—James Evander Deerfield—so I reciprocated with inquiries regarding Jamie.

At some point along the way, our letters had become the genuine exchanges of mothers in the thick of the nursery years. Worry and frustration figured prominently in our narratives, as did hope, fear, and humor.

Sebastian interrupted me before I could append news of his homecoming to my epistle. He strode into the library, looking robust and a bit tousled in his riding attire, and bestowed a kiss to my cheek before wrestling once again with the squeaky window.

"Good morning, *mo chridhe gràdhach.*" He wrenched a second loudly protesting window open. "You might have a word with Mrs. Baird about these windows. Intimate that the footmen are lax and that the laird of the manor remarked it. She'll have the boot-boy in here with an oilcan before you can say, 'By Saint Andrew's cross.'"

My husband had referred to me as *his dear heart*, and with that passing endearment, the sun shone more brightly, and the birds chorusing beyond the windows sang more sweetly.

"MacRae will hate that."

Sebastian took a seat across from me at the reading table. "Precisely."

"You could simply tell MacRae you'll sack him if he doesn't do as I say."

Sebastian studied the molding, which like the great hall was decorated at intervals with shields and targes and other impedimenta of war. "Then I would be bound by my word to sack him if he's too stupid to cede the battle. He is the support of a good dozen youngsters and pensioners, and he's an otherwise fine butler. I can't think what's got into him."

Sebastian swiveled his gaze from the ancestral armaments to me. "Besides, you haven't asked me to intercede. I suspect our staff has been in revolt since I brought you here, but you haven't said a word until now."

I pretended to study my letter, a tale of mashed peas, embroidery, and the challenges of learning Gaelic.

"Violet?"

I rose and closed the library door. "You suspect correctly. At first, I was too tired and too fretful about Maeve to notice. The maids and footmen are all uniformly polite and helpful. They respond to direct orders with alacrity. It's the senior staff who have taken me into dislike."

Sebastian ambled over to the desk and picked up a stack of letters. I'd had occasion to admire the last of the sunset from my balcony the previous evening, and light flickering in the library windows had caught my eye.

"You sorted your mail last night?" I asked, resuming my seat at the reading table.

Sebastian took the place next to me and set a sizable pile of opened letters before us. "I did. Sooner begun is sooner done, which brings us to my house steward. Danny Duff was an understeward during the old marquess's time. His responsibilities have always included sorting the correspondence in my absence. He knows at a glance if a piece of mail is social, business, or something in between. This excuse of not intruding is rankest tripe."

"Or Mr. Duff was challenging me, tempting me to read your mail. A test of some sort." I did not care for that notion, but I did very much like Sebastian's scent. He favored a cedary, woodsy fragrance that at the moment was pleasantly blended with the aromas of horse and piney morning air.

"You are a great one for solving puzzles, Violet Marie. What's afoot in our castle?"

That question had been nagging at the back of my mind since I'd first noticed MacRae's intermittent hearing problems.

"Something other than spontaneous Scottish pigheadedness. Shall I send for a tray?"

Sebastian withdrew a pair of spectacles from an inside pocket of his riding jacket. "You don't mind that I've come straight from the stable? Annis acquitted herself wonderfully, by the way. I let her off the lead line for the last hundred yards, and you'd have thought she and Hannibal had been hacking the bridle paths for years."

"Any daughter of ours will be at home in the saddle. When did you start wearing glasses, my lord?"

He settled his spectacles on his nose. "Would you mind, very much, if we kept the my-lording for when we are in company?"

That was the second time he'd lodged that request.

The glasses revealed a scholarly air Sebastian usually kept hidden. As a boy, he'd been a voracious reader, the type to memorize poems simply because they sounded so lovely in the ear. He'd watched clouds with me by the hour and could quote whole scenes from Shakespeare's Scottish play.

And then he'd gone off to war, a rejected suitor who'd never consulted me regarding my feelings for him.

"Would you like a tea tray, *Sebastian*? Noon is some time off, and I'm a bit peckish myself." I was no longer constantly ravenous, as I had been when Maeve had first arrived. I doubtless owed my reduced appetite to gustatory glories of mashed peas.

He rose again and tugged the bell-pull three times. "Cannot have my lady wife peckish. She gets to starting arguments when she goes without her tucker for too long."

"You have correspondence to see to, sir. I advise you to be about it."

The boyish smile came again, muted, but just as sweet. I hoped he might kiss my cheek, but he settled in to his task and was hard at it ten minutes later when the tray arrived. I poured out, and Sebastian demolished sandwiches, tea cakes, shortbread, strawberries, and goat cheese.

My brothers could eat with the same focus, and Hugh St. Sevier had also enjoyed a very hearty appetite. Appetites, rather.

"What is that look about?" Sebastian said, placing the half-full bowl of strawberries before me. "You look amused and a little wistful. Are you homesick?"

I took a few little berries, feeling slightly guilty for my recollections and resentful of the guilt. "This is my home."

"This is the MacHeath family seat. Not quite the same thing when the staff is selectively deaf, dithering, and disrespectful."

"I'm managing."

Sebastian poured me a second cup of tea. "You managed with that lot of hooligans referred to as your brothers. You managed despite the titled reprobate who calls himself your father. You managed with the buffoon you were married off to. I want better than that for you, Violet."

He stirred in a dash and a dollop, just as I preferred my tea, and passed over the cup and saucer.

"It's early days," I said, the same reassurance I'd offered myself a thousand times. "The staff will give up, and twenty years on, I will still be your marchioness. Why did you leave, Sebastian?"

"I've told you. I wanted to give you room to breathe."

"You wanted to give yourself room to breathe." A shot in the dark.

He rose, and I had the thought that marriage to Sebastian would be vicariously tiring. He'd always been bristling with energy, both physical and intellectual, and once upon a time, I could have kept up with him.

Now? I nibbled strawberries and already knew, halfway through the morning, that this would be a nap day.

"I called on the St. Seviers several times before coming back north," Sebastian said. "They are managing splendidly, if fatuous looks and sweet French nothings signify. I hope that news doesn't upset you."

"To the contrary. They have been through much, and I wish them well." How did this figure into room to breathe?

Sebastian studied me as I studied my tea. "Ye mean that."

"I absolutely do." And to my surprise, that was the truth. I had had *such* plans for Hugh St. Sevier. When I'd completed second mourning, Hugh had wrested me from the grip of melancholia, or something very like it. I'd become unwilling to set foot in even my own dreary garden, and he had coaxed, teased, challenged, and forti-fied me enough that I had been able to put a sad and disturbing chapter of my life behind me.

We had become friends and lovers, and—eventually—an engaged couple. The progression had been gradual, stealing up on us both.

"Do you miss him?"

Once upon a time, I'd been able to tell Sebastian anything. I summoned my courage and hoped we'd make our way back to that place.

"I did miss him," I said slowly. "We'd become good companions. When you went off to Spain, I was cursed with loneliness. Felix went with you, and he is the brother I like best. My friends from school were getting married, and I had hoped Freddie might... In any case, Hugh was good company, and I was that for him."

Sebastian shined his glasses on his coat sleeve and held them up to the window light. "You haven't quite answered the question, Violet."

"I think of him," I said. "Not of him as I knew him, but of him and Ann and Fiona at Belle Terre, brangling with their neighbors, roaming that enchanted forest. I think of them and wish them well."

Sebastian returned his glasses to their perch on his nose. "Ann St. Sevier told me I was daft to leave you fending for yourself here in Perthshire. She all but saddled Hannibal for me and pointed him north. St. Sevier approved of her scold."

"How could you tell?"

"He told me to attempt to argue with his wife, please, because he did so enjoy the spectacle of another man making a fool of himself in such a regard. *Très amusant.*"

I could hear Hugh saying exactly that, the wry humor dancing in his eyes. "So you came north."

"Ashmore has been put to rights," Sebastian said, "at least by my standards. My marchioness might see it differently."

And exactly what had that... ah. What fool had hoped that honesty between Sebastian and me might be restored to its adolescent heights?

"Are asking me to take Maeve and dwell in England, Sebastian?"

The birds were still singing, the sunshine was still streaming through the windows, and the clock on the mantel was ticking away just as steadily as it had a quarter hour ago, but the morning had lost a great deal of its sweetness.

~

"Come," Sebastian said, rising and extending his hand to me.

I glowered up at him, and why did he have to be so majestically tall, anyway?

"Please," he said, letting his hand fall. "Please come with me as far as the sofa, Violet. Is that asking too much?"

"Yes," I retorted, keeping my seat, "if this discussion on the sofa is to be a sermon from you about fashionable couples these days, separate households, and an annual sighting of you in London for form's sake."

He ambled away to take the window seat. "Is that what you want?"

Half the library separated us, and that would not do when I was ready to lecture his lordship about holy matrimony, pride, and vows.

"I want a cordial, loyal, faithful union with you. A real marriage, not some fashionable exercise in civility. Did you have to see for yourself that the St. Seviers are no threat to us?" Even were Hugh and I still attracted to each other—which we were not, not *like that*—we were honorable people. Sebastian had to know that. "I would not play you false, Husband, and though I cannot speak for the man, I suspect Hugh is similarly loyal to Ann."

"Settle your feathers, Violet Marie." Sebastian patted the place beside him. "I am jealous of your Frenchman, but I am not a fool."

The admission surprised me enough that I joined Sebastian on the thin cushion of the window seat. "You have no cause for jealousy. Hugh is not *my* Frenchman. I saw for myself that he and Ann are getting on swimmingly. I doubt Fiona will be an only child."

"I don't want to talk about Hugh and Ann just now," Sebastian said, "but I don't want them to be a forbidden topic either. They deserve to know Maeve, and at some point, the whole situation will have to be explained to Fiona too."

"I had not thought that far." Though Sebastian was right. The girls were half-sisters. "Sweet powers, I need a nap."

"You were up with Maeve last night?"

"Every night, sometimes two or three times. Twice last night. She hasn't had a fussy night for some weeks, but Bevins says teething can turn the sweetest baby into a tyrant. Why are you jealous of St. Sevier? I've known you much longer, and in some senses, you know me better."

Not in the biblical sense, though Sebastian's focus at present did not seem to lie in that direction.

"He courted you," Sebastian said, retrieving the bowl of strawberries from the reading table. "Stood up with you at all the Mayfair gatherings, escorted you the length and breadth of the realm, waltzed with you, and strolled with you under the stars."

"You and I swam together under the stars, you daft man. St. Sevier escorted me out of pity at first. I was so... so... cowardly that I feared to leave my house. His interest was as medical as it was social."

"If you believe that, *mo chridhe gràdhach,* you've finally taken up the art of lying to yourself."

"St. Sevier's interest was kindly rather than amorous, then, and lying to oneself can be a necessary comfort."

Sebastian took the place next to me and held out the bowl of strawberries. I was still hungry, and the fruit was luscious, so I helped myself to more.

"A comfort? Such as when a penniless Scottish boy tells himself that his marital aspirations toward an earl's daughter have hope?"

"They did have hope. I would have married you gladly, Sebastian. Papa should not have interfered, and I have had the satisfaction of telling him that. Don't let me have all these strawberries."

He took a few. "I envy St. Sevier the time with you, Violet. The time haring about, the time socializing, the time when you confided in him because he was a physician or a friend or something in between, and I was... nursing a grudge and coming to terms with a title."

A man who wanted time with his wife did not decamp for parts hundreds of miles to the south, but then, Sebastian was right that Maeve and I had needed to find our balance.

"If you seek to consummate the marriage, Sebastian, I am prepared to accommodate that agenda." I managed this pronouncement without blushing, though I did find it necessary to study the berry stains on my fingers.

"I absolutely seek to consummate the marriage, ye wee besom, but not if that means we awkwardly accommodate some notion of duty or legal requirements. We make love if, as, and when we please to, but..."

Sebastian wasn't blushing either—I doubted he could blush—but he was staring off into the distance as if trying to recall some poetical quote lost to the mists of memory.

"But what?"

"But we need time and privacy, and while we might have the one here at the castle, I doubt we'll have the other."

I took his hand and dumped the last of the strawberries into his palm. I'd always loved Sebastian's hands. Capable, masculine, but also gentle when braiding a girl's hair or petting a cat.

"We cannot sack the whole staff, Sebastian, but we can banish the aunties to Clemmie's for the rest of the summer. Make a point to them that stealing mail and fomenting insurrection will not be tolerated."

"They're Scottish. Insurrection is their birthright. I had another solution in mind."

I put the empty bowl on the floor, unwilling to leave my perch beside my husband. The conversation—a little awkward, a lot honest —was also a comforting reprise of discussions we'd had in our youth. About biology, marriage, wagering, spirits, naughty songs... No topic had been beyond the pale for us then.

I'd even practiced my schoolgirl kisses on Sebastian, and he—ever gallant—had stoically consented to endure my experiments. I'd been so dangerously innocent, and he'd been so kind.

"How do we find time and privacy here, my—Sebastian? Even if we banish the aunties, there's still the staff, the neighbors panting to call upon you, the churchyard drill every Sunday... I had more privacy in the middle of London than I have in the wilds of Perthshire."

"I envied St. Sevier all the time he had to court you," Sebastian said. "I also envy him all the time he had you to himself."

"For your information, St. Sevier was oblivious to my charms until I all but threw myself at him. He claimed he was waiting for ideal circumstances or some such rot, but I disabused him of the notion that coyness was attractive or acceptable."

Sebastian took my hand and kissed my knuckles. "Did you now?

Told the poor laddie to get on with it or to pack his sweet nothings and dose himself with a few bottles of fine French brandy?"

"Something like that, but not... It's none of your business and has nothing to do with us."

Sebastian kept hold of my hand. "We have received an invitation to a house party in Kent. Mrs. Clothilda Gillespie was a friend of my mother's and particularly kind to Clemmie after Mama died. Mrs. Gillespie is something of a literary hostess, knows everybody—"

"I've met her," I said, picturing a statuesque blonde with a pretty smile and hearty laughter. "She's well liked, and her support would have smoothed Clemmie's way considerably. Are you inclined to attend, Sebastian?"

I had learned to appreciate house parties, for the social challenge they represented, the possibilities of new acquaintances, and the change of scene. I had solved the occasional mystery at such gatherings, and that, too, had been enjoyable.

One did want to be of use, after all.

"Clemmie would like us to attend, I'm sure," Sebastian said, stroking my knuckles absently. "We could take a packet from Edinburgh to Portsmouth, and Maeve seems to be a good traveler."

His tone was casual, as if he were considering these travel arrangements for the first time, but I knew the significance of that diffident tone when Sebastian used it.

"You want to travel with me, a baby, a mountain of luggage, and in the worst of the summer heat?"

He nudged the empty bowl with the toe of a dusty boot, and in my head, I heard what he was too shy to repeat: *You traveled the length and breadth of the realm with St. Sevier...*

"I certainly don't want to travel alone, Violet. Not again so soon."

He'd been traveling alone since his boyhood. The realization landed like a cuff to the back of my head.

"Kent is a long way off, Sebastian, and it's not far from Derwent Hall." My meddling family, in other words, but also my sisters-in-law and... the St. Seviers.

"I'm asking too much," Sebastian said. "Forgive me. It was a daft notion, and the castle is at its best in the summer. You were gracious enough to come all the way to Perthshire with a babe in arms, and I can't possibly expect that you'd want to travel again so soon."

I wanted what Sebastian wanted: time and privacy with my spouse, a chance to get our marriage off on the footing of our choosing—to get *our family* off on the footing of our choosing.

"You are right," I said slowly. "You ask a lot, and the traveling might well be tedious, but if you are asking me whether I want to bide here in the midst of a domestic rebellion or sail back to England with you, I prefer the prospect of a holiday with you."

"A holiday? We won't exactly be holidaying, Violet, but we'll be away from this place, and together. Is that what you want?"

"*I do.*" And it felt good to say what I wanted, to be *asked* what I wanted. "I will need some time to pack, to tend to my wardrobe, and to convince Bevins to join us, but I do want to attend this house party with you. We can enjoy a respite at Ashmore and pop up to London for some shopping. My wardrobe hasn't had much attention in recent years."

Sebastian enveloped my hand in both of his. "Then we're as good as there. Hannibal's a good sailor, and I've always enjoyed time on the water myself. I'll send an acceptance, though we don't have to leave for another week."

He badly wanted to go and had barely let me see any of that. "Annis will enjoy the journey too," I said, "though we probably can't expect Mrs. Yancy to be half as enthusiastic. She might well sail south with us and then give notice."

And that might be a good thing all around, given what I'd observed of her governessing thus far.

Sebastian withdrew his hands. "Annis? You want to bring Annis with us? Have fairies stolen your wits, Violet Marie?"

CHAPTER FOUR

Sebastian

I had loved Violet Marie Deerfield from the moment she'd informed me that I occupied *her* tree on *her* papa's land. She'd been all big blue eyes and indignation, and when I'd invited her to join me—taunted her, more like—she'd scampered up the tree as nimbly as a cat.

She'd been as wary as a cat, too, but also fair-minded enough to actually *listen* to what a homesick Scottish boy thought about the Irish question, raspberries, and crop rotation. Her own views were surprisingly well thought out, and she had been ferociously articulate when defending them.

From time to time, she'd also been ferocious about defending me. On the occasion of our reunion after my time in Spain, Violet had been all that had stood between my valet, Upjohn, and a noose he had not deserved.

My wife was a woman of strong principles. She had declared that we were to have a real marriage, and that meant my own marital aspirations had hope—though not if the Terror of Castle MacHeath came with us on our journey.

"Annis might have sad associations with sailing," I said, scrabbling about for credible excuses to leave a dramatic, moody child out of our travel plans. The plain truth was, I wanted Violet to myself. I could not ask her to part from Maeve—not and preserve any hope of cordial relations with my spouse—but Annis was another matter.

"Was she inconsolable when you took her from Spain?" Violet asked, all limpid concern.

"She was ravenous and wanted nothing more than to soak in a steaming tub of bubbles for the whole journey, eating like an infantry recruit even as she pickled her fingers and toes. I could not oblige her whims, and she grew cross—very loudly cross."

The memory amused now—the sprite bellowing away in Spanish to one of His Majesty's duly commissioned officers about oranges and cheese and fresh cow's milk.

"Was Mrs. Yancy on board the same ship?"

"Aye, and she addressed Annis as I was accustomed to addressing recruits—the same tone, more ladylike vocabulary—and the result was astonishing. Annis apparently had had some contact with the Sisters of Saint Somebody, and she settled right down." *Temporarily.*

"The poor child was exhausted, Sebastian, in spirit as well as body. I'm so glad you brought her home with you." Violet took my hand, the first such occasion I could recall since our wedding. "I had wondered what exactly Mrs. Yancy's credentials as a governess are. She is not exactly creative about Annis's curriculum."

I mentally kicked myself, because I had not foreseen that Violet would become an advocate for Annis. That eventuality should have presented itself to me as a foregone conclusion, given that Violet herself had been the odd sibling out at Derwent Hall.

"Mrs. Yancy is patient, and she speaks Spanish. Those qualities recommended her highly at the time. I'm sure she'd agree that Annis will be better off enjoying her summer at the castle rather than racketing around with us."

Violet rose and took the empty strawberry bowl back to the tray on the reading table. "If I, as your wife and a reasoning adult, felt abandoned when you took a notion to travel south, how do you think Annis has felt during your frequent, protracted absences?"

Nobody could wield logic with more ruthlessness than Violet. I had never thought of her as Violet Belmaine, and I was having a similarly difficult time applying the title Lady Dunkeld to her. She was simply Violet—my Violet, I hoped.

"Annis has objected strongly to my absences, and she admonishes me without limit in her letters that I must come home. She has to learn that she does not call the tune and that I *always* come home. Traveling to my other holdings is not abandoning her."

I felt a fool, being jealous of a child, but Violet did not know how disruptive Annis could be. The girl had a genius for hiding in impossible places and for making up wild tales designed to elicit the sympathies of strangers.

I rose from the window seat and came around the reading table. Violet was gathering up her writing implements and stowing them in a lap desk that bore the Earl of Derwent's family crest. She had doubtless written many a letter to me on that lap desk, some of them recently.

"Trust me on this, Violet. We all will be better off if Annis is allowed to remain in Scotland." I honestly believed this, though I knew Annis would disagree with me in three languages and at the highest possible volume.

"Do you suppose," Violet mused with suspicious sweetness, "that your parents told themselves something similar, that young Sebastian was truly better off hundreds of miles away in Kent, surrounded by only English tutors, English staff, and English neighbors? No summers home in Scotland—the tail didn't wag the dog, the child should not call the tune, of course —and his homesickness would only grow worse for being reminded of all he missed. No Gaelic speakers for him to chat with, even in the stable. That was all for the best, though, clearly."

I knew what was coming next, and yet, I had to make one last effort to forestall disaster. "Annis isn't me, and she isn't you. This is her home. She barely remembers Spain, and that's a mercy."

Violet closed the writing desk with a snap of the latch. "Perhaps it's a mercy we're having this discussion now rather than the day before we're scheduled to depart for Edinburgh. You know what it is to be a pawn in adult schemes, Sebastian. You know the hopelessness and frustration, and so do I. You married me in part because your resentment of the Dunkeld title and all it cost you as a boy is so great that you would not have begrudged another man's child the inheritance of the marquessate. Maybe you were even hoping that Maeve would be a boy."

What flight of female illogic was this? "I *hoped* Maeve would be a healthy baby and that you would come through your travail unscathed. My prayers in that regard have so far been answered."

A younger Violet would have come back at me with some flaming arrow of a retort, but my wife regarded me with a chilling degree of detachment.

"Annis comes with us, or Maeve and I will stay here at the castle with her. Gallivant around the house parties, Sebastian, put it about that motherhood is taking a toll on me—because it is—but Maeve and Annis are to be siblings. If we distinguish between them now, they will take their cue from us, and that harm cannot be undone by fancy bonnets or ponies or other bribes. When we are old and gray—when we are *dead*—the wound we deal them now will still cause pain."

I'd left two cheese sandwiches on the tray in case Violet's appetite had run in that direction. She'd chosen beef instead and half an orange. I wanted to resume snacking, to take up again scrubbing at the Aegean stables of my correspondence, to brush off this difference of opinion as so much marital noise.

I could not, because Violet had raised a point I'd overlooked. I'd been banished to England, and Clemmie and I had become fiercely devoted correspondents as a result. We were still close, despite all the distance that had been imposed between us.

Violet's brothers, by contrast, had excluded her from every

activity that protocol and convention hadn't already foreclosed her from, and they had done so with their father's tacit assent. They had not needed a fifth at cards, rowing, hacking out, in their amateur parlor dramas, or in holiday pranking.

The two middle brothers—Hector and Ajax—had ridiculed Violet behind her back, mimicked her, and teased her without mercy, behavior I had not understood at the time and still recalled with disgust. Derwent, if he had known of it, hadn't intervened.

"Is this my punishment for journeying to England this spring?" I asked, trying not to sound like an arrogant fool.

"My decision is based on what I believe is best for our children, Sebastian. You and I haven't had a wedding journey, and I'd hoped... Well, never mind that. Annis has adjusted fairly well to a baby in the nursery, all things considered, but if you leave her behind now, we will all regret it."

I had regrets already where Violet was concerned. I should not have asked for her father's permission to court her. I should have consulted Violet, and Violet alone, and charted my course according to her feelings for me. Without the title and its wealth, my path to wooing her would have been long and arduous, but I'd have trod it gladly if I'd known I had her blessing.

I'd bungled instead, trying to observe English courting protocol to the letter and getting laughed to scorn—to Spain, rather—by Lord Derwent.

Then I had bungled further, and without Derwent's aid. I should have renewed a cordial acquaintance with Violet during her marriage to Belmaine—she had needed allies and had had none. Clemmie had known that much. I'd been too arrogant and too busy preventing my uncle from destroying my birthright to swallow my pride where Violet was concerned.

I should not have deposited Violet and Maeve at the castle earlier in the year and jaunted off to England again, but that maneuver had been in defense of my masculine sanity.

"You have made up your mind on this?" I asked.

She collected a tea cake from the tray. "I have. I'm off to the nursery. I'll see you at luncheon, and good luck with the correspondence."

She smiled a convincingly genial smile, and a riot of emotions coursed through me. Grief, because the ability to cast off a disagreement and soldier on was a skill Violet had acquired in a hard school. She'd given up some sort of innocence in the years when she'd been lost to me, and that broke my heart.

Damn Freddie Belmaine to the loneliest corner of the pit.

As Violet munched her tea cake, I also felt the frustration of a man whose romantic plans had been thwarted—again—by pragmatic concerns. Violet was right, and our daughters would benefit from their mother's wisdom.

And I felt admiration for my wife. She'd once upon a time been desperate for approval and acceptance from the men in her life. Violet walked her own path now, and damned be to any husband who disrespected her choices.

"I concede to your reasoning," I said. "Annis comes with us, as does Mrs. Yancy if she's willing. I'd like to leave a week from tomorrow, if you can manage it."

Violet dusted her hands over the tray. "Thank you, Sebastian. We will have a wonderful adventure, and you will not regret traveling with all your ladies. Say the word, and I will be ready to depart by nightfall."

She kissed my cheek, swiped another tea cake, and sashayed from the library with her traveling desk under her arm.

I resumed my place at the reading table, idly finishing off the food on the tray and staring at a bill from the chandler in Perth. I was uncertain what had just transpired between my wife and me, but the lady had kissed my cheek in parting, and that was cause for rejoicing.

~

I spent the morning and half the afternoon battling the forces of epistolary chaos and had a sizable stack of letters, memoranda to

Duff, and completed bank drafts to show for my heroics. Also a sore backside, the result of sitting for too long after traveling too far.

Aunt Hibernia stuck her head in the door just as I decided I was entitled to ramble some damn where that involved fresh air, beautiful scenery, and solitude.

"There you are!" she said, bustling forward. "One did wonder if the fairies hadn't made off with you. I looked for you in the laird's study and in your apartment, and here you are hiding in plain sight." She eyed the stacks of correspondence. "Coming home is such sweet sorrow, isn't it?"

"I am overjoyed to be home, Aunt, though I will have some very stern words for Danny Duff. I've never known him to be negligent in his duties before."

That was a warning shot, and a slight dimming of Aunt's good cheer suggested she took it as such. "Spring is a busy time, Sebastian, especially for stewards. You must not judge him too harshly when he had so little notice of your planned departure. Mags and I are off to call upon the MacKellans and are hoping you will escort us. Fanny is such a dear girl and always such pleasant company."

Fanny MacKellan, née MacPherson, had attended a posh finishing school with Violet—another Scot banished to the south for the sake of social advancement. I liked Fanny and got on well with Iain, her taciturn, hardworking husband. The previous year, Violet had come north to attend Fanny's nuptials, though the occasion had become complicated by intrigue. Violet and—it must be said—St. Sevier had sorted out the secrets, aided to a modest degree by myself.

The timing of that visit was such that I could credibly claim to be Maeve's father in a biological sense, which would matter once the gossips set to work.

"You don't need an escort, Hibernia, and Danny Duff does need a serious dressing down."

Something furtive flitted through her faded blue eyes. "You can scold him when we get back, though good stewards do not grow on trees. Come as you are. The MacKellans don't stand on ceremony."

Our nearest neighbors were blessedly informal. They worked hard to keep a rambling old pile from crumbling into the River Tay and worked even harder at a fledging whisky export business. I had considered letting Iain handle commercial sales of my own inventory and wanted to open that discussion with him in person.

"I'd rather change into proper morning attire," I said, mostly to needle my aunt. She was up to something, but then, the aunties were always up to something.

"You'll take half the afternoon primping, and that will not serve. Put on a fresh cravat like all the fribbles do, and let's be on our way. I vow you are turning into your uncle."

For Hibernia, that came near to insulting me, suggesting she was desperate to get me off the property.

"Uncle cared nothing for fashion. Give me a quarter hour, and I will meet you out front. Oh, and I have an invitation to a house party hosted by Mrs. Clothilda Gillespie. Is that Clemmie's doing?"

"Tilda Gillespie was an honorary fairy godmother to our Clemmie, Sebastian. Is it so unusual that Tilda would invite you south? You *do* have a title after all, and you cut a fetching figure in your kilt."

To the bottom of the North Sea with my kilt. "Why don't I ever hear of a Mr. Gillespie?"

"Because he's a quiet sort. Nathan Gillespie doesn't intrude on his wife's affairs, as it were. In their way, they are devoted, but the money came from her side of the family. He manages the wealth, of course, but the whole social whirl that Tilda thrives on was never of much interest to him. Very down-to-earth fellow. You'll like him. He's conscientious and responsible and doesn't involve himself in politics."

Mr. Gillespie sounded like all that was dull and respectable about English gentry, and at that moment, I did not like my aunt.

"They have a daughter." An unmarried daughter, as best I recalled. "Aunt, what were you thinking? I am the husband of a woman whom I have esteemed for more than half my life. Tossing heiresses at me now makes no sense."

"Heiresses are not cabers, Sebastian. Really, how you do go on sometimes. Dorothy Gillespie is a lovely girl, and house parties are where lovely girls learn to be lovely, confident girls. She has no siblings, nobody on hand her own age save some ward of Nathan's and a lot of Kentish yokels. A marquess is a feather in any hostess's cap, and the MacHeaths owe Tilda for her kindness to Clemmie. Do the decent thing and grace Tilda's gathering with your presence."

"And you would have me believe this is Clemmie's doing?"

Aunt treated me to a frowning perusal, which was rather like being inspected by one of her cats. "Honestly, Sebastian. Mags and I despair of you sometimes."

The scold fell flat. I was no longer that homesick boy, desperate for any word from home. My aunts had been faithful, if dull, correspondents, and they had been part of the reason why the castle had run smoothly during my uncle's decline.

Uncle's much younger wife had promptly decamped upon his death. The only place gloomier than a Highland castle was a Highland castle in mourning, according to the dowager marchioness. She was said to be frittering away her enormous funds on the Continent, and I wished her the well-earned joy of her frolics.

"Fifteen minutes," Aunt called as she quit the library. "Not one second more."

I made my way not to my apartment, but to Violet's. I found her drowsing on the bed and realized with some trepidation that I had not only an opportunity, but also the right to join her there.

"Come in," she said, sitting up. "Is it the children? What could possibly bring you *here* at this hour? Sebastian, what's amiss?"

"Nothing," I said, unless pounding desire for this tousled, rosy, barely dressed version of my wife could be considered *amiss*. "I am off with the aunts to call on Fanny and Iain MacKellan. Shall you come with us?"

Violet knuckled her eyes and glanced at the curtain flapping gently in the summer breeze. "What time is it?"

"Going on three."

"I've slept more than an hour. Ye perishing..." She flipped the covers back with the same air of determination any soldier displayed when the bugler sounded "Boots and Saddles."

"Violet... no." I took the place at her hip, which made the bed dip. "If you need more rest, then rest. You can jaunt down the hill to see Fanny tomorrow, and I will happily go with you."

She had dark half circles under her eyes, which hadn't been there in the morning. Or perhaps they had, and I hadn't noticed.

"The aunties planned this outing for when I was napping, Sebastian. What the hell are they up to?" Violet was not generally inclined to profanity, but she was clearly learning new vocabulary as a mother.

"I suspect you are right. They sought to drag me along, and you'd learn at supper that I'd gone calling without you."

She flopped back against the pillows. "Which you will. I feel as if I could sleep for a week, though I mustn't. What brings you to my bedroom, Husband?"

Arrant foolishness, now that I beheld my darling Violet abed. "I wasn't about to fall in with any scheme that could be interpreted as snubbing my wife, but I want to talk whisky with Iain—in person and, I hope, in private. I'm sorry I disturbed you." I meant to get off the bed before I did something truly clodpated, like start kissing my wife, but Violet seized me in a hug.

"Thank you, Sebastian."

I allowed myself to stroke her hair, twice. "For?"

"For asking me if I'd like to come with you." She let me go and shoved my arm. "Be off with you. My regards to Fanny, and I will call on her before we leave for Edinburgh. See you at supper."

"At supper, then." I risked a kiss to her cheek and then blew retreat. A hug and kiss were progress, and that progress had apparently resulted simply because I'd asked Violet to accompany me on a call.

We were on the path to the happy marriage Violet and I both apparently wanted. I took my time washing up and changing into morning attire and kept the aunties waiting for a good thirty minutes.

~

"Fanny says if the customer has a choice of products, they're more likely to buy from you than if you can offer only the one whisky." Iain MacKellan ambled along the graveled walk of his walled garden, as unwilling as I to sit idly by the teapot with the ladies. "My Fan is a shrewd woman, though you don't realize it for all her sweetness."

He spoke in Gaelic as he cut a late rose and affixed it to his lapel. Had anybody told me a year ago that Iain MacKellan would willingly adorn himself with a delicate pink flower, I would have scoffed. He began to gather more roses, a careful undertaking, given their myriad tiny thorns.

I'd known Iain for years, while he'd served as the unpaid estate manager, poor relation, and general factotum on his wife's property. He had, in fact, held the property together and even made it prosper while Fanny's step-father had meddled, criticized, and swaggered about as the ineffectual laird of the manor.

Iain was a hard worker and also, apparently, a man besotted. He wasn't quite strutting along the walkway in his kilt, but he did move purposefully to the lavender border and add a few sprigs to his roses.

"Might you have a use for a few bottles of MacHeath's?" I asked.

"Aye. Fan was on about making cordials—something for the ladies —in addition to the whisky, but the ladies don't frequent the clubs and pubs where the whisky is most likely to sell. I'm happy to offer the cordials, but I don't expect to sell much of them."

"Selling whisky to the English strikes me as a thankless job. They generally regard the water of life as little better than gin."

"And they drink oceans of gin," Iain said, rolling a lavender bud between his fingers and releasing a rich aroma. "The difficulty is that we're aiming between, ye see. Between the gin and the brandy, a step above the ale, a step aside from the Continental wines. An adventure and an indulgence—and just a wee bit of wildness too."

Since I'd known him, I had not heard Iain MacKellan rhapsodize about anything other than a plow horse's stamina, though in his defense, aged MacKellan whisky was worthy of his panegyric.

"Marriage agrees with you." An understatement, but Iain was shy, and one did not want to embarrass one's host.

He gestured to a bench and reposed himself upon it, his somewhat lopsided bouquet of a piece with craggy features, a stern countenance, and callused hands.

"Marriage will be the making of me, Dunkeld. I will always do my job to the best of my ability, but for Fan and the wean, I will exert myself to the utmost. She's bloomed in the last year. She smiles at nothing, and when I see her with our baby... You must think me daft."

I took the place beside him and let the peace and beauty of the garden have its moment. A tiered fountain at the intersection of the walkways trickled gently, and the summer air was redolent of earth and blossoms.

"I think you happy, MacKellan, and it's about damned time."

Iain took a whiff of his bouquet and made a futile attempt to impose some symmetry upon it. "Fan wants another baby, but I'm telling her to be patient. A woman's health can be delicate."

We had always been friends of a sort, but it dawned on me that we were now two young married fellows, and that created a fraternity both peculiar and fascinating.

"Are you warning me to leave my marchioness in peace for the nonce, MacKellan?"

Iain began cutting the stems of his flowers with his folding knife. He was careful to let the trimmings fall to his lap rather than to the gravel walkway, and he cut at a slant, something Fanny had likely taught him.

"Your marchioness strikes me as a lady who can do her own warning, Dunkeld. Fan has loved having a dear friend up the hill, and we do see her ladyship fairly often."

"What of the aunties?"

He gathered up the detritus on his lap and tossed it into the border behind our bench. "They do their regular patrols."

"And?"

He passed me his bouquet, rose, and shook out his kilt, then plucked the flowers from my hand.

"They damn your marchioness with faint praise, Dunkeld. 'Lady Violet means well, but she hasn't the energy to take on the running of a castle just yet. New babies can be so exhausting.' Or, 'Violet needs time to grasp how a Scottish household functions. She canna help that's she's so blessed English.' Fan says that's rot. You've good help in the nursery, and Lady Violet could manage Windsor Castle if she'd a mind to. Did you cut yourself?"

A thorn had bitten me as MacKellan had appropriated his bouquet. I wrapped a handkerchief around my bleeding finger.

"It's nothing, and I agree with you. Violet could run Windsor Castle blindfolded, with one hand while serving tea with the other." We resumed our perambulations, moving in the direction of the house.

"Why'd you scamper off to London if you think so highly of her ladyship?"

"Kent. I have properties in Kent."

"You have a damned pretty wife in Perthshire."

Violet was not only pretty, she was smart, loyal, had a fine sense of humor, and had stolen my heart years ago.

"She needed time with our daughter."

Iain was among the few who knew exactly who had been sleeping with whom at the time of Maeve's conception. He'd support any fiction Violet and I cared to put forth, as would Fanny and the whole shire.

"Dunkeld, if you claim the child as your own, why desert your wife when she dearly needs you?"

I had no answer for him. Desire had figured in my flight, but so had... uncertainty. I shied away from the word *cowardice*, though it might apply.

"I needed sorting out, and Maeve is my daughter. Make no mistake about that."

"You've a talent for acquiring daughters without the usual preliminaries, apparently. I'd best put these in water, and—"

He stopped as the ladies emerged from the house, Fanny flanked by the two aunties. She was an elfin woman made beautiful by joy. Her strawberry-blond hair, spritely gait, and pale blue attire contrasted with the aunties' dark colors and careful descent of the steps.

"Iain, my darling," she called, striding along the walk. "Did you pick those for me?"

"Aye. The thorns were too small to trim, so you'll not be handling them."

"I'll kiss you," she said, suiting deed to words, "for your thoughtfulness. Did you and Dunkeld plan your domination of the London whisky market?"

"London, among its many other shortcomings, has no whisky market to dominate, my dear."

"Yet," she said, beaming up at him. "Dunkeld, are you through neglecting your wife? Violet has been stoically loyal in your absence, would not hear a word against you, but strand her in the castle again like that, and you and I will come to blows."

"Violet is loyal," Aunt Mags said, as if conceding a minor point to an unworthy debating partner.

"She had better be," Aunt Bernie added darkly.

I was unwilling to let that pass, not before neighbors. "Mind your tongue, Hibernia, and your tone, and recall that I am loyal to my wife and daughters."

A look passed between Fanny and Iain, one decipherable only to them.

"I mean her ladyship no disrespect," Bernie countered, "and we really must be getting back to the castle. Fanny, a pleasure as always. Iain, you'll want to put that bouquet in water. Come, Mags. You too, Sebastian."

The ladies went into the sort of flutters necessitated by friendly farewells while Iain walked me to the coach.

"So are you all sorted out now?" Iain asked. "Did retreating to Kent work the desired miracle?"

I wanted to smack him, but the inquiry was meant kindly—and a little bit to annoy me. "I'm a work in progress."

Iain glanced over his shoulder at the ladies, fussing and hugging one another. "Don't drag your feet, Dunkeld. Life is short, and if your marchioness has no use for you, deal with that and get on as best you can. You married her fully aware of her circumstances, and she married you when she could doubtless have found some prancing younger son to do the pretty."

"Fix bayonets and charge?"

"Pick her a damned bouquet and leave it on her pillow. Memorize some of Walter Scott's drivel, or if ye can't stomach that, Burns will do. Tell her your dreams, and when she tells you hers, *listen* to her. Must I make you a list?"

Iain MacKellan dispensing advice to the lovelorn. Next, unicorns would come waltzing out of the woods.

"I listen to her."

He shook his head as Fanny and the aunts came along the walkway arm in arm. "No, you don't. You nod politely and smile at the appropriate moments, all the while wondering if you can drain some wetland and put the acreage in wheat, or whether that will just create a bog in the next field."

I had created a bog—that was a problem. "My wife did not marry me because she was madly in love with me, MacKellan. I was a known quantity, of suitable rank, and we were friendly in our youth."

He shoved me stoutly on the shoulder. "And such a doddering old mon you are now."

I disdained to shove him back, though I did return his smile. "Wish me luck."

"You don't need luck. You're in love, and love conquers all."

On that patently silly note, we took our leave. The aunties, united in disapproval of me for shaming Hibernia in public, held a lovely silence on the forward-facing seat. I handed them down in the castle courtyard and got more wordless disdain in return for my good manners.

The coach clattered off to the carriage house, and I turned my steps for the gardens.

"And where are you off to?" Aunt Mags asked.

"I've business to see to. Until supper, ladies." I bowed and walked away while they doubtless glared daggers at my back.

"What business?" Bernie bellowed.

I waved a hand without turning. What I was about was none of *their* business, and the sooner they learned to cease their meddling, the more likely they were to escape banishment to some dower property in Glasgow.

An undergardener, a sturdy, towheaded MacRae nephew traveling under the Gibson banner, met me as I ambled along a rainbow border of towering hollyhocks.

"My lord, good day." He greeted me cheerfully, though the Marquesses of Dunkeld were not known for wandering among the posies, and Gibson's eyes betrayed a hint of wariness.

I took out my folding knife. "I need a bouquet," I said, "and I must gather it myself. Not too dramatic, a pleasant scent, and pleasing symbolism, but nothing too... too..."

"Sentimental?"

I inspected the hollyhocks most thoroughly. "Aye. Nothing too sentimental." Violet was not, after all, a sentimental woman.

"Lavender is for devotion," Gibson said, studying the opposite border. "We've plenty of that. Keeps the bugs away, good for healing wounds. Cut all the lavender you like, sir."

"What do pink roses symbolize?"

He looked at me curiously. "Getting late for roses, but we do have some along the south wall. The pink is for appreciation, gratitude. 'Thank you,' but more genteel."

"Then pink roses and lavender will do." I marched off on my quest, silently thanking MacKellan for his example and reminding myself to trim off the thorns, no matter how small.

CHAPTER FIVE

Violet

"You were quiet at supper, *mo chridhe*. Are you weary of the aunties' rudeness?" Sebastian posed his question with studied casualness.

In truth, I'd been all but silent over a long and tedious meal.

We ascended the main staircase after having endured a final pot of tea with Hibernia and Maighread. I'd poured out, allowed the aunties to chatter, and watched the hands of the clock remain all but frozen for multiple eternities.

"I am weary," I replied. "I well know how to prepare for a journey, but I've never had to figure a small child into those preparations before. Lucy is very pleased we're returning to England."

Lucy, my bulldog-cum-guardian-angel of a lady's maid, was very pleased that Upjohn, Sebastian's valet, would be traveling to England with us.

"Why were you so remote at supper, Violet? Not merely remote, withdrawn, preoccupied, almost as if you've already climbed into a mental coach and quit the castle."

I paused outside the nursery suite door and regarded my husband in the gloom of the corridor. He'd always been a noticing fellow, annoyingly so at times, but this was not one of them.

"I found three of your letters."

"I wrote you many more than three letters."

"Almost all of them sterling examples of how to bore a lady with the written word, when I know you to be a gifted correspondent. Come in. The situation wants discussion, and we'll have privacy here."

I ducked into the nursery, and Sebastian followed. We were seldom in these rooms at the same time, which struck me as sad.

"Bevins," I said to the yawning nurserymaid, "I'll put Maeve down when we're finished. You can pay a visit to the kitchen and then turn in. Is Annis asleep?"

"Aye, milady," Bevins replied. "Mrs. Yancy fair wore the child out with packing and repacking her little satchel. Lord help us if anything happens to that Bella."

Bella had once been a stuffed cat and, according to Mrs. Yancy, Annis's sole possession when Sebastian had come upon the child in Spain, other than a pathetically thin, filthy dress. He hadn't had the heart to pitch the wad of rags into the sea, and Mrs. Yancy hadn't had the skills to restore Bella to a recognizable feline form.

"Bella will come to no harm," I said, scooping Maeve up from a blanket on the floor. My back, after sitting at the table for so long, protested the movement. "Make your farewells in the servants' hall when you're belowstairs. We leave at first light."

While I situated myself with Maeve in a rocking chair, Sebastian blew out the candelabra on the mantel and went to the doorway that led to Annis's bedroom. He was accommodating my modesty, though after months of nursing my baby, I ought not to have any modesty left.

I did, though. Heaps of it. I arranged a shawl over Maeve, opened my bodice, and covered up more carefully than the situation warranted.

"Annis is asleep," Sebastian said, taking the second rocker. "she has Bella clutched about the neck and half squashed beneath her. Tell me about these letters you've found."

I appreciated that he'd get straight to business. "Two mentioned books you thought I might enjoy and also stated that you missed me and kept me in your prayers. The third informed me of your planned return."

"And?"

"And I found them tucked at the bottom of Hibernia's workbasket. I lent her a thimble that my aunt Florence gave me when I went away to finishing school. I sought to retrieve my possession and came upon the purloined letters."

Sebastian said something in Gaelic about *the bottom of the loch.* "They are banished," he went on, rising to pace before the dying fire. "The pair of them. I understand they're worried about what passes for their consequence in this household now that I've married, but thievery and mischief are inexcusable."

He'd kept his voice down, the natural instinct of a man attuned to the presence of children.

"You can't banish them just yet, Sebastian. We are leaving for Edinburgh in a few hours, and Clemmie deserves notice before we foist them off on her. If you think to establish the aunts in Glasgow or Edinburgh, a household will have to be prepared for them."

"I'll establish them on Hirta, and they can manage in a goatherd's hut."

"Hirta?"

"An island off the Outer Hebrides. Why in the world...?" He dropped back into the second rocker and scrubbed a hand over a tired face. "I cannot tolerate this, Violet. They've come between husband and wife, and we've troubles enough without their damned mischief. *We* cannot tolerate this."

We did not have troubles, not truly. We had a bit of understandable awkwardness. Some challenges.

"I have considered the evidence, Sebastian, and I doubt they were trying to come between us."

He closed his eyes and leaned his head against the back of the rocker. "Explain. Please, explain."

The Marquess of Dunkeld had a patrician profile, complete with a slightly aquiline nose. In contrast to a jaw sculpted of determination, the dark hair curling over his forehead was silky, a trifle unkempt, and... tempting.

"What if the aunties were trying to reunite us?"

He opened his eyes and swung his gaze on me. "We aren't at daggers drawn, Violet Marie. I have missed you and believe you are glad to see me as well, or do I mistake the matter?"

A loch full of banked pride lay behind that question. "You do not mistake the matter, but if the aunties believed we were out of charity with each other, they might have hoped I'd summon you home when I faced untenable domestic opposition."

He rubbed his forehead, a certain sign that a headache stalked him. "Apologies, my lady, but given the lateness of the hour and the deviousness of my near relations, my powers of divination are not equal to the puzzle. What exactly was that pair up to?"

The very question I'd been asking myself for half the day. "If I am correct, they wanted me to send for reinforcements. They put the staff up to disrespecting me, let the neighbors think ill of me, and subjected me to petty slights all in the hope that I would demand that you return home and set all to rights."

He looked skeptical but intrigued. "I did return home."

"Not at my request. If they read your letters to me, they likely read mine to you, and for that disrespect, I can second your motion regarding Hirta." My letters had been superficial and reserved, thank heavens, but they were still my private correspondence to *my husband*. As a girl, I had poured out my heart to Sebastian in any number of epistles while he'd been off at university, or while I'd been doing penance at Miss Harmon's Academy.

I'd resisted the temptation to pen dreams and wishes now that we were married, but in another few weeks, who could say what confidences I might have included with my weather reports?

I busied myself switching Maeve to the second breast, an awkward undertaking, given that I was manipulating matters beneath a shawl that must not slip.

"She has a good appetite?" Sebastian asked, staring at his boots.

"She has a good appetite, and she's a sound sleeper. Bevins says Maeve is a saint among babies. Mashed peas seem to have resulted in less interest in what I have to offer, and Bevins is agitating to try some thin porridge."

"And you're... recovering well?"

Gracious days. Maeve was nearly half a year old, but the question was relevant. I was still recovering—from the birth, from the onset of motherhood, from speaking my wedding vows.

"I am in excellent health. You'll allow the aunties to stay?"

"I don't know. Your theory, that they were backing you into a corner so you'd summon the watch, makes some sense, but if so, why didn't they cease annoying you once it became apparent you would not yield to their tactics?"

"They were barely getting started, Sebastian."

He frowned at the fire. "You say this went on for months."

And he, a seasoned soldier, expected battles to be over in a matter of hours. Sieges might last several weeks, and they were a hated ordeal. The notion that a household could be a battlefield for decades was foreign to his experience.

"Freddie's staff tested my resolve for two years, and then they offered a truce, not an alliance, because Freddie's behavior exceeded even their indulgent standards for the head of the household." The morning after we'd returned from our wedding journey, the pot of tea at Freddie's end of the table had been swaddled in linen. The one at my elbow had not—by no means an oversight—and my marriage had thus begun with a symbolically tepid cup of tea.

Sebastian had never heard that story, and I hoped he never would.

"Hibernia led the neighbors to believe you are some die-away English rose who can't be bothered to manage her own household."

This offended Sebastian on my behalf, and maybe on his own. "They spoke disparagingly of me only to Fanny and Iain, and of all the neighbors, the MacKellans are the only ones who would take issue with such gossip. Fanny brought that tale straight to me the first time Hibernia aired it. The aunties were trying to rile me."

"They've riled me."

And whatever his other faults, Sebastian was slow to anger.

"I would like to give them the benefit of the doubt and a stern warning. If they ever tamper with the mail again, you are free to banish them to wherever you please, but this once, I will assume they meant well and took desperate measures."

Sebastian rose and muttered something.

"I beg your pardon?" Beneath the shawl, Maeve let my nipple slip from her mouth on a contented sigh.

"I said, 'Not desperate enough.' If the ghost of Butcher Cumberland himself had begun stalking the halls, you'd have contended with him on your own, wouldn't you?"

"What *are* you going on about?" I could not manage the baby, do up my bodice, and keep the shawl from slipping, though I tried.

"Violet Marie MacHeath... for the love of good whisky." Sebastian extracted Maeve from my grasp, and while my wares were not exactly on display, his hand brushed my sternum. Another couple—besotted or even merely fond—would have made nothing of such a moment, but for me, the occasion was awkward.

"I've gone swimming with you when you wore only your shift," Sebastian said, putting Maeve to his shoulder. "As a lad, I heard about your female bodily woes until I wanted to clap my hands over my ears while belting 'Scots Wha Hae' at the top of my lungs. I walked the length and breadth of Ashmore with you when the birth pangs began, and you did not spare my blushes with your commentary when Maeve grew intent on arriving."

"I don't make a habit of sparing your blushes in the general case." I passed him a piece of toweling, which he arranged on his shoulder as if he'd been burping babies for years.

He patted Maeve's little back ever so gently as he made a circuit of the nursery. "Do you know why I went south, Violet? Back to the scene of my own banishment?"

I finished doing up what needed doing up and rose from the rocking chair. "You've said you went to England to give me time to get acquainted with Maeve." And in Sebastian's absence, I had become well acquainted with both Maeve and Annis. I had healed from the birth and begun to adjust to the exalted, exhausting office of motherhood.

The status of marchioness had yet to become real to me.

Maeve let go with a tiny eructation. Sebastian smiled at her and kissed her temple as his patting turned to slow circles.

"I went south because I didn't know what else to do," he said as he halted before the fire and took up a slow swaying in rhythm with the movements of his hand. "Both St. Sevier and his wife admonished me in blunt terms to leave you in peace for at least three months following the birth. Not pestering you was easier if I was hundreds of miles away."

The St. Seviers had, on separate occasions, delivered the same lecture to me, which might be amusing some distant day. For now, it was merely ironic.

"Is pestering me a delicate way to refer to marital intimacies?"

"Aye, but not only that. She's falling asleep."

"Give her another few minutes." I draped the shawl over Maeve and around Sebastian's broad shoulders. "She can make you think she's lost in slumber, but she's only having you on. Little wretch."

"Why didn't you send for me, Violet?"

Because you might not have come. "The problem wasn't yours to solve and, in the grand scheme of things, not much of a problem. Maeve, Annis, and I were in good health and well cared for. Why complain about trivialities?"

He held the baby with one arm and slipped the other around my waist. "Promise me something please, *bean mo ghràidh.*"

My *something* wife—stubborn, perhaps, or difficult. "I've already

spoken vows with you. What more do you want?" I resisted the urge
to lay my head on his shoulder, because I needed my wits about me if
Sebastian was intent on wheedling promises.

"Promise me that if you ever need reinforcements, or an ally, or
somebody to vent frustrations upon, you will send for me. I don't care
if you regard me as the most contemptible man ever to blight your
acquaintance. If you are being disrespected, that is not a triviality to
me and never will be."

I slipped free of his half embrace. "I could never regard you as
contemptible."

"Promise me, Violet."

His insistence made me wary. Sebastian had gone off to war just
as I had been poised to make my come out, and I'd had no idea why.
My best friend had deserted me without explanation, and I'd been
reduced to begging my brother Felix for news of him. Sebastian hadn't
sent so much as a perfunctory note when Freddie had died. Had not
paid a condolence call, or a courtesy call when I'd emerged from
mourning. I had spent a good portion of my adulthood wondering
where Sebastian had gone and what I'd done to offend him, and now...

He wanted me to *rely* on him? "Will you make me the same
promise?"

His hand went still on Maeve's back. "Yes. Yes, I will. If am ever
without allies and in need of same, I will prevail upon you."

We put Maeve to bed, drew the covers over her, and stole toward
the door with that combination of determination and hope known to
all parents of infants. She obliged us by remaining asleep, and Sebastian walked me to my apartment.

He kissed my forehead again—I was growing to hate that gesture
—and exhaustion deluged me.

Dawn came obscenely early and, with it, our departure for Edinburgh. We had barely lost sight of the castle before I was regretting
that I'd gainsaid my husband's wishes regarding that small human
banshee known as Annis MacHeath.

The child, my nerves, and the peace of the realm would all have fared much better if she'd remained at the castle, but I'd made up my mind we were to travel as a family, and the tail would not wag the dog.

~

Sebastian was an excellent travel manager, and his decisions were entirely at variance with the stereotype of the thrifty Scot. His objective was a swift, commodious journey to the south of England, and we nearly achieved that goal.

Annis was the sole obstacle to a pleasant passage down the coast. She was like no child I had ever encountered—wise beyond her years, though we weren't sure precisely how many years she had, vexatious beyond all bearing, and then, when I was at the very end of my tether, as winsome as a kitten.

She staged impromptu games of hide-and-seek all over the packet Sebastian had hired for our exclusive use. She "forgot" to speak English, then "forgot" she wasn't to play lost-at-sea in the lifeboat. She refused to part with the disreputable Bella even at meals and clung to my skirts whenever I brought Maeve on deck for some sunshine and fresh air.

After nearly a week of sailing, the magnificent prospect of Dover's white cliffs loomed off the starboard rail. I had never been to sea, and the whole experience would have delighted me, but for Annis's exasperating behaviors. Even the feel of her fingers entwined in my skirts had grown annoying.

"Does heaven look like that?" she asked, studying the gleaming chalk precipices.

"I suppose heaven is however we envision it. For a sailor who has been years at sea, those cliffs might look like a bit of heaven. For a child who has known too much of hunger and cold, heaven might be a bakery."

Annis peered up at me, her dark eyes unreadable. "What will your heaven look like?"

Maeve was cradled in my arms, fussing slightly in the bright sunlight. I gave the standard answer. "My family safe and happy. My health and the health of my loved ones in good repair. My country prosperous and at peace."

"But what does that *look* like?" Annis asked. "Sometimes I was happy in Spain, when the weather was good and the sisters had bread and honey for us. If I forgot to wash my hands, and Sister slapped me, I could be unhappy even while my belly was full."

"What does heaven look like for you?" I asked, genuinely curious as to the answer.

Annis was not an affectionate child, but she had a wonderful smile. "I will ride Hannibal there, and Bella will have all her fur, and Rory will be with us too."

Rory was the ship's cat, a marmalade tom with an enormous head who liked to sharpen his claws on the base of the mast.

"Rory," said Sebastian, coming up on my right, "will go straight to perdition for dereliction of his mousing duties. I have never met a fellow more inclined to laze about in the sun when there's work to be done. We'll put in to Folkestone in another hour or so. Annis, best gather up your things. Mrs. Yancy won't do that for you."

Annis sent a worried look in the direction of the cat, then decamped for the steps that led to the staterooms. She held on to my skirt until the fabric would stretch no farther, let go, then darted to the railing along the stairway.

"Was Mrs. Yancy this poor of a sailor on the journey from Spain?" I asked. She had barely stirred from her bed to take meals, though the captain had put out to sea only in fair weather. Otherwise, at Sebastian's direction, we had twice bided in commodious harbor-side inns and waited overnight for the skies to clear.

"On the journey from Spain," Sebastian said, taking Maeve from me, "Mrs. Yancy was an excellent sailor, but Annis was younger then, and half a battalion of soldiers were on board to take turns nannying the child."

"You like sea travel, don't you?" I would not have suspected this of Sebastian. I was reminded that, though I'd known him more than half my life, he was in many ways still a stranger to me.

"When I go to sea," he said, gaze on the Channel sparkling off to port, "most of my troubles remain on shore. The squabbling aunties, the exorbitant price of good timber, the stupidity of Parliament, and the social gauntlet we will face at this house party... The sea is a safe place, in some regards."

I drew Maeve's blanket over her head, lest the sun burn her fair skin. "We will not face a gauntlet. Our hostess is renowned for her graciousness, and if we don't enjoy the company, we will plead a teething baby and repair to Ashmore."

He kissed Maeve's nose, and she beamed at him. "Will we?"

"You are the ranking title on the guest list, Sebastian. If every footman, groom, and underbutler doesn't exert himself to see to your smallest whim, I will be very much surprised."

The cliffs were receding in our wake, though the shoreline continued in an endless green undulation to the southeast. William the Conqueror's armada of some six hundred ships had doubtless sailed these same waters, and what on earth had the coastal communities made of such a sight?

Nothing good.

"We face a gauntlet nonetheless," Sebastian said. "Our first outing as a married couple."

"As a family. You and I are long-acquainted, and I was well past mourning when we became engaged. That you would marry a formerly childless widow speaks to a true attachment between us. I will comport myself so as to support that conclusion, and so shall you."

He nuzzled Maeve's cheek, inspiring a hearty baby-chortle. "Your confidence never fails to amaze me, Violet Marie."

What confidence? "Maeve and I should probably go below. Lucy and Bevins are more than competent to prepare for our disembarkation, but God help the king's peace if we forget Bella."

Sebastian winged his arm, when I had expected him to simply surrender the baby. "Somebody should rouse Mrs. Yancy. The mere sight of distant land often helps with seasickness."

"I'll see to it." We had been in sight of land for much of our voyage, and Mrs. Yancy had nonetheless been afflicted. Sebastian, Bevins, the nurserymaids, Lucy, and Upjohn had all pitched in to keep Annis from inciting a mutiny.

I settled Maeve with Bevins, knocked on Mrs. Yancy's door, and peeked into her room. I expected to find her napping, but she was sitting in her wing chair, fully dressed, and reading some letter or other.

"We'll soon be at Folkestone," I said. "Annis is with me and Bevins for the nonce. If you have any final packing to do, now's the time."

She remained in her chair, an understandable breach of manners, given her *mal de mer*. "Thanks be to God for a safe journey. Never have I known such protracted discomfort. If the good Lord had wanted us to cross open water, He'd have given us fins or feathers and webbed feet."

"He gave us sails instead." Steam power was also looking very promising, and balloons had been crossing the Channel for more than two decades. "Not long now, and we'll be on our way inland."

I was wrong about that. Dealing with harbor protocol, maneuvering lighters from dockside to the moored ship, and getting our baggage organized and then stacked on the quay took nearly two hours. Annis whined, Maeve wailed, and Sebastian cursed in Gaelic, while Lucy, Bevins, and Upjohn exchanged baleful glances.

We were eventually sorted into two enormous traveling coaches. Sebastian handed me and Maeve into the one, as Upjohn took the bench beside John Coachman. Lucy and Bevins, with Annis between them, made for the second coach.

Not until we were ready to take on the challenge of a port town's traffic did I realize that Mrs. Yancy was nowhere to be found.

~

Sebastian, with an air of command I still found surprising, ordered the coaches to return with us to Ashmore, though our scheduled destination had been the Gillespie estate. While the children and I were being dispatched inland, he would remain in Folkestone, searching for Annis's errant governess.

My frustration with those arrangements was boundless. A missing governess was a mystery, and I was keen to get my teeth into another one of those. I had climbed from the coach rather than risk Sebastian banishing me to the countryside before I was ready to go.

"Mrs. Yancy has doubtless wandered away in search of the necessary," I said, swaying slowly with Maeve in my arms. "If we wait a bit, she'll find her way back to the quay." The harbor wasn't that large, and Mrs. Yancy certainly knew to look for coaches bearing the Dunkeld crest on the quayside.

Annis's fingers were again fisted in my skirts, just as if we were still on board ship, and that incessant tug—symbolic of every maternal frustration—plucked at my last nerve.

"She might have fallen into the water," Lucy said. "Wasn't too steady on her pins aboard ship, and my own balance is still a bit off." My lady's maid was outspoken, a quality I usually treasured about her.

"Mrs. Y didn't fall into the water," Upjohn retorted. Sebastian's valet was a diminutive young fellow who hailed from Nottinghamshire. What he lacked in size, he made up for in devotion to his marquess. "She would have set up a hue and cry and made a great splash, and his lordship woulda had to dive in after her."

Annis's grasp of my skirts had become an insistent tugging.

"Annis," I began, "you will please desist—what's that?" She held up a slim epistle, a single piece of folded foolscap.

"Mrs. Yancy said I was to give this to you before we boarded the coaches. I thought it was another one of her do-as-I-say tests. I hope she did fall into the harbor."

As did I—almost—at that moment, and what on earth was a *do-as-I-say test*? "If she'd fallen in, and she could not swim, you'd have just wished a long-suffering woman to her death. Hardly a becoming sentiment."

Sebastian listened to this exchange, but said nothing. I sounded like every annoyed mother in the history of motherhood, which did not reflect well on me.

"She didn't fall in," Annis said. "She went off that way and got into one of those little carriages. She was carrying her satchel and her valise."

The little carriages Annis pointed to were hansom cabs, lined up at a stand to take disembarking passengers to local destinations.

The letter was terse.

My lady, I hereby quit the post of governess to a thoroughly ungovernable child. May God help you as you search for my successor in the days to come. Eunice Yancy.

Well that was plain speaking. "How long ago did she leave, Annis?"

"The lighters were still unloading our trunks."

"Why didn't you say something?"

Annis muttered a few words in Spanish. I looked to Sebastian for a translation.

"Annis followed Mrs. Yancy's orders, more or less," he said. "Let's be on our way. I'll send word to the harbormaster and ask him to alert the innkeepers, but Mrs. Yancy has deserted. Provided she didn't steal the silver, we wish her Godspeed. Into the coaches with us."

"I do not wish her Godspeed," I murmured as Sebastian handed me up into the coach. He passed Maeve to me and climbed in after us. "I gave that woman a generous allotment of traveling money, Sebastian, in addition to her usual pay, and she's likely saved her wages the whole time she's been at the castle. She planned this desertion when we've been nothing but reasonable to her."

"Annis would try the nerves of a saint. We'll find her a new governess, and she can wear that one down too."

I would be the one finding that new governess. "Are we traveling to Ashmore?"

"The Falls," he said. "Might as well keep to the schedule. Mrs. Gillespie will doubtless have domestics on hand who can assist Bevins in the nursery while we send to the agencies and so forth."

"One doesn't," I said. "Not in the country. One asks the neighbors and sends word to the aunties and mentions the situation when chatting in the churchyard." And one hoped that somebody among one's acquaintances would come across a suitably skilled woman who didn't mind the prospect of a permanent remove to Scotland.

A challenge for another day.

Sebastian sat beside me on the forward-facing seat, his presence in the coach a novelty. For most of our journey north to Perthshire, he'd remained in the saddle. When I'd traveled with St. Sevier, Hugh had bided with me in the coach, a pleasant conversationalist, reading companion, and—as our regard had progressed—lover.

What *had* I been thinking? I had proved something to myself by instigating those bold encounters, but the notion of folding down the benches of Sebastian's rolling monstrosity and frolicking... I craved a nap, and only a nap.

The route to The Falls would pass within a few miles of Belle Terre, the elegant behemoth county house where Hugh and Ann now bided. I did not particularly want to look in on them—not without giving them fair warning—but had Hugh been my escort, he would have consulted my wishes regarding the perishing schedule.

"You know how to find a successor governess," Sebastian said, pulling a shade the better to stop the sun from annoying Maeve. "Might I ask how?"

"I ran mine off regularly, if you'll recall, most of them lasting less than six months." All of Papa's wages, his rank, his efforts to charm and intimidate by turns had been insufficient to keep my governesses at their appointed task.

Sebastian took the baby from me, I lost the battle to keep my eyes open, and when I awoke, the afternoon was waning, my breasts were full, and Maeve was fussing.

"Did we just turn between the gateposts?" I asked, sitting up.

"Aye. We've arrived at The Falls, and I believe her ladyship could do with fresh linens."

"Wet or stinky?"

"Wet."

"Stinky will soon follow. I cannot tarry over the introductions, Sebastian. I'll start leaking."

His expression went through a predictable progression—puzzled, appalled, amused, and then... sweet and reserved.

"Your shawl," he said, retrieving from the opposite bench that item of apparel no nursing mother was ever willingly without.

I need not have worried about lengthy introductions. Our hostess, according to the handsomest young butler south of Mayfair, was unavoidably detained, but would greet us at the evening buffet. A gracious, smiling housekeeper offered to show us to our rooms.

Sebastian carried Maeve, which was fortunate, because despite my nap, I was yet fatigued. My legs still felt the effects of being on solid land, and my mind was oppressed by Mrs. Yancy's departure.

Why not give proper notice, a fortnight at least or a month? Why not ask for and receive a character? Why drag poor Annis into the drama? Why not leave on good terms and spare the child a sense of failure?

Why did I care, when we were clearly better off without such a creature?

"You'll be very comfortable in the Hyacinth Suite," the house-keeper said, her good cheer coming across as a bit too hearty. "Lovely views of the river and the park. The balcony is quite private, and you need only use the bell-pull—"

A very loud male voice from behind a closed door interrupted. "For God's sake, Tilda, why do you never *think?*"

We had all stopped, because a shout bearing that much frustration was utterly incongruous amid The Falls' gracious appointments and the quiet of a peaceful summer afternoon.

"House parties," our guide murmured. "The heat, young people on the property, all very challenging."

She moved off, but not before a female voice returned fire. "For God's sake, Nathan, why do you never do me the basic courtesy of consulting me? Need I remind you…"

Sebastian put a hand to my lower back and tactilely suggested that I cease eavesdropping. I yielded to his guidance—this time—but realized before we reached our rooms that the raised voices belonged to our host and hostess.

A blazing row, and with a house filling up with guests. *How interesting.*

The Hyacinth Suite was named for the pattern on the wallpaper, a lovely blue and green imitation of a border of hyacinths in full bloom under a blue and white sky. The sitting room was upholstered in more blue, green, and white, and a lovely view of the park fell away beneath a long balcony.

Maeve was beginning to fuss, so I retreated to the bedroom while Sebastian engaged the housekeeper in some murmured exchange. The baby latched on greedily—thank God for a healthy infant—and I arranged the shawl to protect my modesty.

Not until I'd heard a door close and Sebastian sauntered into the bedroom did I notice that our hostess had housed us in an apartment with a single bed. An enormous bed, hung with blue and green linens, but only the one to be seen.

And, apparently, to be shared.

CHAPTER SIX

Sebastian

The Hyacinth Suite, for all its overdone flowers, had commodious appointments, a lovely view, and one bed.

I saw the moment when Violet came to that realization. She was ensconced in a wing chair by the window, the afternoon sun slanting over her shoulder, the baby tucked close beneath the lacy shawl. I'd received my instructions from the housekeeper—buffet meal at seven, one tug on the bell-pull for a tea tray, two for something more substantial—and a vague reference to strain on the host and hostess being understandable *in light of the circumstances.*

Trying to give Violet instructions—*stay put until I return, avoid provoking riots*—would earn me a drop over the balcony into the bed of roses below. She had kept her powder dry for the duration of the journey, but I had seen a telltale set to her mouth in Folkestone, a temptation to argue as only Violet could argue, with half the merchant navy and our entire retinue looking on.

"I'll find the nursery," I said, "and send Bevins to retrieve Maeve."

"I can find the nursery on my own, and I need to know where it is, in any case."

I wanted to protest. Violet had been up and down half the night since we'd left Edinburgh. If she wasn't tending to Maeve, she'd been soothing Annis's nightmares, or examining the ship's stores for a tisane to quiet Mrs. Yancy's *mal de mer*. My wife had paced the deck with a fussy Maeve by the hour and settled squabbles among the staff without appearing to even notice an altercation was in progress.

At some point between when I'd bought my commission and when Violet and I had spoken our vows, the darling, exasperating hoyden I'd known in my youth had disappeared, leaving a competent, self-possessed *lady* in her place.

I missed the hoyden and wasn't at all sure how to go on with the lady.

"I napped for most of the journey up from the coast, Sebastian. If you want to patrol the perimeter, please be about it. I will doubtless do likewise once Maeve is finished."

"I'll find Upjohn and ensure Hannibal is settled. We can patrol the perimeter together."

She tended to the baby, managing to switch breasts beneath the shawl without exposing an inch of flesh. I regretted her self-consciousness, but I understood it too.

"I have attended house parties since I was sixteen years old, sir. You need not nanny me."

How I hated that patient, dismissive tone. "I'll have you know, Violet Marie, that I have attended exactly three house parties in all my years on earth. I stand before you, ignorant of whether I should change into morning clothes for a trip to the stable, remain in my traveling ensemble, or dig up riding attire. When will our trunks arrive, for that matter, and is it rude to order a bath when the house is at sixes and sevens, or will the staff anticipate such requests?"

I'd begun to pace, and Violet was watching me as if she'd arrived in the middle of the second act of a poorly written comedy and hadn't quite caught on to the plot.

"Shouldn't my lady have first crack at any baths," I went on, "and how the hell will I find Upjohn in this rural labyrinth?"

And how, I silently ranted, did I convey to Mrs. Gillespie that Violet and I did not share a bed, when admitting that to anybody was beyond me?

"Until the buffet this evening," Violet said, "wardrobe protocols need not be observed. Ask any footman to send Upjohn to you. His rank belowstairs derives from yours, so the lot of them will toady to him. Our trunks will arrive within the hour, and I bathed at the inn this morning. If you'd like a bath, you should have one, but you don't need one."

"I don't?" How could she possibly...?

Violet busied herself rearranging the shawl and the baby. "I slept plastered to your side for most of two hours, Sebastian. You do not need a bath."

Marriage to Violet was just full of surprises. "Then I'm off to the stable, and if I'm not back in three days, organize a searching party."

Violet speared me with a look that said, quite clearly, my humor had fallen flat. I had the damnedest urge to salute her before I took my leave, but settled for bowing to my wife.

The Falls was named for a set of natural cataracts that spilled from the uplands onto the plateau of cultivated acres belonging to the estate. The arched and recessed main entrance to the house suggested the dwelling had begun its life as a medieval manor. The front gallery opening off the foyer was a chilly, vaulted space about twenty yards long that looked to have been the main hall of the earlier structure.

Elizabethan prosperity was doubtless to blame for three imposing wings. Passing style and more wasted coin had left their stamp in follies, an attached conservatory, an orangery, fruit walls, the occasional picturesque ruin, and the obligatory hermit's grotto.

The building material of choice was native blue-gray ragstone, which gave the whole a settled, antique feel, only slightly leavened by ubiquitous pots of pink and white geraniums.

I was lost within five minutes of leaving the Hyacinth Suite.

Violet had an uncanny sense not only of direction, but of physical organization. She had doubtless taken one look at The Falls and known exactly which was the family wing, where the nursery was situated, and where staircases for maids and footmen were secreted behind the paneling.

I managed well enough in the outdoors. I could reckon by the stars, the moon, and the sun. Violet navigated by an internal compass I could only envy.

I came around a corner that looked as if I might have come around it before, only this time, a dark-haired young man was rummaging in the drawers of a sideboard under a portrait of Queen Charlotte.

He rose, his bearing exuding polite patience. "You have the look of a fellow who's been taken captive by the fairies. One of Clothilda's guests, I presume? I'm Greer Nicholson, bachelor-at-large when same are in short supply, tour guide if need be, and Mr. Gillespie's former ward."

He exuded the testy humor of the unwilling volunteer, making a jest not of himself, but of the situation he found himself in. Dark brown eyes gave his face an air of gravity, and his countenance, for all his surly good cheer, was attractive. Excellent bones, the ladies would have said, no feature out of proportion with the others.

A good-looking if sober fellow, a touch on the tall side, rangy, and —in riding attire—a credit to his tailor.

"Mr. Nicholson. Dunkeld, at your service."

He bowed to me, and I returned the courtesy. The whole business was beyond tedious, but Violet was entitled to expect best behavior from me, so bow, I would.

"Clothilda refuses to hand out maps to the guests," Nicholson went on. "She says it's more fun to explore The Falls willy-nilly, but I and countless bewildered visitors beg to differ. People get lost for hours in this old mausoleum, or so they claim. Where are you headed?"

"The stable."

"I've just come from there. This way," he said, striding in the direction I'd traveled, "and we can stop by the library, where you will find a floor plan of the house if you know where to look. That will come in handy for the scavenger hunt."

I loathed scavenger hunts, and Mr. Nicholson's tone said he was none too fond of them either. Glorified excuses for canoodling in the conservatory and frolicking among the follies.

"Perhaps we can save the library for another time, Mr. Nicholson. I'm in something of a hurry." Violet would settle Maeve in the nursery and then go on reconnaissance without my escort, given half a chance.

"Of course," Nicholson said, turning down yet another corridor. "The scavenger hunt isn't until next week. This week, we'll have the pall-mall contest, a whist tournament, a musicale, cricket, and—doubtless—several domestic dramas. Clothilda does not permit any real scandal at her house parties, but that rule is sometimes honored in the breach."

He might have been reciting the weekday menu at an unpre-suming gentlemen's club. "No steeplechases on the program?"

"None that involve horses, my lord. The daughter of the house is to be launched next spring, which presages all manner of jockeying among the eligibles. Through here," he said, opening a paneled door and leading me into a parlor done up in red and green. "We call this the Christmas Parlor." He continued out a set of French doors. In the distance, I beheld a long, low, gray stone building with walls punctu-ated by wooden half doors. "Your objective. If you'd like to hack out tomorrow morning, I'm happy to join you."

Mr. Nicholson was polite and informative, but I doubted he was happy.

"Will you be doing any steeplechasing at this house party, Mr. Nicholson?"

His air of masculine gravitas faltered. "Not if I can help it. Clothilda's sense of what constitutes entertainment and my own diverge in many particulars. She must have her little games and intrigues—a friendly warning, if you need one—while I am fond of books and quiet walks by the river. I'll bid you good day, Dunkeld. A pleasure to make your acquaintance."

As I took the path leading to the stable, I tried to imagine what Violet would make of Greer Nicholson: restless, reserved, handsome enough to make up the numbers, and loyal enough to his former guardian to do so, but not best pleased to serve in that capacity.

Violet might, in a completely clinical manner, find Greer Nicholson *interesting*.

I was lost in thought and hurrying toward my destination when a majestic traveling coach rattled past on the drive between the house and the stable. An equally imposing chestnut gelding trotted beside the coach, the rider posting along with the relaxed grace of the born equestrian.

The horse—Charlemagne—was a magnificent specimen. The rider—Hugh St. Sevier—wasn't bad looking either, if one preferred tall, chestnut-haired Frenchmen with soulful brown eyes.

Which, for a time, Violet had. I raised an arm and hailed him. He slowed the horse to the walk and then made a path across the grass.

"Dunkeld. An unexpected pleasure." St. Sevier swung down. He did not shake my hand or offer a smile in welcome. "The ladies are with you?"

"Violet and Maeve are with me, as is young Annis. They all weathered the journey well. What of Ann?"

"Madame and Fiona are already at the house, though we were not aware that you'd intended to join the gathering." St. Sevier was too much of a gentleman to put his dismay any more clearly than that.

"Violet and I had no idea you and Ann had been invited, but this answers one question."

"And that would be?"

"What fun and games Clothilda Gillespie has scheduled for her own amusement over the next two weeks."

~

"I do not care for these fun and games." St. Sevier's words, spoken with that particular Gallic precision, conveyed that an outbreak of the plague would suit him better than being a guest at The Falls.

A groom jogged out from the stable and hovered a few yards off. The banked curiosity in his gaze suggested that word of Mrs. Gillespie's little game had spread among the staff. St. Sevier and I were doubtless supposed to have first set eyes on each other at the buffet, with an audience of at least thirty goggling at the encounter.

Better still if Violet and St. Sevier had been taken aback to find each other on opposite sides of the punchbowl.

I slapped on my Highland Laddie smile and extended a hand to St. Sevier. "Let the groom take your beast. The ladies are doubtless already settled in with a pot of tea, and I know Violet will be very pleased to see you."

St. Sevier returned fire with his best Charming Frenchman grin. For good measure, he treated me to that half embrace—one hand grasping my arm, another thumping my shoulder—which grown men engaged in when they lacked the fortitude to engage in a proper hug.

"*Mon ami. C'est une merveilleuse journée!*" He prattled on in French, about taking a dull blade to the fool who thought staging social ambushes amusing. The English were ever lacking in civility, and he— Hugh St. Sevier—would delight in administering a lesson in manners to any who sought to make a fool of him or his friends. He knew of tisanes for loosening the bowels that were undetectable in wine punch...

A marvelous day, indeed.

To any busybody peering out of the manor's windows, St. Sevier and I, strutting arm in arm for the house, were the picture of masculine amiability. I offered him my flask, he flourished his own, and as long as we were within earshot of the stables, we argued good-naturedly in English over the merits of brandy versus whisky.

I was married to St. Sevier's former fiancée. I was raising his daughter. We might well have hated each other, but the opposite was true.

If Clothilda Gillespie had schemed to create scenes between Violet, myself, Hugh, and Ann, she would be sorely disappointed. St. Sevier might not like me, he might resent that I was raising his daughter, but I trusted him and knew my respect in that regard was reciprocated.

"So why did you come?" I asked in French. Some of the upper servants and certainly the guests were familiar with that language. French nonetheless afforded some privacy over English.

"Because Ann says it is time," St. Sevier said as we reached the steps at the bottom of the back terrace. "We have made progress with the neighbors. We have held an open house, two Venetian breakfasts, and innumerable informal dinners. We have called on every neighbor within fifteen miles of Belle Terre and even upon that disgrace to the peerage known as the Earl of Derwent."

Violet's father was a wily old-school aristocrat, much respected by his peers. For years, I'd hated him. "He received you?"

"The earl was all that was gracious, which was prudent of him. Ann was ready to bring up pots and kettles if he proved difficult. Violet cannot help her circumstances, but Derwent's peccadilloes were many and public. He is in your debt, and he knows it."

Guests were milling about on the terrace above, so I gestured for St. Sevier to walk with me among the roses.

"I ought to enjoy having him in my debt," I said, "but I don't. He was a miserable father to Violet, and he shows no remorse over his treatment of me."

"He will be here," St. Sevier said, plucking a small red rose. "Next week. Ann's spies at Derwent Hall warned her."

Mallachd air an iarla. "Violet says Maeve's teething might require that we repair to Ashmore, but we can't snub his lordship."

"Hence you curse him instead." St. Sevier smiled evilly, a reminder that he was married to a native Gaelic speaker and had been educated in Scotland. His Gaelic was doubtless the equal of my French.

"The decision to attend was sudden for Violet and me. I'm already regretting it. I ran into a Mr. Greer Nicholson, who was some sort of ward to Nathan Gillespie. Nicholson warned me to avoid follies, as it were."

St. Sevier presumed to affix the rose to my lapel, and he accomplished his objective before I sensed what he was about.

"Better," he said. "Softens that Highland scowl."

"I know some tisanes too, St. Sevier. A dash of left hook followed by a distillation of right cross."

He patted my lapel. "Keep your recipes handy, and I shall do likewise. We may need them. I must report news of your presence to Ann. What room are you in?"

The one with a single bed. "The wallpaper is full of blue flowers. Insipid blue, puffy clouds, bilious green foliage. The view of the park from the balcony is peaceful."

"If I am not mistaken, we are in the Rose Suite, next door to yours. Our balconies adjoin, or nearly so. Mrs. Gillespie's schemes lack subtlety, but that's the English for you."

Upjohn stood at the foot of the terrace steps. He was former military, and his posture suggested my valet had taken up guard duty over the parterres.

"We will see you at supper," I said, giving my boutonniere a nudge. "Upjohn has a report, unless I miss my guess, and Violet intends to go on reconnaissance before we change for the evening meal."

"She feels safer when she knows her way around," St. Sevier said. "I'd forgotten that."

While I had never realized this about my own wife. "So do I. We are in for a long two weeks."

St. Sevier ambled with me back toward the steps. "What cannot be changed must be endured, as Ann would say. She has no use for intrigues and gossip, but we do this for Fiona's sake. We visit the vicar, we socialize, we are gracious neighbors. After Derwent returned our call, the supper invitations started, though this is our first house party. I am determined to be charming, and so, I'd suppose, are you, to the best of your limited ability."

"Charming, yes. A fool, no. Avoid the follies, St. Sevier. Until supper."

We bowed jauntily, exchanged toothy smiles, and strode away from each other with every appearance of great good cheer.

One look at Upjohn's expression, and I ceased my playacting.

~

I found my way to the library, inquired of a footman as to where the estate maps were, then continued on to the temporary quarters I shared with Violet. She was walking the balcony with a dozing Maeve when I returned and looking pensive and restless.

"I was about to explore on my own," she said quietly. "I have news, but it will keep. What's amiss?"

"What makes you think something's amiss?" I kept my voice down, too, though Maeve was doubtless exhausted by the day's upheaval.

"You wear a trying-not-to-scowl expression when something vexes you, and you've been running your hands through your hair. Both hands at the same time. Gives you a dash of Byronic appeal."

"Hannibal is acting colicky."

"Drat and damnation. Has he had colic before?"

"Never." Not across Spain and into France. Not at sea, not in the middle of a Highland winter. "He's getting on, though, and I ask much of him."

Violet shifted Maeve to the other shoulder. "He can't be but twelve years old, Sebastian. A fellow in his prime. He doubtless neglected his water bucket on board ship and will come right soon enough. I will make your excuses at supper. I'm sure I know one or two people here. In fact..."

Maeve chose then to squirm and kick, as infants sometimes did in sleep.

"I know," I said, taking the baby. "I ran into Monsieur on my way to the stable. The St. Seviers are not only guests, we share a balcony with them. Our hostess apparently has an odd sense of humor. This child grows heavier by the day."

"For which we are grateful," Violet said, quitting the balcony. "Lucy came by and gave me directions to the nursery. I will look in on Annis, and you can see to your horse."

I followed Violet into the bedroom as Maeve sighed and snuggled against my shoulder. "Upjohn is doing what's needed for Hannibal. I will accompany you to the nursery."

Violet regarded me, and what a picture I must have presented: travel-stained, hair disheveled, the baby in my arms, worry in my eyes.

"I suppose a united marital front is the best response," Violet said, finger-combing my hair, "but you needn't accompany me to supper if you'd rather be in the stable. What on earth could Tilda Gillespie have been thinking? We are cordial with Hugh and Ann, more than cordial, but still... I don't care to be manipulated."

"Neither do I. St. Sevier and I are agreed that we will be pattern cards of mutual goodwill for the duration."

This apparently amused Violet, though her smile was fleeting. "While Ann and I will be bosom bows. I've never had a bosom bow before, and I daresay Ann hasn't either. The nursery is only one floor up."

She bustled out the door, and I followed with Maeve. In our entire exchange, neither one of us had so much as glanced at the bed, but much like an off smell or an argument in the next room, the bed had dominated at least my awareness.

If I knew anything about Violet, Marchioness of Dunkeld, it was that she should not be hurried, teased, wheedled, or negotiated into intimacies with me. The decision had to be hers. When I'd first broached marriage with her, she had been newly aware of her pregnancy, and our conversation had remained mostly theoretical.

She had allowed that she'd like to see more of Scotland. I had been amenable to finding us a home near her family in Sussex. Violet had posited that I needed heirs. I had rejoined that the title could revert to the crown for all I cared, but the esteem of my wife would be a treasure beyond price.

All very indirect, which for us had been a step back from the blunt exchanges of our youth and a step forward in our adult rapprochement.

Annis had made the acquaintance of the St. Seviers' daughter, Fiona, a coltish sprite who had St. Sevier's brown eyes and Ann's flaming tresses. We handed Maeve off to a cheerful Bevins, and Violet made the appropriate exclamations about how much Fiona had grown in the past six months.

"Bevins has sent a footman for a deck of cards," Fiona said, "because Annis and I are holding a patience tournament. I am teaching her French, and she is teaching me Spanish. We will have a secret language that's half of each, and nobody will be able to understand us."

"And we both know English and Gaelic," Annis added, "for speaking to grown-ups. I told Fee Mrs. Yancy quit, and Fee said her governess is very nice. I want a nice governess."

The footman arrived with the deck of cards and a tray of lemonade, and Violet and I made our escape.

"They have known each other less than an hour," Violet said, "and already they are fast friends. Why didn't I see this?"

"See what?"

"*Annis needs friends*, Sebastian. Children her own age who are her equal for mischief and imagination. I suppose I did not notice the lack because friends were not a prominent feature of my own early upbringing."

I thought to offer my arm as we strode along, but Violet clearly did not need that courtesy. "You made friends at Miss Hairball's Academy. You and Fanny MacKellan met there, as I recall."

Violet slowed her step, snickered, and then stopped and laughed outright. "Poor Miss Harmon. I'd forgotten that nickname, but she did wear the most frightful coiffures. Miss Hairball. Miss Charm-None. We were so naughty and so blasted bored."

Violet had perfected the art of maintaining a circumspect, proper appearance to such an extent that I'd forgotten how she could sparkle with high spirits. As we circumnavigated the exterior of the whole house and then studied the maps in the library, I made a mental note to provoke her laughter as much as possible.

I was perusing the shelves of biographies while Violet did a sketch of the manor's floor plan when we were interrupted by no less personage than our hostess.

"There you are," she said, advancing on Violet, who sat at the reading table. "My lady, I am so abjectly sorry to have missed your arrival."

Clothilda Gillespie was what some referred to as a handsome woman. Statuesque, blond, maturing splendidly, and very much aware of her own charms. I put her age at fortyish and determined to advance no further in terms of her appearance. At my sister Clementine's suggestion, I'd kept a distance from Mrs. Gillespie despite repeated invitations whenever I bided in Town.

Clemmie had been unforthcoming regarding details other than to suggest that Mrs. Gillespie was something of a matchmaker and possessed of a tolerant husband. I had wondered if Clemmie's late spouse had been smitten with Mrs. Gillespie's charms, but one did not pry.

"Mrs. Gillespie." Violet stood, and curtseys were exchanged. "Your staff has been all that is gracious, and our rooms are lovely. House parties can be such a whirlwind for the hostess, can't they?"

"Oh, my lady! A whirlwind wrapped in a tempest tied up with a typhoon, but such fun, too, don't you agree?"

"I'm sure this one will be." Violet's words were pleasant, but some undercurrent in her tone delivered a warning.

"With you and the marquess as our honored guests, I dearly hope so. I don't suppose you've come across Greer Nicholson as you've acquainted yourself with The Falls?"

"I have not. His lordship and I took the air after seeing the children settled, and we'll shortly go up to change for supper."

"I ran into Nicholson," I said, stepping from between the bookshelves. "He had just come from the stable and was good enough to give me directions."

"My lord." Mrs. Gillespie offered me a curtsey worthy of a court presentation. "*Such* a pleasure. We are so very honored that you'd make the journey to join our little gathering. You must allow me to give you a personal tour of the house and grounds later this week, and you, too, of course, Lady Violet, assuming you are up to the exertion."

I bowed over my hostess's hand. At the least indication from Violet, I would have corrected Mrs. Gillespie's form of address—my wife was Lady Dunkeld—but Violet appeared, if anything, amused.

"Is there any particular reason you're looking for Nicholson?" I asked.

"A small domestic matter. Nothing of any import. Nathan does rely on Greer, perhaps a bit too much, but the boy has been like a son to us." She blinked several times at a landscape over the mantel of The Falls in autumn plumage.

Nicholson was not, that I knew of, sailing to Cathay, buying his colors, or battling a dread disease, but Mrs. Gillespie's performance suggested all of the above.

"We won't keep you," Violet said, taking my arm. "If we see Mr. Nicholson, where should we send him?"

"To the study, if you please, though of course Greer will join us at supper, as will my darling Dottie. Dorothy, I mean. I must remember to call her Dorothy, lest she disown me before she's launched. Daughters are the very devil, don't you agree?"

"Ours have yet to reach the devilish stage," Violet said, patting my arm. "I'm rather looking forward to it. One doesn't want to be the only lady in the household with a mind of her own, does she?"

She offered Mrs. Gillespie a feline smile, and our hostess took her leave of us.

"Remind me not to cross social swords with you," I said, because the exchange had revealed an aspect of Violet I had not seen before, an impressive formidableness that was slightly intimidating and—to me—attractive.

"She knew Freddie," Violet said, dropping my arm. "I suspect the biblical sense of the word might apply, but Freddie was discreet about his Society amours."

Not discreet enough, apparently. "Then why are we here? Why subject yourself to that saber-rattling and posturing and twenty paces with a smile?"

She closed the estate atlas and collected a book from the mantel. "Freddie's tomcatting doesn't signify. I came to that conclusion before our first anniversary. If I cowered before my late husband's passing fancies, I'd have no time for anything else. Tilda Gillespie did not figure prominently on a very long list, and we need not discuss this again."

A long and devastating list. "If you want to leave," I said, "we leave. We're the ranking guests, and we do as we please. Snub Tilda Gillespie, wreck her name over the teapot, imply that her hospitality was wanting. She wronged you and has not made amends."

Violet, to my shock, set aside her book and slipped her arms around my waist. "You are so wonderfully fierce. Freddie had needs I could not meet, Tilda wronged nobody according to polite society's rules, and if I am not to fall asleep facedown in my aspic this evening, I need another nap before we change for supper."

Anybody could walk into the library without warning, and I almost wished they would. My wife was confiding in me, after a fashion, and seeking comfort in my arms. The moment probably looked unremarkable from the outside, but I hugged Violet to me with a sense of hope.

"I could make your excuses at supper."

She stepped away and collected her book. "We have a farce to put on with Hugh and Ann, lest you forget. I will dote upon you shamelessly and anticipate copious fawning in return. I expect you will want to look in on your Hannibal while I catch forty winks."

She expected correctly—for the most part. "I meant what I said, Violet. We endure this gathering only so long as you see fit to do so."

She returned to my side, kissed my cheek, and headed for the door. "And I meant what I said too."

I let her have the last words, though they were ambiguous words: To what pronouncement did she refer? Freddie's tomcatting did not signify? The fawning and doting? Or...

Finding her husband *wonderfully fierce?*

CHAPTER SEVEN

Violet

Sebastian, veteran of both battlefields and ballrooms, had been ready to go to war for me over some minor bad form from our hostess. Mrs. Gillespie had referred to me as Lady Violet, as if Freddie were still alive or as if my status were that of widow rather than marchioness.

She had referred to daughters—plural—a tacit reminder that I was perhaps raising Sebastian's by-blow in the nursery along with my own.

Not a subtle woman, and I was relieved to quit her company, though she seemed to genuinely care for her offspring. I moved along the upstairs corridor, approaching the closed door behind which I'd previously heard raised voices. Before I passed, a young woman emerged. She was tall, blond, and red-eyed.

"You must be Miss Gillespie," I said, fishing a handkerchief from a pocket. Motherhood had reduced me to carrying several at all times. "I am Lady Dunkeld, and I apologize for presuming, but you look as if you could use this."

"My lady." Her curtsey was graceful, though marred by sniffling.

"I am sorry. Mama will be mortified, but I have lost my rabbit. Scipio is upset at all the commotion—who wouldn't be?—and some fool left the door to my sitting room open, and he's slipped away, and now I c-can't f-find him *anywhere.*"

A man emerged from the same door, a pleasant-looking ruddy-cheeked fellow going handsomely gray at the temples.

"Dot, you must pull yourself together. The rabbit will be found, and your mother will not be best pleased by all this drama."

Miss Gillespie whirled on him. "The drama is entirely of Mama's making. I told her we needn't have this perishing party. I told her spring was soon enough to fire me off. I told her..."

Mr. Gillespie—for who else would address the young lady as Dot?—sent me a pleading glance. "I well know what you told her, my dear, but your mother is a force of nature when she's set upon an objective. We shall find the blasted bunny, though I daresay we needn't air any more family linen before our guests."

"Shall we organize a searching party?" I asked. "Lady Dunkeld, by the way."

"My lady." A gracious bow. "Nathan Gillespie, at your service, though I'm fairly sure our paths crossed in London. Welcome to The Falls. Please excuse..." He waved a manicured hand in the direction of his daughter. "The rabbit means much to Dorothy."

"Scipio means *everything*, and we cannot organize a searching party, because that will be yet more commotion, and Skippy is a very sensitive creature. He will hide harder than ever if we send all the footmen racketing about calling his name."

"Lady Dunkeld," Mr. Gillespie began, "you must ignore this display. We are regularly cast into the bows over bunnies, hair ribbons, and harp solos. Think nothing of it, and please accept my apologies."

He was trying, albeit charmingly, to hasten me on my way, but I well knew the disproportionate upset Miss Gillespie suffered. After years in the schoolroom, she was to be introduced to Society and presented at court—ready or not.

She would be subjected to the ordeal of a London come out and had likely already begun the fittings for her spring wardrobe. All the new frocks in Mayfair could not disguise the fact that a very young lady was being thrust into adulthood. If she was well received, marriage would follow. Her home, her friendships, her name, her appearance, her bodily privacy—all caught up in the tempest of courtship and marriage, never to be the same again.

For a young lady staring into that abyss of uncertainty, grief, and excitement, the loss of a treasured pet could fall into the straw-on-the-camel's-back category.

"Could Scipio be lonely?" I asked.

Mr. Gillespie looked at me as if I'd begun imitating birdcalls. "I beg your pardon?"

"If Scipio is a healthy adult male, then a female visitor to his usual haunts might lure him home."

As a girl, I'd had a pet rabbit, a pet duck, cats without number, the occasional dog, and—mostly to vex my brothers—I'd spent a whole summer befriending toads and extending to them the hospitality of our conservatory.

I certainly knew where baby bunnies came from and so apparently did Miss Gillespie. She beamed at me, showing a resemblance to her mother.

"That is brilliant. A Mrs. Scipio might be just the thing if Greer cannot lure Skippy from hiding. My lady, you are brilliant."

"Greer has an affinity for animals," Mr. Gillespie said. "Greer Nicholson, my former ward. The rabbit likes him."

"As I understand it, Mr. Nicholson has recently returned from the stable," I said. "He might be changing for supper."

"Thank you, my lady." Miss Gillespie shook my hand in an alarmingly familiar manner and strode off down the corridor. "I will haul Greer out of his lair by the heels if I have to. Skippy is all alone and frightened, and I'm not having it."

She disappeared around a corner, her skirts swishing with purpose.

"Takes after her mother," Mr. Gillespie said with a slight smile. "I do apologize for the bother, my lady."

"Mr. Gillespie, if you knew how many times the hue and cry was raised at Derwent Hall over a missing pair of gloves, a pair of eyeglasses, or a hat, you would make no apology."

His smile bloomed into genuine friendliness. "I suppose we're all a bit flighty in our youth."

"I was referring to my father's behavior."

Mr. Gillespie laughed, though I had not made a jest. "Just so, my lady. Just so. We fellows have our little crotchets, don't we? I dearly hope a missing rabbit is the worst of the dramas you'll witness here at The Falls. Tilda delights in the role of hostess, and I am helpless to deny her anything. Will we see you at supper, or will you do as the seasoned guests do and recover from your travels for a day or so?"

He was either unaware of the particulars involving the St. Seviers, or he was a gifted thespian. "I will see you at supper. Good luck finding Skippy."

He offered a jaunty bow, and I went upon my way. Nathan Gillespie was the gracious host, complete with self-deprecating humor, unprepossessing honesty, and exasperated familial affection.

Nonetheless, he was the same man who'd been shouting angrily at his wife barely two hours ago, and thus I was pleased to take my leave of him. I had every intention of stealing a nap—another nap—when I returned to the Hyacinth Suite, though circumstances conspired to foil my plans.

As seemed to be the usual case in my life of late.

~

Lucy was in the mood to relay intelligence as she put together my evening ensemble, and because my lady's maid was adept at making friends belowstairs, I put off my nap.

"Mrs. Gillespie didn't know the marquess had gone back to Scotland," Lucy said, laying a brown velvet evening dress on the bed. The frock was as comfortable as it was unremarkable. "She believed Dunkeld yet bided in Kent, but she sent the invitations out early enough that his was forwarded to Perthshire."

"How could an accomplished Society hostess not know where a marquess whose manor isn't half a day's...?"

Well, that was the point of Lucy's recitation, wasn't it? Sebastian had apparently lurked at Ashmore, no lairdly pennant in sight, and thus the neighbors had remained largely ignorant of his departure. Though why invite that peer when his marchioness was unlikely to accompany him to the gathering?

As Freddie Belmaine's widow, I knew exactly why. Somebody, perhaps Mrs. Gillespie herself or one of her bosom bows, had been intent on a frolic with my husband.

I considered the brown velvet, which was in the nature of an old sartorial friend. "You are saying Mrs. Gillespie had no intention of making me or the children a part of this gathering. Not the brown, please. I'm making a first impression in many regards, and my turnout must befit my husband's station. We will aim for gracious splendor."

"Your turnout must befit *your* station, my lady, and about time, if you ask me."

"Which I did not."

Lucy smirked, shoved the brown velvet back into the wardrobe, and retrieved a high-waisted raspberry silk creation I hadn't worn for two years.

"A bit out of date," I said, running my hand over cool, luscious fabric, "but I love this dress. I'd forgotten about it."

"You've had a bit on your mind lately. Shall we make sure it still fits? Might be a bit snug in the bodice, though some prefer their dresses that way."

"Shame on you, Lucy Hewitt. Where did that shawl come from?"

She'd produced a shimmery confection of lacy damask roses, with glints of gold threaded among the flowers.

"Mr. Belmaine gave it to you by way of an apology, and you never wore it."

Freddie's husbandly bungling had included trying to buy forgiveness for transgressions he had no intention of forgoing in the future. By the time he'd died, my jewelry box had overflowed with testaments to his passing sense of contrition.

That Maeve and Annis would inherit the lot of it pleased me greatly.

I wrapped the shawl around me and considered my reflection in the mirror. "Freddie did have good taste in fashion, didn't he?" The colors flattered my complexion and did nice things for unremarkable blue eyes.

"The worst bounders do, if they have money. Money is apparently a problem for the Gillespies."

"Fast work, Lucy." We got me out of my traveling attire and into the raspberry silk, which was just a trifle snug in the bodice.

"I like it," Lucy said, eyeing me critically. "Fits you better now than it did before motherhood befell you. Fits you perfectly."

Lucy was opinionated and outspoken for a lady's maid—when we were private. She had seen me through the worst years of my marriage and the worse-in-a-different-way years of mourning. If I'd referred to her in her hearing as more friend than employee, she would have been horrified, though she had taken my welfare to heart more than any friend or family member had.

She was ferociously loyal, full of common sense, and got on *quite well* with Sebastian's valet.

"If the Gillespies are in dun territory," I said, "why throw this lavish house party?" The reflection in the mirror confirmed that the dress was flattering. More significantly, it *felt* wonderful. Graciously splendid was a stretch, but maybe with pink pearl earbobs...

Though I didn't generally care for pearls, or for pink pearls especially.

"The Gillespies aren't skint," Lucy said, rummaging in the wardrobe, "but the money came from Mrs. Gillespie's family. Mister manages the funds, of course, and he always has enough for a new hunter or a few weeks of shooting in the north. He has a yacht at

Folkestone that he uses about three times a year. The stables are pala-
tial, according to Rhys... Upjohn, rather, and Mister collects and
commissions hunt scenes by the dozen."

"And this vexes Mrs. Gillespie?"

"Opinion is divided. Does the extravagance vex her, or is she
more jealous of the time spent on the hunters and the grouse moors?
Both? They have only the one child, and Missus has already stuck her
oar in about the settlements for Miss Gillespie."

Somebody belowstairs had been talking very much out of turn.
"Settlements are complicated."

The young lady must have enough means to assure her security
later in life and enough to attract suitable *partis.* Enormous settlements also attracted unsuitable *partis,* and distinguishing between
the two varieties of bachelor was a challenge. The heirs, widowers,
and wealthy scions were charming and bold, the fortune hunters
were charming and bolder.

And, as mother to both Annis and Maeve, sorting the rams and
billy goats would one day fall to *me.* A daunting realization.

"Garnets," I said, standing taller. "This ensemble wants garnets.
Did we bring any?"

Lucy set a pair of gold slippers on the cedar chest at the foot of
the bed. "Now you insult me. Of course we brought the garnets,
unless that Mrs. Yancy piked off with them."

"Why do you suppose she scarpered?"

"She was never meant to be a governess, I can tell you that. An
officer's widow fallen on hard times. His lordship took pity on her
and offered her a post, from what I hear. Her people hailed from
Canterbury, and Scottish winters did not agree with her. She learned
not a word of Gaelic the whole time she was in Perthshire."

While Annis had learned English and Gaelic both.

I held still as Lucy unfastened my hooks. "Why not give notice,
Lucy? To abandon a post in a marquess's household is not the done
thing."

"Folkestone is less than twenty miles from Canterbury, ma'am.

Maybe she was afraid she'd lose her nerve if she didn't do a bunk when the doing was good. You should have a lie-down."

"A short lie-down. I'll need to make another visit to the nursery before we go to supper."

Lucy carefully lifted the dress over my head and hung it on the inside of the wardrobe door. "I'll leave you, then and come back in, say, an hour?"

"That will suit. Before you go, Lucy, did you hear any mention of Mr. Nicholson while you were making friends among the maids? Greer Nicholson?"

Lucy tucked the slippers inside the wardrobe, draped the shawl over the vanity stool, and closed the wardrobe door.

"The footmen are the worst gossips, if you want to know the truth. A regular mischief of magpies in livery. They did mention Mr. Nicholson, and while they don't exactly like him, they seem to respect him. He's often the referee when Mister and Missus get to spatting. Has pots of money, and much of it fell into his hands when he turned eighteen. The rest comes to him year by year, until he's five-and-twenty."

"And Mr. Gillespie is the trustee of that fortune?"

"That did not come up. Mr. Nicholson is apparently the last of his line on both sides, and the Gillespies are all the family he has. After his mama died, he was raised here, when he wasn't off at a fancy public school. Shall I wait up for you after supper, my lady?"

Her tone had turned diffident, suggesting she was asking the question now so she could make plans with Upjohn for later in the evening.

"No need. I can get myself undressed." More to the point, I would make my bed on the cot in the dressing closet, and that was nobody's business but mine—and Sebastian's. "Be off with you, and should you happen to overhear the whereabouts of a certain tame rabbit, Miss Gillespie would be most interested."

"The first underfootman says Mr. Nicholas caught the bunny, or found it in his rooms. Cause for general rejoicing. To bed with you, my lady." Lucy took her leave, off to plan her assignation with Upjohn.

The cot would be my fate overnight, but I could catch my forty winks in the great hyacinth barge dominating the bedroom. I had peeled out of my stockings and turned back the covers when I heard the bedroom door open.

"Not another loose bunny?" I asked, expecting Lucy had returned on some forgotten errand.

"More in the nature of a marquess without supervision," Sebastian said. "You are intent on a nap?"

Surprise alone preserved me from a blush.

He had seen me in the early throes of childbirth. Years ago, he had seen me sopping wet in my shift by moonlight. We were husband and wife, and truth be told, I was powerfully attracted to my husband. I had hoped this journey might free us from familiar constraints to the point that we leaped the hurdle into marital intimacy, though I did not know precisely how to make that leap.

"I have become a prodigiously gifted napper," I said, tossing a pillow into the reading chair, "and this day has been wearying. Perhaps you'd care to join me?"

He closed the door, locked it, and prowled into the room. "Perhaps I would."

～

Sebastian tugged at his cravat, and my first instinct was to unknot his neckcloth for him. I instead retrieved a dressing gown from the wardrobe and belted it loosely.

"How is Hannibal?" I asked, taking the wrinkled linen from him and hanging it over the privacy screen.

"Not good. My boy is stoic. When another horse would be kicking down the walls of his stall or rolling incessantly, Hannibal merely gazes into the distance as if contemplating his final arrangements."

"Let me do that," I said, taking hold of the cuff of Sebastian's shirt. I extracted the right sleeve button, then the left, and held out my hand for his jacket.

"You must hang the coat over a chair," Sebastian said, shrugging out of his riding jacket. "Upjohn grows downright loquacious about the ill effects of mistreating good tailoring."

Neither heat nor humor infused Sebastian's warning, and it occurred to me that Hannibal was not the only stoic in the family.

"You are exhausted. Sit down, Sebastian. Did you not sleep well on board ship?"

He sank onto the cedar chest at the foot of the bed. "I generally sleep well enough at sea, but I heard you with Maeve and Annis, I checked on Hannibal, I watched the starry night sky and wondered when I'd be homesick for Perthshire."

He was half out of his mind with worry for the horse, else he'd never have shared even that much. "Are you homesick?"

"Not for that drafty old castle and my scheming relations. You are not removing my boots, Violet Marie."

"Then remove them yourself." What or who was he homesick for if not the magnificent dwelling and its spectacular views? "Lucy says all is not marital accord here at The Falls."

"Upjohn reports similarly." Sebastian pulled off his boots and set them in the dressing closet, then settled into the reading chair by the cold hearth. "Mrs. Gillespie is a heedless spendthrift, and her husband retaliates by indulging himself in gentlemanly pursuits. It's her family's money, and she'd have burned through the lot of it but for Mr. Gillespie's steadying hand."

"While the maids claim Mister is the spendthrift, and Missus is consoling herself as best she can with social pursuits. I met Miss Gillespie."

Sebastian undid his garters and peeled out of his stockings. Part of me was shocked—*naked*, muscular calves so casually displayed!— but I was oddly comforted by what was a maritally mundane moment.

Couples in charity with each other chatted amiably while dressing and undressing. I knew this because in the first year of my previous marriage, I had tried my utmost to be in charity with Freddie, who had been at all times amiable.

Amiably selfish.

Amiably snide about his friends.

Amiably determined to indulge his every whim and wickedness.

"Tell me of Miss Gillespie," Sebastian said, holding out a hand.

What did he want? I thought to take a seat on the cedar chest or the vanity stool when I found myself abruptly pulled into my husband's lap.

"Better," he said, arranging my legs over the arm of the chair. "Will the young lady take London by storm next spring?"

For about five seconds, I tried to sit up straight, then abandoned the undertaking as futile. "What is this indignity in aid of, Sebastian?"

"Our comfort. Cuddle up."

This spontaneous display of husbandly familiarity had to be a result of worry for the horse. I cuddled up anyway, because I was worried for Hannibal too.

"Miss Gillespie is so young, Sebastian. Painfully young."

"As young as you were when you spoke your vows with Belmaine?"

"Yes." The insight left me angry, sad, and so sorry for my younger self. "Lambs to slaughter come to mind."

"You are married to me now," Sebastian said, cradling my jaw against his palm. "A much happier state of affairs, aye? Miss Gillespie will have a field of admirers at this house party. I've met a few of them."

I closed my eyes when Sebastian slid his hand back to massage the nape of my neck. "Because the best way to impress a young lady is to lounge about the stables with the other fellows, smoking and making vulgar jokes?"

"The best way to assess the competition is to lounge about the stables, evaluating the other fellows' cattle and conveyances, and letting it be known that you are in the running for the lady's hand. If I were a betting man, I'd put a fiver on Lord Jasper Blenrith, a marquess's spare, though Mr. Aristotle Dinwiddie will give him a run for his—note the term—*money*. The Dinwiddies have made an obscenely large fortune in shipping, and young Aristotle cuts quite a golden dash."

Tension I'd carried with me all the way south from Perthshire floated away with the gentle caresses of Sebastian's fingers. He made a warm and comfy chaise, and I sensed no intimate agenda on his part. I was too tired and too aware of the clock ticking relentlessly forward to have any designs on him. Lucy would return in less than an hour. Maeve would need my attention as well.

Sebastian had simply wanted to hold me, and I... Sleep beckoned, but the pleasure of cuddling with my husband was too delicious to part with.

"Any dark-horse bachelors in the field?" I asked.

"Several. Sir Miniver Holmes is widowed and well-heeled. Experience and guile are on his side, and his estate is only eight miles to the west. He's a fine-looking specimen, if you don't mind red hair, and his horses are in excellent condition."

"Good to know. Who else? A few of the more presentable fortune hunters must be making up the numbers." I did not care in the least which bachelors vied for Miss Gillespie's hand. The young lady deserved to make her come out free of romantic obligations, after all. I did, though, treasure the sound of Sebastian's voice and the pleasure of his embrace.

I realized with some dismay that I'd never known a moment like this with Freddie, nor anything quite like it with St. Sevier. We'd been affectionate, but most of that affection had been of the sort enjoyed in bed.

"In terms of presentable," Sebastian said, shifting deeper into the chair, "we have Lord Cranston, new to his honors as a viscount, but alas, pockets to let and barely shaving. His horses are high-strung and lacking weight, but he probably inherited them along with the title."

"Skinny horses are a sure sign of pockets to let. I know his sister. She's high-strung and used to be quite trim as well. Married a beer baron." Which had nothing to do with anything.

"And then there's Mr. Leo Fontaine, late of Paris. He serves as our unknown quantity, which is always useful for keeping the front-runners on their toes. His sister has accompanied him, and I'm told she's comely."

"We won't be of any moment, will we? The race is truly on for Miss Gillespie's hand. The rabbits are assembled at the starting line." What I'd just said had made no sense.

"Go to sleep, Violet. I'll wake you in half an hour."

"I'm too heavy."

"You are perfect. Go to sleep."

"Do not presume to give me orders, Sebastian."

He kissed my temple, and I fell asleep.

~

"Last I heard from Upjohn, Hannibal was sinking slowly," Lucy said, her ominous tone at odds with the brilliant morning sunshine streaming through the bedroom windows. "Said the beast was fighting in his own way, to no avail. Horses are delicate when it comes to their tummies, according to him. This would have been about two in the morning, judging by the moon."

I withheld comment on assignations by moonlight among the staff, because Lucy was as cheerful as ever, while I was suffering the ill effects of a short and restless night. Sebastian had spent the dark watches with his horse, so what slumber I'd managed had occurred in the vast and somewhat lumpy bed.

"Will Upjohn see that the marquess gets something to eat?" I sat at the table near the open French doors and poured myself a cup of tea. Stubborn Scotsmen were no more invincible than their horses, and Sebastian had to be as exhausted as I was.

The evening buffet had been the predictable gauntlet, with sidelong glances and knowing smiles aimed at me, St. Sevier, and Ann. The whole company doubtless knew that St. Sevier had been my traveling companion on various excursions after I'd emerged from mourning.

Had I taken to travel unaccompanied, they'd have exchanged the same nudges and winks, though nobody had dared smirk at Sebastian.

We had endured with smiles, air kisses, and half-genuine inquiries about mutual acquaintances. Then we had drifted apart, according to the expected choreography of congeniality. At Ann's suggestion, we had enjoyed supper *à quatre* on the back terrace in full view of the other guests. Those worthies had discreetly goggled at us until whispering about the execrable dessert punch provided better entertainment.

"Upjohn took his lordship a plate at first light," Lucy said, laying one of my prettier morning dresses on the bed. "Was the punch truly as awful as all that?"

"Wormwood and gall would have compared favorably to what was on offer in that crystal bowl. The first few guests who partook said nothing, because they did not want to be rude, but when Mr. Gillespie tried his portion, he spewed it all over the roses. Then everybody had to take a taste, lest they miss out on the horror."

The truly appalling aspect of the evening had been Mr. Gillespie ranting at his wife before a terrace full of guests. St. Sevier had interrupted to suggest an unsoundly corked batch of champagne was to blame, though I'd never known champagne to turn a punch to purple brine. The bachelors in particular had taken up maligning champagne, and they'd done so with a suspiciously merry air.

Lucy set out stockings and heeled slippers to go with the dress. "First footman—name is Peters—says he and Cook can both vouch for the quality of the punch when it left the kitchen."

"As can half the kitchen staff, would be my guess. Easy enough to dump a flask of vinegar into the punchbowl once service is set up on the terrace." Or several flasks, if the prank had resulted from a conspiracy. The punch had been absolutely ruined.

"Nasty business, if you ask me. Champagne comes dear, that raspberry cordial was lovely, and somebody wasted a fair lot of both. What shall we do with your hair?"

My hair had become a force of nature—thick, shiny, and fast-growing. Lucy was ever in favor of cropping it short and letting "the natural curl" manifest. I passionately defended my braids and buns.

For summer, short hair would have doubtless been more comfortable, and curls were certainly fashionable, but I vividly recalled Sebastian, once upon a long-ago summer, telling me that he liked long hair on a female. He'd come back from his first year at university and had rendered that opinion with disconcerting confidence.

I dispatched two croissants with butter and jam and two more cups of tea—I was that short of sleep—while Lucy tidied up the bedroom. When Lucy had made me presentable, I rapped on the door to the St. Seviers' apartment. Ann opened it, looking composed and pale, but then, she was a redhead with a complexion the archangels would envy.

"Good morning," I said. "Shall we to the nursery?"

She stepped back, admitting me into a parlor all done up in damask roses—the curtains, the carpet, the upholstery. The effect was busy, and the color scheme—pink, pale green, and cream—wanted contrast.

Ann closed the door. "Must you be so obnoxiously coherent at such an early hour?"

"Must you be so ungracious? When I've paid my call on the nursery, I need to retrieve my husband from the stable, where he kept vigil over his ailing horse. *Tempus fugit*, and Maeve has yet to learn much patience when it comes to regular sustenance."

St. Sevier emerged from the bedroom, looking dapper and tidy in breeches and waistcoat. He was fastening a cuff, but gave up on that endeavor to offer me a bow. "My lady, good morning. You look radiant."

I looked tired, as did he, to a lesser extent. Nonetheless, his smile was friendly, as was mine. Hugh was a treat for the eye, even if he was no longer my treat.

"Her ladyship is determined," Ann said, taking her husband by the wrist and doing up his sleeve button. "She is bound for the nursery. I am bound for the teapot. You two go along, and I will follow when I've been reunited with my faultless good manners."

As Ann did up Hugh's second sleeve button, he murmured something to her in French. I didn't catch the words, but I knew the tone, equal parts solicitous and admonitory.

"Don't fuss," Ann replied—in Gaelic—as she held his riding jacket for him. "Off to the nursery with you."

"I have my orders," Hugh said, winging his arm at me. "Fiona will doubtless add to my responsibilities for the day. We did not bring her mount, you see, and thus I am in her bad books."

We departed. and I dropped Hugh's arm as soon as we gained the corridor. "Stow the Gallic charm, sir. Is Ann well?"

"My wife enjoys the greatest of good health, thank you. What of you?" On the landing, Hugh nodded cordially to Miss Gillespie, who was haranguing Mr. Nicholson in whispers and gesticulations.

"I'm well," I said, "though Maeve does not sleep through the night, and naps are still a necessity for us both."

Hugh paused at the top of the steps. "The child... thrives?"

Ann had exhibited tremendous generosity of spirit by sending Hugh to the nursery with me. We were not husband and wife, but we were father and mother. Hugh had been parted from Maeve for months, and being Hugh, that mattered to him—and to me.

"When you were younger," I said, eyeing his chestnut locks, "was your hair a brighter red?"

"*Comme un feu de joie,*" he said. "Like a bonfire, a conflagration, when I was a very small boy. Fortunately for me, time moderated nature's excess."

Well, that explained our daughter's flaming tresses. "Maeve thrives. She is charming and merry, and I adore her, as does Sebastian."

St. Sevier's smile was mischievous. "Then she gets her disposition from her papa, clearly."

I smacked his arm and experienced an unexpected relief. St. Sevier could joke about the situation, even as his heart was doubtless aching, as was mine. Maeve had been conceived in love, and she was very much loved still, but matters had not gone according to anybody's plans.

I settled in to provide Maeve her breakfast, while Hugh joined Fiona and Annis on the balcony. The girls were already finishing each other's sentences—they had English and Gaelic in common— and making great plans for a child's scavenger hunt.

"They are mad keen on that scavenger hunt," Bevins said, tidying up a game of carpet marbles. "One of the other nurserymaids mentioned a children's scavenger hunt she'd helped with at some Yuletide gathering, and Annis and Fiona immediately began making lists."

"The idea has merit," I said as Maeve concluded her meal. "I'll mention it to Mrs. Gillespie and volunteer to coordinate it. How many young guests are there?"

Bevins lacked something of her usual good cheer, but she rattled off four other names. Sir Miniver Holmes had brought his two boys— eight and ten—and another family had brought a boy and a girl of nine and eleven, respectively.

"A well-behaved lot," Bevins said. "The older children are playing patience in the schoolroom with Sir Miniver's governess. Shall I take the baby?"

"No need." I managed to put my bodice to rights mostly one-handed, then rose with Maeve in my arms. Bevins passed me a soft cotton cloth, and I took Her Highness to the balcony.

"If I'm to manage the children's scavenger hunt," I said, "I will need some ideas to get me started. What are we to search for?"

LADY VIOLET SAYS I DO

Hugh's gaze was on Maeve, though he was trying not to stare. I draped the cloth over his shoulder and passed him the baby.

"Make yourself useful. The young ladies and I have matters to discuss."

He sent me one fleeting, unfathomable glance, then broke into the sweetest, most pleased smile I had ever seen from him.

"Useful. Of course." He rearranged the cloth on his shoulder and cradled Maeve gently. "*Salutations, mon ange. Comme tu es adorable.*" He pattered on, murmuring to his daughter and gently patting her little back.

"Come along, you two." I took Annis by one hand and Fiona by the other. "I need pencil and paper and a pair of lively imaginations."

We settled on a bench facing the park and made lists of items to hide and possible hiding places. Annis insisted on a list of places that must be out of bounds and places that were too easy.

"You mustn't hide anything near the foot of the falls," Fiona said. "Mama would hang me by my toes if I went there without a grown-up."

"My papa would hang me by my hair," Annis added, though I was certain the topic of wandering to the falls had not come up between Sebastian and the child.

"You cannot see the falls from the balcony," Fiona went on, "but we can see everything else."

"Not everything," Annis retorted, sending Fiona a portentous look. "A lot of things. Not everything."

Clearly, they had seen *something*. I considered the park, stretching away from the formal parterres below. The stable was visible through some trees to the left. The park gave way to wilderness to the right and rolled down to the river in the near distance.

And immediately below us was the terrace.

"You spied on the guests last night?" I asked.

"We don't spy," Annis said, her little chin coming up. "Spies are wicked. We watch and learn." She executed a gracious curtsey, and Fiona obliged her with a bow, followed by peals of giggles.

St. Sevier smiled at me from the far end of the balcony, Maeve now asleep against his shoulder. Some tiny, hard knot of worry in my heart eased.

The laughter of children was good medicine indeed.

"And we saw Mr. Gillespie spit punch on the roses," Fiona added, miming that undignified moment over the railing. "He was very loud."

"He yelled at Mrs. Gillespie," Annis said, striking a pose. "'Good God, madam. What were you thinking?'"

"And then Papa blamed the champagne, and everybody started talking. Was the punch truly bad?"

"It was awful, but you are not to ridicule people when they are upset, Fee."

St. Sevier was listening to this recitation, though he remained in his corner of the balcony.

"We aren't to make fun of anybody, ever," Annis said, sounding not the least bit contrite. "But Mr. Gillespie wasn't very nice to his wife."

"And the champagne wasn't to blame," Fiona added. "We saw a fellow dump something into the punchbowl when the footmen went back to the kitchen to fetch the rest of the glasses."

"Can you describe this fellow?" Hugh asked.

"*Oui*," Fiona replied. "*Il avait les cheveux bruns, et—*"

Annis smacked Fiona's shoulder. "English, Fee, and then the French. We agreed."

"He had brown hair," Fiona said, "*cheveux bruns*, and he was tall —*grand*." She stretched her hand up high. "He wore a part right down the middle of his head—*au centre de sa tête*. When Mr. Gillespie began yelling, the tall fellow stood next to Mrs. Gillespie."

"She's blond," Annis observed, "and the tall fellow put his arm around her waist, like a promenade." She and Fiona demonstrated that posture. "Then Bevins made us come inside, and she read us a story."

"About *The Tortoise and the Hare*, which we already knew, but it's a good tale. Slow and steady wins the race!"

If this recitation was accurate, Greer Nicholson had ruined the punch and then attempted to console the hostess whom he had humiliated. That made no sense to me. None at all.

"What do you make of it?" I asked St. Sevier when Bevins had retrieved Maeve and shepherded the girls back inside.

"Odd business, but then, Nicholson isn't quite family to the Gillespies, and he apparently doesn't want to be here. I still wouldn't have said he was the sort to play cruel jests. We say nothing of this?"

"I suppose not, unless more nasty pranks crop up."

We fell silent as the glory of a brilliant morning bathed the park before us. Summer in the south of England was a mellower, more placid season than in Perthshire, and I was abruptly glad I'd made the journey.

"Your husband returns from the stable," St. Sevier said, nodding in the direction of the long, low, stone building. "His lordship moves as if exhausted."

"Hannibal has colic, or is trying to colic or trying not to colic. Sebastian loves that horse. I'd best go to him."

"Warn him of Nicholson's prank, and I will tell Ann. I don't like it."

"Neither do I. Anybody who'd pull a stunt like that in plain view of four dozen windows is not a skilled schemer, though. We can take heart from the clumsiness of the mischief."

He bowed over my hand and murmured, very softly, "*Merci*, Violet. *Merci beaucoup*."

That was the first direct contact we'd had... since... in a very long time. That we could touch was another indicator of progress.

"Visit the nursery as often as you please, St. Sevier. You don't need my permission to enjoy the company of our daughters."

I took my leave on that note and met my weary, rumpled husband on the terrace steps.

CHAPTER EIGHT

Sebastian

Violet was her usual brisk, poised self when she met me on the terrace, but around her eyes, I detected signs of fatigue. When she gave me her hand, her fingers were uncharacteristically cool.

"Hannibal has turned the corner," I said, wanting to whoop the words loudly enough for every guest to hear me. "Nicholson came out at first light for an early hack and found me half asleep on a pile of straw. He asked if Hannibal had served with me on the Peninsula, and when I replied in the affirmative, Nicholson suggested we try a beer mash."

Violet began brushing at my hair, not the done thing in public, but I was too tired and relieved—and pleased that she'd fuss me at all —to care.

"What on earth is a beer mash? Now you do need a bath."

I caught her hands, in love with her and with the day. "My pony has come right. Insult me all you please, ye wee besom, and I will still be in charity with all of creation."

She was trying not to smile. How well I knew the look.

"You reek of the stable, my lord. I make an observation based on fact, and you are insulted. I have married a fanciful man prone to imagined slights. I'm told Upjohn took you a tray to break your fast, but did you eat or merely thank him and resume praying for your horse? Be honest, Sebastian. I have my informants."

"You worried about me." I was at risk for kissing my wife, truly kissing her, with half the company gawking at us. To avoid that spectacle, I put Violet's hand on my arm and escorted her into the house. She came along docilely enough, until we were out of view of the guests.

"Upjohn doubtless brought you weak tea and cold toast, as if a man of your Brobdingnagian proportions can maintain his vigor on mere snacks. As if you can travel the length of the realm twice in the space of weeks, go without sleep, worry yourself sick over dear Hannibal, and make do on crumbs."

She started up the steps, and I trailed along behind, marveling at her stamina. She had always had a flair for a scold, and I was delighted to think she'd honed her skills on Belmaine and St. Sevier.

"Upjohn is a good fellow," she went on, "but he has yet to grasp that his consequence derives from your own. Unless there's a duke underfoot, Upjohn is the reigning monarch belowstairs, provided he doesn't insult the Gillespies' butler or housekeeper."

Violet rounded the landing, gaining momentum as we climbed the second flight. "Lucy has tried to elucidate the particulars to Mr. Upjohn, but his humility is a granite edifice. Humility is all to the good, of course, but he should also exercise the perquisites of his post on your behalf. He should have brought you a steaming platter, carried by a footman—the plate covered, of course—with a tea tray carried by a second footman."

She reached the upper floor and marched on toward the green-and-blue bower. "Sustenance matters, my lord. A woman who has endured gestation, parturition, and their aftermath learns that lesson well. Wellington knew how important provisions were to the success of his endeavors, as did Napoleon. Dry toast and tepid teal will not do."

She opened the door to our sitting room herself—such was her momentum when in full sail—and I closed the door behind us.

The click of the latch ushered in a silence, during which Violet began rearranging pillows on the sofa. When she had exhausted that dilatory tactic, she shifted the candle on the mantel, then stood blinking at the cold hearth.

"Violet Marie, come here." I held out my arms, and she bundled close. "Hannibal is grazing as I speak. We didn't lose him, and God willing, he'll be swishing his tail at flies into a great old age."

Violet was apparently not in the mood for half measures. She clung to me tightly, her nose mashed against my chest.

"He's such a good, dear fellow, Sebastian. I wanted to go to you, and yet, I dared not imply the situation was beyond you. You love that horse. I love that horse because he loves you. You never did explain this beer mash business."

Even in her upset, Violet stopped short of telling me she loved me. That she would use the word was comfort enough.

"A beer mash," I said, "is like a bran mash, military style. It's basically horse porridge liberally supplemented with applesauce or chopped apples, chopped or grated carrots, a dollop of honey, and a dash of salt. In addition to soaked wheat bran, some of the grooms would add a few handfuls of oats. The lot of it is stirred up with a portion of beer or ale, and half the cavalry swore by it."

She peered up at me. "*Beer* for horses?"

"The military watched its stores of beer and ale as closely as it did the stores of ammunition and seldom ran out of either."

Violet relaxed against me. "You are sure he'll be well?"

"As certain as one can be. How did St. Sevier weather his visit to the nursery?"

She eased away and yanked the bell-pull. "You saw us on the balcony?"

"Anybody on the terrace could have seen you, but what does that matter? A conscientious papa looks in on his daughters." I purposely emphasized the plural, which earned me a different kind of smile from Violet.

"I told him as much. I appreciate your understanding."

Now that we were private, I was aware of crushing fatigue, roaring hunger, and a need to get clean. I was also aware, though, that the discussion was awkward for Violet.

"Somewhere in Spain," I said, "Annis has a father and a mother, or she could. The nuns had no information to give me, and Annis hasn't mentioned parents by name. Mother Superior suggested Annis might have been born a Garcia, which in that region was comparable to being a Smith in England or a Jones in Wales."

Violet smoothed my sleeve, an unnecessary gesture, not quite affectionate, but wifely. "Go on."

"If Annis has family, then they worry for her. Every night, they offer a desperate prayer for her wellbeing. Maybe they learned that a Scottish officer took her to England, and they can only hope he's a decent fellow and not some scoundrel. Could you imagine not knowing if Maeve was safe? Not knowing if she was alive?"

"St. Sevier can rely on us—both of us—to take good care of Maeve."

"We would die for her, but Hugh St. Sevier is her father. In his mind, if anybody must die for that child, it should be he, and yet, he is relegated to the status of doting godpapa."

Violet sank onto the sofa, something about her movements suggesting she'd had as little sleep the previous night as I had.

"Do the sisters in Spain know how to contact you?"

"Of course, but it has been years. I send a quarterly inquiry with a donation in appreciation for their efforts where Annis was concerned, but they've heard nothing."

She wedged a pillow behind her back, putting me in mind of the second half of her pregnancy. She'd slept amid a fortress of pillows, sat with pillows, and put her feet up on pillows.

"You support Papists?" she asked.

"I'd support Lucifer himself if he'd done for those orphans what the sisters did." I didn't talk much about my time in the military, though I'd served with one of Violet's brothers. She'd doubtless heard from Felix of the dubious glories of war.

A knock sounded on the door.

"Come in," Violet called.

A domestic parade ensued, footmen and maids bearing a tub, steaming buckets, two trays, and a pile of toweling, suggesting she'd had the staff on high alert.

"Fast work, my lady," I said when the tub was filled and the tray set out on the raised hearth. "Much-appreciated fast work."

The footmen and maids had left, and I was alone with my wife.

"Unless you favor cold baths," she said, "we'd best get you into the tub. Upjohn will want that coat and your boots, and you will leave me at least one of those sandwiches."

"You eschewed the breakfast buffet?" I pulled off my boots, which were much the worse for the night's activities.

"I had to get to the nursery. Maeve is on something of a schedule, and thus bantering with the bachelors over breakfast had to wait. Give me your jewelry."

She took my sleeve buttons, cravat pin, and signet ring and disappeared into the bedroom. I used her absence to finish disrobing and sink into the bliss of a warm bath. I closed my eyes and listened to the sound of Violet in the next room. Opening drawers, the wardrobe, smacking pillows...

When I awoke, the water was cold and our room silent. The distinctive sound of a wooden bat whacking a ball drifted in from the park along with shouts indicative of a morning cricket match.

I rose and dressed, demolishing the offerings on the tray save for one sandwich. Violet had again abandoned me at my ablutions, and this time she hadn't peeked in on me when all danger of nudity was past.

Or perhaps she had and had left me to pickle in the cooling water. I went into the bedroom, thinking to find clean footwear, and instead came upon my wife, fast asleep in the great bed. She slept on her side, the back of her hand resting on her pillow in a posture I recalled from the occasional youthful picnic. Violet was a sound sleeper, and to see her devoid of her usual starch and purpose tugged at my heart.

Worn out by worry, apparently. The room itself looked in need of a thorough tidying. The wardrobe was open, two drawers on the clothes press were not quite closed, pillows were strewn on chairs, and the tail of a blanket trailed from beneath the lid of the cedar chest.

Lucy Hewitt would never have allowed Violet's bedroom to remain in this condition, meaning Violet had been rummaging about in here while I'd soaked. I sat on the bed and brushed an errant lock from her forehead.

Out in the park, another batter connected with the ball, and a cheer went up.

Violet's eyes opened before I could decide whether she'd wallop me for kissing her awake or appreciate that I'd taken the initiative.

"Ye ministers and angels of grace," she muttered, "I hate it when I doze off. I'm not a tipsy dowager yet. What time is it?"

"Not yet ten of the clock. You might have slept for forty-five minutes. I fell asleep in the tub."

She pushed to sitting and eyed me up and down. "You do clean up nicely."

While she looked cross and had parted with a few hairpins. "What were you searching for, Violet?"

Her expression went puzzled and then carefully composed. "What makes you think I was conducting a search?"

My wife was deciding whether or not to lie to me. Despite the miracle of Hannibal's recovery, despite the glorious summer day and the fact that I was, after a fashion, in bed with my wife, my joy in the morning dimmed.

"Don't lie to me, Violet. I have my informants." My attempt at levity fell flat, though Violet didn't appear to take offense.

"You trust me with St. Sevier, but interrogate me about missing slippers?"

I rose from the bed. "Of course I trust you with St. Sevier and him with you. You did not mislay your slippers, and you would never have rifled my clothing without a good reason. Has Miss Gillespie's rabbit escaped again, or did Mrs. Yancy purloin a tiara that you hope to find in my second pair of boots?"

She left the bed and set about straightening the covers. "I've lost my mother's diary, and I feel as if I've misplaced my wits. That one volume, written in her hand, is all I have of her, and I've read it constantly. The dates correspond with when I was conceived through my first year of life, and I should have it memorized by now."

Violet hurled pillows one after the other onto the tidied bed. "I had it, Sebastian. I know I had it with me when we left Folkestone. I did not leave that journal on board ship. I packed it myself in the largest trunk, and Lucy claims she set it on the bedside table, because I kept it on the bedside table at the castle. Lucy abhors mendacity, and what would the point of such a fabrication be?"

Slamming of drawers commenced, along with a firm closing of the wardrobe doors.

"You were up half the night looking for this diary?"

"You were up half the night worrying for your horse. I could not go to you, and my dearest possession had gone missing. One tries to be p-productive."

Her features were still entirely composed, but I'd heard the catch in her breath, and I would have bet Hannibal's saddle that she was silently counting backward from twenty in Latin. I knew better than to tell Violet not to cry.

Her only link with her mother was gone, and she blamed herself.

"We'll find it," I said. "The damned thing has to be here somewhere. Nobody has any reason to steal it. Where did you last see it?"

Violet sank onto the newly made bed. "On the packet when I put it among my belongings in the trunk, right along the side. Lucy says she retrieved it from that same location and set it on the bedside table yesterday while you and I strolled the grounds. I think I recall seeing the journal before we went down to dinner, but it's not there now, and I'm so upset that I doubt my own recollections."

I took the place beside her and wrapped an arm around her waist. The mattress was more of the old, thin, and lumpy variety than soft and bouncy.

"You did not want to bother me with this?"

She laid her head against my shoulder. "I don't want to bother anybody, and I hate looking so foolish. How hard can it be to keep track of one small diary? I want to nap and be your wife and eat sandwiches all day—just as soon as I find Mama's journal."

I dearly hoped our lovemaking ranked above sandwiches and naps on Violet's list of pleasures, though there was certainly more to being husband and wife than dancing the mattress hornpipe.

"You searched the wardrobe?"

"Of course, and the balcony, and the cedar chest. I feel as if Mama has abandoned me all over again."

Something was nagging at me, some detail, some burr under my mental saddle. "Is anything else missing?"

"I hadn't thought to look. Are you suggesting we have another thief?"

At a different house party, shortly after Violet had emerged from mourning, a string of thefts had marred an otherwise pleasant gathering. Violet had solved that riddle, and in time to save Upjohn from transportation, or worse.

"We'd have heard a hue and cry if larceny were afoot," I said. "You searched all the hatboxes and shoe bags and such? As I recall, the diary is a smallish volume."

"I searched everywhere, twice, and then I sat down on the bed to think and woke up when Lucy brought my morning tray. This bed looks more comfortable than it is, I'll have you know. I swear there are rocks in the batting."

The sense of a prodding detail nagged at me again. "Stand for a moment," I said, offering my hand. "Please."

She rose, and I reverted to schoolboy instincts, which had become army instincts. Though it was the most obvious hiding place in the world, boys and men far from home would hide treasures beneath their mattresses.

"Got it," I said after a moment of poking about. I held out the little bound volume, and Violet reached for it, then reached for me. She tossed the journal on the mattress, grabbed me by the hair, and commenced kissing me witless.

Or perhaps not quite witless, because in the next instant, I was kissing her back with equal ardor.

❧

I owed Violet many things, not the least of which were my earliest lessons in masculine restraint. She'd come home from her first year at Miss Hairball's academy for incorrigible hoydens determined to learn as much about kissing as the older girls had purported to know.

Fortunately for me, the older girls must have been blessedly ignorant. Violet had dragooned me into being her practice partner for a few short weeks that in hindsight struck me as sweet and hilarious. At the time, all I'd known was that if I did not sacrifice my sanity on the altar of Violet's education, she'd recruit another pair of lips.

I hadn't dared put her at risk for the sort of mischief *that* might entail, and thus I had learned to endure. What she'd lacked in skill, she'd made for up in diligence. She concluded her explorations when she'd decided that I was abysmally untalented in the kissing department.

"One cannot make a silk purse and so forth," she'd informed me with her usual confidence in her own judgment. We'd retreated for the rest of the summer into bickering and bantering, which should have been a relief, but was not.

That I'd disappointed her sat ill with me at the time, but if I'd put her off recreational kissing for another year or two, that had to be all to the good. For my part, I'd learned to separate mind and body, such that even when kissing the female most dear and fascinating to me in the whole world, I could restrain my animal urges.

A lesson no gentleman can neglect.

Since marrying Violet, I had nearly made friends with sexual frustration. To deny oneself a pleasure temporarily is a vast improvement over resigning oneself to never having that pleasure. Now that we were husband and wife, my challenge had become choosing the perfect moment and the perfect mood to consummate our union—or waiting for Violet to make that choice.

As she twined a leg around my flank and brushed her thumb over my ear, I knew that the moment had come and that we had chosen it together. The morning was joyous—a stalwart equine friend on the road to recovery, a treasured legacy found—and we had both time and privacy.

Years of forbearance, philosophizing, and frustration fell away as I scooped Violet into my arms and settled her on the lumpy bed. I came down over her in a close crouch and reignited our kissing bonfire, while some sensible, logical part of me nattered on about *too many clothes* and *lock the damned doors.*

All the while, Violet clutched at my backside with the most glorious enthusiasm.

"Sebastian..." Another clutch, this one with the delicious sharpness of a pinch, even through the chamois of my breeches. "*Sebastian.* Wait."

Why in the name of all that was scrumptious...?

"They need the tub," she said. "That has to be the footmen come back for the wretched tub."

Somebody was rapping, quietly but insistently, on the outer door to the sitting room.

"*Gu ifrinn...*" I managed to lever up on all fours. "*To hell* with them."

"I like it when you curse in Gaelic," Violet said, patting my cheek. "You broaden my vocabulary. They won't go away until they've retrieved their tub. Compose yourself, and I will deal with them."

Her cheeks were flushed, her eyes sparkled, and I'd loosened the chignon at her nape.

"You will remain here, lest the poor footmen expire of unrequited love." As I so nearly had.

I wrenched myself from the bed, tucked in the shirttails some houri had yanked free, and grabbed a pair of clean stockings. My intention was to convey the impression that I'd been interrupted while dressing.

Upjohn was among the worthies loitering in the corridor. While the footmen collected the tray—I swiped the last sandwich just in the nick—and wheeled the tub from the room, Upjohn shifted from foot to foot.

He was a diminutive fellow who saw much more than he let on. He had the knack of being unobtrusive, one of those people who appeared to be a natural and easily overlooked element of his surroundings, no matter what those surroundings might be.

Upjohn would have made a good spy, though I did not insult him by telling him as much.

"Hannibal is napping," he said when the footmen had left us in peace. "Had another helping of mash, did justice to some grass in the park, slurped half a bucket of water, and settled in for a snooze."

"You put some ale in his water?"

"A half pint or so."

"We'll keep that up for a few days. Thank God for Nicholson's suggestion. If Hannibal shows no signs of relapsing, he can enjoy a few hours in a grassy paddock after sundown."

"Right, milord, and I'll graze him in hand throughout the day from time to time. I also have a message from Mr. Gillespie."

To hell with him too. "I was hoping to catch a few winks. Can it wait?"

"He were in a proper taking when I left him. Seems somebody

turned Miss Gillespie's mare out with the stud last night. The filly were lying flat out in the shade when the grooms come upon 'er."

The equine equivalent of a postcoital nap, thought by old grooms to increase the chances of conception. Violet had once suggested that a mare lying on the ground after mating ensured the stud left her in peace for a time.

Even her brothers had had no response to that insight. "Why does Gillespie want to see me?"

"You were in the stable all night, mostly awake, and you might have seen or heard something."

Whereas grooms playing a prank would never peach on one another. I'd been focused exclusively on Hannibal's distress, but my host would need me to convey that in person.

Even Gaelic curses were inadequate to express my frustration. "I'll be along presently, and please send Hewitt up to tidy the bedroom. Her ladyship lost track of a favorite pair of slippers, and the search was thorough."

Upjohn gave me a look, half pitying, half commiserating. "Ladies do set powerful store by their slippers, my lord. If Hannibal's recovery falters, I'll let you know."

He marched off with the impressive posture of the former infantryman, and I closed the door behind him.

"Is that my sandwich?" Violet asked.

She was all spruce and tidy, not a hair out of place. I passed her the sandwich. "Somebody put Miss Gillespie's mare in with the stud colt last night. Mr. Gillespie is not best pleased."

Violet took a nibble of sandwich. "Miss Gillespie won't be best pleased either. If the mare catches now, accompanying Miss Gillespie to Town next spring is out of the question. Aurora was a tremendous comfort to me when I made my come out. A much-needed ally."

My wife had doubtless not intended her observation as a reproach, but I felt it as such. When she'd been navigating the ballrooms without benefit of a mother's guidance or a sister's support, I'd been in Spain, taking stupid risks on the battlefields because the woman I loved had rejected me.

Or so Violet's father had led me to believe. "I should have written to you," I said.

"Papa would have intercepted your letters, and you are too honorable to have asked Felix to sneak correspondence behind enemy lines for you." She passed me the last quarter of the sandwich. "What an odd thing to do—turn a riding mare loose with the colt. Could the mare have got free on her own?"

"One supposes not."

"We'll have a look around, shall we? This is the second creature on the property going absent without leave. Once you've settled Mr. Gillespie's feathers, he should also have a chat with Mr. Nicholson."

I finished the sandwich in two bites, though I wasn't particularly hungry for food. "Why Nicholson?"

"You said he came around at first light spouting suggestions. He's apparently at home in the stable, and if he slipped the bolt on the mare's door, and she's in season... A determined female would think nothing of leaping a fence or two to reach a worthy suitor. I don't recall hearing the stud screaming last night, but then, I was preoccupied."

"How do you do this?" I said, taking Violet in a loose embrace. "How do you drive me mad one moment and then spout deductions the next? I didn't hear the stud scream either, but then, not all stallions trumpet their passion to the heavens."

"No," she said, patting my bum, "they do not. I might sound logical to you—anybody could have slipped the bolt on a stall door— but part of me is plotting the ruin of whoever demanded that tub."

"That would be Sir Miniver, if the footmen can be believed."

Violet eased away. "Let's do have a look around the stable, Sebastian. The children claim they saw Mr. Nicholson doctoring the dessert punch last evening, the rabbit turned up in Nicholson's quarters, and now there's mischief with the mare. Nicholson is not a happy fellow, from what I can see, and we are only on the second day of this gathering."

"I'll meet you on the terrace in twenty minutes or so." Rather than get myself in difficulties, I bowed my leave to her.

"Sebastian?"

I paused before opening the door. "My lady?"

"Your kissing has improved."

"So, by God, has yours."

I quit the apartment with Violet's laughter ringing in my ears.

～

"The foal will be exquisite," Nathan Gillespie said, gesturing for me to take a seat. "That's some consolation, but Dorothy and her mother will take little comfort from that."

Ladies had personal parlors, but men—important, busy fellows— had studies and offices. Gillespie's private retreat made a few gestures in the direction of industry—a desk in the corner, an abacus upon the mantel—but the dominant sense of the room was comfort.

Next to the abacus was a rack of pipes, and the bookshelves were full not of ledgers, but of novels, newspapers, and agricultural pamphlets. Over the mantel hung a depiction of the hunt pageant coming in from a run—an unsuccessful run, fortunately for my artistic sensibilities—and the open French doors admitted a lovely view of the park. The sideboard was serviceable rather than a show-piece, and the mirror above it was going a trifle speckled in one corner.

The sofa was long, well cushioned, and slightly worn. A nap would be more easily enjoyed there than in the bed Violet and I had been assigned. No gigantic flowers on the placid green wallpaper, and the several pillows on the sofa were covered in plain, sturdy maroon linen. The carpet was similarly unprepossessing, a muted pattern of green, gold, and maroon.

"I know the hour is early," Gillespie said, "but would you care for a drink?"

"Too early for me, given that I'm short of sleep."

"About that..." Gillespie poured himself a neat brandy at the sideboard and remained across the room. "You were on hand in the stable all night. Any unusual recollections, my lord?"

Gillespie was caught between the morning sun slanting through the windows and the reflection from the mirror. That much illumination revealed him to be well past the first blush of youth, perhaps ten years older than his wife.

"I'm afraid I cannot add much to what you already know," I said, taking in the view of the park. As inviting as the sofa was, I would avoid it. "I was concerned for my horse."

"Who's coming right, I hear, thanks be."

"Hannibal is recovering, and I am indebted to Greer Nicholson for his suggestion that we try a beer mash."

Gillespie's genial expression shuttered. "Fancies himself a squire, does our Greer. Would rather hack out than entertain the ladies at breakfast. What's the point of having a bachelor underfoot at a house party if he ain't prepared to be charming?"

"He makes up the numbers, and he very likely saved my horse." And for that reason, I would keep to myself what the children claimed they'd seen. The perspective from the nursery did not allow easy recognition of faces in evening shadows, and nobody had corroborated the girls' recounting.

"I love Greer as if he were my own son," Gillespie said. "His mama was Tilda's best friend, and she was widowed much too young. Then Greer came along, a consolation in her bereavement, and Tilda and I did what we could for mother and child. He was always a serious little lad, and then his mother succumbed to pleurisy when he was nine or ten. I don't believe he's laughed since."

"Do you suspect him of turning the mare out with the colt?"

Gillespie took a sip of his drink. "One must investigate all the avenues, though I admit a house party turns everything inside out for the staff. Coaches coming and going, horses everywhere and taking exception to the uproar, grooms run off their feet. If the somebody hadn't quite secured the bolt on the stall door, if the mare took to worrying the latch... Mares are ingenious and determined creatures, as I'm sure you will agree."

He took another sip. "But I ask myself: Why *that* mare? Any other horse, and the repercussions would have been insignificant. My own breeding stock was put to the stud earlier this year, and a loose gelding is concerned only with grazing by the hour. Dottie's filly is riding stock for the nonce—her mother's mare is the only other riding mare in the stable, save for a few guest horses—and Greer knows every horse on the property as none of the guests would."

What would Violet say to these musings? Did Gillespie *want* his former ward to be guilty of pulling this stunt?

"If the mare was in season," I said, "every groom would know that, and besides, what motive could inspire such a prank? Miss Gillespie and her mama are likely upset, but there's every chance the mare won't catch. If she does, Miss Gillespie can ride another. I wouldn't make too much of what might well be a mishap."

Particularly not so early in the house party.

Gillespie finished his drink. "You saw nothing, then? Heard nothing? The grooms weren't being furtive or..." He gestured with his empty glass. "Acting mischievous? They are good fellows, but many are former military. Their sense of humor can be peculiar."

I thought back to the long, worrisome night. "I was preoccupied with my horse, and yet, I recall nothing out of order. Your stable lads were concerned for Hannibal, and they mostly left me and my man, Upjohn, to it. I would point out, though, that a number of bachelors grace your guest list. When young men get to wagering over drinks, foolishness can result."

Gillespie set his glass on the sideboard and propped a hip against his desk. "And then they wake up one morning and notice a strand of gray among their curling locks. They realize years they should have spent building a legacy were instead frittered away over whist and wenches, or in Greer's case, conferring with the stewards or solicitors and avoiding Tilda's guests."

Somebody had to confer with the stewards and solicitors, as I well knew. "He's been to university?"

"Took a first in Greek and in fiddling with his investments on 'Change. The boy's wealthy, and he's not bad-looking... As a young man, I was bent on frivolity and frolic. Tilda's parents and mine were great friends, and I'd always thought of young Tilda as a comely little thing. Then she wasn't so little, but she was every bit as comely, and my father was putting his affairs in order. I was not the best choice of husband for her, but what young lady could possibly be smitten with Greer? He needs to sow wild oats, or even some tame oats, and get free of The Falls."

"A grand tour?" Nicholson was several years past when that exercise might have been appropriate.

"Something like that. For a man of his means, life offers much more than Tilda's house parties and the annual harvest."

How many brandies had Gillespie treated himself to on this fine summer morning? "And yet, you think Nicholson might have turned the mare loose?"

Gillespie rubbed his fingers across his forehead, abruptly looking not merely mature, but aged.

"Greer is an odd duck, Dunkeld. Never knew his father, lost his mother while he was yet a boy, then he was thrust into this household where the only other child was a female somewhat his junior... I have never pretended to understand him, but I did try to do my best by my ward."

"Perhaps the other bachelors will be a leavening influence on young Nicholson."

"Now that is a cheering thought. Did you know your father-in-law is also on the guest list? Derwent might not be a leavening influence, precisely, but he always adds a certain dash to any gathering, even at his age. He'll join us next week. Tilda adores the old boy and considers having you both at The Falls to be quite a coup."

While Derwent and I would doubtless consider each other's company a penance. "I'm sure Lady Dunkeld will enjoy spending time with her father." Fifteen minutes or so, provided Derwent behaved himself. "If you will excuse me, I've promised her ladyship a stroll out of doors before the day grows too warm."

"That's the thing about house parties," Gillespie said, accompanying me to the door. "We comport ourselves as guests just as we ought to do at home. A morning or evening stroll with the ladies, a hack with the fellows, a hand of cards, a picnic, an hour or two of mental combat over the chessboard. I chide Tilda for the extravagance, but her gatherings are always enormously successful."

"And this gathering is intended to ready Miss Gillespie for a London Season?"

"So my wife tells me." Gillespie closed and—this caught my notice—locked his door with a key kept on the end of his watch chain. "My lord, might I put one more question to you?"

"Of course."

"You were on the terrace last night when that awful punch was served."

I saw no point in defending what had been truly execrable potation. "I was."

Gillespie glanced up and down the deserted corridor. "I'd nipped inside when the desserts were brought out. Needed to freshen up, so to speak. When I returned to the terrace, the punchbowl was set up, and the footman was ladling out the drinks. Was Greer underfoot then? I know he was on hand about ten minutes later, when I picked up my glass, but earlier...?"

What to say? "The marchioness and I were off to the side, dining with St. Sevier and his lady. Mr. Nicholson was among the guests, but I did not see him hovering near the punchbowl." Because my seat had faced the park—and Violet. "I might add, though, that Lord Jasper has been known to indulge in high spirits, and he and Mr. Dinwiddie might be in some sort of outrageous-behavior competition."

"That pair. Tilda insisted on having them—*prime contenders*, according to her—because it's time both of them settled down. Neither one is good enough for my Dottie."

I thought of Maeve, Annis, and Fiona. "Is anybody good enough for your Dottie?"

He clapped me on the shoulder. "No, they are not. Not a one of them. My regards to your lady, Dunkeld, and thank you for your time —and your discretion."

He strode off, exuding congenial self-possession. Nathan Gillespie was nonetheless a man with doubts and fears, and—more to the point—regrets. I turned my steps toward the stable, intent on enjoying a pleasant hour with my wife, though, of course, I found no sign of Violet in the stable, the formal garden, or the conservatory.

She hadn't fallen asleep on the lumpy bed, she wasn't in the nursery or the library, and the footmen professed not to have seen her at all that morning.

CHAPTER NINE

Violet

I made the mistake of pausing on my way to the stable to enjoy the cricket tableau. Several young swains in shirt-sleeves and waistcoats jogged about, two others manfully swung bats at nothing, and the bowler conferred with an older fellow, tossing the ball from hand to hand as he did.

The spectators occupied blankets, benches, and—in the case of Sir Miniver—a shooting stick pressed into service as a temporary chair. The ladies wore wide straw hats and pale colors, the footmen in their livery a dark, and likely sweltering, contrast to the guests in repose.

Monsieur Leo Fontaine also stood out because of his darker complexion and the exquisite peacock embroidery of his waistcoat.

Young Lord Cranston's distinction—other than shoulders of considerably lesser breadth than when he wore his coats and jackets —was an overly hearty laugh and hair so blond as to be nearly white.

Off to one side, Miss Gillespie stood arm in arm with Mr. Nicholson, who cut a dash in his riding attire. They, along with the solitary

Sir Miniver, looked at ease rather than on display, unlike the rest of the guests.

Mademoiselle Fontaine was holding Mr. Dinwiddie's coat and gazing up at him raptly, while a few yards away, lanky Lord Jasper was guzzling from an ale mug and trying to turn that exercise into posturing worthy of an ancient Athenian athlete.

The grass stain on the seat of his breeches rather ruined that aspiration.

Cricket was a game, but no female with four brothers would mistake any public athletic undertaking for mere entertainment. While the guests were generally occupied with displaying prowess and appreciating such displays, Sebastian and I could execute a thorough examination of the stable.

"Do they not make the most attractive couple?" Mrs. Gillespie accosted me just as I started back toward the path leading away from the park.

I considered Mademoiselle Fontaine and Mr. Dinwiddie. "They are young, innocent, and in great good health. Anybody would find them lovely to behold." I certainly did, though I wasn't much older than either party.

"We mothers see things differently, don't we, my lady?" Mrs. Gillespie said, slipping her arm through mine. "I must tell you how much I appreciate the effort you made to accompany his lordship to our little gathering. I honestly did not expect either of you to attend, but the courtesies are to be observed, and we are neighbors—and here you are!"

Her eyes sparkled, and her air was that of a pleased confidante. A talented hostess had this ability to make every guest feel honored, and Mrs. Gillespie was accounted a very skilled hostess.

"We came by sea," I said, "a new experience for me and, for the most part, enjoyable."

We fell silent as Mr. Dinwiddie took up a bat, swung a few times, and stepped up to the crease. He handled the bat as if he knew what he was about.

"Who is the bowler?" I asked, because he, too, seemed well suited to his job. Blond, trim, slightly above medium height, with a quality of being at home in his body that the strutting specimens lacked.

"Cyrus Thurmont. His younger brother Thomas is the wicket-keeper. One either recruits the neighbors on such an occasion, or the older male guests get involved. As they injure knees and strain their backs, the footmen are pressed into service. Not the done thing, so needs must. The Thurmonts are well respected, and Greer and Nathan are firm proponents of cordiality toward the neighbors."

My father had often remarked that the gentry were greater snobs than the peerage, and shopkeepers were the worst snobs of all. One dreaded to think Papa could be right about anything, but he was a keen observer of society and had traveled its metes and bounds far longer than I had.

Miss Gillespie called encouragement to Cyrus Thurmont. Mademoiselle Fontaine retaliated by blowing a kiss to Mr. Dinwiddie.

"Greer is so patient with her," Mrs. Gillespie said just as I would have extricated my arm from hers. "Far more patient than Nathan ever was with me."

I wanted to meet Sebastian in the stable, and I did not want to be drawn into Mrs. Gillespie's matchmaking dramas. Nonetheless, I was the Marchioness of Dunkeld making my first public appearance after my confinement, and rudeness on my part would be remarked.

"I beg your pardon?" was the best I could do.

"Greer and Dorothy. They are so perfectly suited, notwithstanding that one must allow them to discover that fact for themselves."

Mr. Nicholson stood politely at Miss Gillespie's side, while Miss Gillespie appeared intent upon the batsman and bowler.

"You'll aid the cause of such discovery?" I asked.

Mrs. Gillespie's smile was wistful. "Greer's mother was my oldest and dearest friend, my lady. We talked about our children one day marrying, as mothers do. Then Greer came to us, and he has doted on

Dorothy since he was a boy. We have not been blessed with sons, but Greer has been like a son to us."

And somehow this did not make him *like a brother to Dorothy?* True, Dorothy did seem close to Mr. Nicholson, but not amorously so.

"You think I'm being sentimental," Mrs. Gillespie went on. "I doubtless am, but Greer is also well-fixed, and his mama was a baronet's daughter. Nathan was Greer's guardian, and the trustees managed the inheritance *quite* competently. He's a bright young man, if short on charm, and Dorothy adores him. With time and the right circumstances, I'm sure we'll hear wedding bells."

This was more—far more—than I wanted to know. "You will see to it that Dorothy has her come out, though, won't you?" Mr. Nicholson was as short on charm as Hannibal was short on table manners.

Mrs. Gillespie's mouth acquired a grim set as Mr. Dinwiddie made an awkward swipe at the ball, which glanced off his arm.

An out on the first pitch. One for the gentry swain.

"Of course Dorothy will be presented," Mrs. Gillespie said as the spectators politely applauded Cyrus's skill. "She will have her waltzes and meet the right people, and Greer will escort her to all the right functions. To strike a man out on the first pitch is hardly sporting."

Miss Gillespie was clapping madly nonetheless, and even Mr. Nicholson was smiling. Dinwiddie retired with good grace, and I tried to do the same.

"You will excuse me," I said, slipping my arm free at last. "Dunkeld invited me for a stroll, and after days on board ship, I do feel a need to move."

"You won't stay for the punch and sandwiches? I'm serving the raspberry cordial and champagne so the guests will know my recipe was not at fault."

Brave of her. I spied St. Sevier and Ann on the terrace and waved to them. "Some exercise first," I said, "and I dare not keep my husband waiting."

Ann started down the steps, St. Sevier trailing while he took in the cricket match. Lord Jasper assayed a few swings of the bat, and Cyrus looked to be enjoying himself.

"Nathan is the same way," Mrs. Gillespie said. "Sets great store by punctuality and manners. My parents thought an older husband would mean a patient husband, but the patience took years to come along. I love him dearly, but I do not always understand my spouse."

"Thus sayeth we all." Would this woman never let me go?

"You heard about Dorothy's mare?"

"A mishap, I'm sure. My first mare was something of an escape artist." As I had been in my youth, though I'd apparently lost my touch. Thank heavens, Ann approached with Hugh in tow.

"Madame St. Sevier, a pleasure to see you. I am taking a constitutional with Dunkeld, who awaits me in the stable. Shall you and Monsieur join us?"

Mrs. Gillespie looked as if she might well have ensnared Ann and Hugh, but for a footman hovering several yards off.

"Good morning, madame, monsieur," she said, treating the recent arrivals to a gracious smile. "I trust you both slept well?"

An interminable round of small talk ensued. When our hostess finally took herself off to confer with the footman, I made directly for the stable.

"She's matchmaking," I said, marching off. "Thinks to pair Dorothy with Mr. Nicholson, and I don't believe either young person is interested in that arrangement."

"Young people can change their minds," Ann said, keeping up with me easily.

"Young people also do what their dunderheaded elders expect of them, with miserable results. I should have braced our hostess on the children's scavenger hunt."

"The girls are taking great delight in planning their contributions to the hunt," Ann replied. "They got up to a game of hide-and-seek while we were at dinner last night and plan to explore The Falls floor by floor. The scavenger hunt might serve best if you hold off for a week or so."

"We must take the children to the actual falls as soon as may be," Hugh said. "I'm told there's an old folly picturesquely falling down the cliffside from neglect and forbidden to all. Curiosity appeased is curiosity that will not result in tragedies."

"Valid point." And somebody had become a conscientious father virtually overnight. "Shall we plan a picnic for later in the week?"

"Sir Miniver might like to join us," Ann said. "His boys are full of high spirits. The Bechtels seem to leave their children mostly to the staff."

"I will confer with Mrs. Bechtel," I said as we reached the stable. "She cannot object to her darlings getting some fresh air in good company. Now, where do you suppose the mares are housed? St. Sevier, might you make some inquiries?"

Ann sent him a look—amused and wifely. Hugh bowed and strode off.

"Does he know?" I asked when St. Sevier was out of earshot.

Ann's smile faded. "I haven't found the right moment to tell him, but Hugh is a noticing sort and quite the medical expert. How did you guess?"

"You were more pale than usual this morning, subdued when you typically hurl thunderbolts as easily as Mr. Thurmont tosses his cricket ball, and you have a look in your eye... as if you contemplate a happy, distant secret." Then too, Ann and Hugh were in love. Not the flaming passion of the young and heedless, but with a quiet, powerful current of trust, esteem, and attraction running between them.

How I longed to hug her, whom I'd once regarded as the author of all my woes. "Hugh will wait until you tell him, and you are waiting until you are sure. Why not carry the worry and hope together?"

Sebastian, in his way, had fretted through my pregnancy along with me. We had alternated duties, with one of us doing the worrying and the other being sensible. When I grew too pensive, Sebastian had jollied me into spatting. When he'd become broody, I'd prodded him into political debates.

And somehow, the time had passed, Maeve had arrived, and Sebastian and I were parents without having become lovers—yet.

Ann watched her departing husband until he disappeared into the dim reaches of the stable.

"Hugh did not think we could have children," she said. "He claims Fiona is one miracle, Maeve another, and we must not dun the Almighty for a third."

"Miracles, because of all the illnesses he suffered in Spain." Children were unlikely for a man who'd endured chickenpox, measles, and God knew what else later in life than most who suffered such afflictions.

"Because of that, and because of some pessimism native to the Gaul. The Scots have it, too, but Hugh and I are both healthy now, and we do have Fiona and Maeve, so my hopes are winning out over my fears."

Yes, *we* did. "You should tell him, not only because he's your husband, but also because he's very knowledgeable about how best to care for a woman in pregnancy. Sebastian asked St. Sevier all manner of unbearable questions, and Hugh set his mind at ease."

And where was Sebastian?

"I will tell Hugh when the right moment comes along."

In all likelihood, St. Sevier had already divined Ann's condition. He was an observant fellow and doubtless a devoted husband in the intimate sense. I could contemplate that reality with all good cheer, in part because I anticipated consummating my own vows with Sebastian.

Though first, I would have to find that good fellow.

We poked around the stable at length, coming to no definitive conclusions regarding the mare's adventure. I parted from Ann and

Hugh and decided to explore the grounds on my own before paying my midday call on the nursery.

I had toured the conservatory—hot and close, even when only half full of greenery—and made my way to the hermit's grotto—shady and commodious, as hermit's grottos went—and was trundling back to the house along a rhododendron walk when I finally encountered my spouse.

Sebastian did not see me, which was fortunate. When I came upon him, Miss Dorothy Gillespie was clinging to my husband more desperately than any barnacle had ever attached itself to a ship of the line, and Sebastian's arms were rather firmly around her too.

~

"Lady Dunkeld," Mr. Nicholson called from ten yards behind me.

I retraced my steps in his direction, lest he come upon the same embrace I had. "Mr. Nicholson, good morning. You've abandoned the cricket match?"

"We all have, due to the increasing heat. We'll resume the game tomorrow and tomorrow and tomorrow, to quote the Bard, weather permitting. Might I ask if you've seen Miss Gillespie?"

What he lacked in small talk, he made up for in directness, a quality I would normally admire. "I have not seen Miss Gillespie's smiling face since I left the match more than an hour ago." Her hands clutching my husband's shoulders were another matter. "I have been exploring the grounds and, in particular, admiring the hermit's grotto."

Mr. Nicholson scowled faintly in the direction of the river. "Aunt Tilda's revenge, or one of them. Uncle Nathan expanded the orangery, though we have enough oranges, lemons, and limes. Tilda turned the grotto into a reading retreat, or so she calls it. I'll probably find Dorothy there. Aunt Tilda is adamant that Dottie assist her to make up teams for a pall-mall tournament."

Or Tilda had seen Dorothy leave the cricket match on the arm of

Lord Jasper, Mr. Dinwiddie, or some other fellow who might enjoy exploring the hermit's grotto with Miss Gillespie all too well.

"You don't care for pall-mall, Mr. Nicholson?"

He didn't smile, but his gaze showed a hint of humor. "I don't care for idleness, my lady. A bit of fun, some pleasant relaxation is all well and good, but my nature isn't suited to day after day of aimless activity. I remember my mother as an invalid..." He ran a hand through wavy dark locks. "Old business. Ancient business. If you see Dorothy, please—"

"My lady!" Dorothy leaned heavily on Sebastian as they came around the bend in the path. "Oh, how fortunate, you have Greer with you. Greer, do stop scowling. I've turned my ankle, and the marquess was good enough to aid me. So silly to take a bad step on a path I've trodden for years. My lady, you must think me the greatest fool ever to nearly fall on her face."

I thought her the worst dissembler ever to make free with the person of another woman's husband. I nonetheless smiled sympathetically.

"Perhaps Mr. Nicholson would be good enough to escort you back to the manor?" I inquired with perfect amiability. "His lordship and I are overdue for our constitutional."

In truth, we were overdue for a nap and a very frank talk, not in that order.

"Come along, Dottie," Mr. Nicholson said. "Aunt Tilda was ready to rouse the watch when she realized you hadn't come in with the other ladies. You know how she gets, and now she's on about pall-mall teams, as if she's deploying troops at Waterloo."

"I have run tame on this property since birth," Dottie retorted, "and now Mama thinks I was lost? Stolen by pirates? Because I wanted to look in on dear Ariadne? Did she and Papa think I would not hear of my poor mare's misadventure? Truly, Greer, I shall go mad before this house party ends."

He muttered what sounded like, "That makes two of us," bowed again to me and then to Sebastian, and offered Dorothy his arm.

Sebastian watched them depart. "Miss Gillespie has miraculously recovered from an ankle that was surely broken five minutes ago."

"The recuperative powers of the young are amazing, perhaps to compensate for a complete inability to lie convincingly."

"You saw us?"

The question was careful, as it should have been. "I saw *her*, wrapped about you as if you were the maypole and she were a village worth of ribbons. You weren't exactly trying to extricate yourself."

Sebastian studied the path in both directions. "Violet, I vow that young woman was trying to kiss me. She pled a turned ankle, and then... What is the point in kissing a man who cannot marry her? If I were an eligible, then her aim might have been a forced engagement."

He seemed not merely puzzled, but disconcerted. I took his hand and led him in the direction of the grotto.

"Perhaps she chose you precisely because you could not offer for her."

"Chose me for *what*?"

"To ruin her?" I was thinking out loud, trying to put myself into the slippers of a young woman with passionately held dreams and little experience of the world in which those dreams must unfold. Not a difficult exercise, but painful. "Dorothy is to take London by storm in the spring, then marry Mr. Nicholson, if Tilda Gillespie's plans are realized."

"That might come as a shock to Mr. Nicholson."

"And to Dorothy."

Sebastian had the knack of holding hands. He matched my pace, neither slowing me down nor dragging me forward, and his grip was easy.

"I inspected the stable, Sebastian, with Hugh and Ann. We started with the mare's stall, and any enterprising horse could have bumped that bolt loose. The half-doors don't swing, they slide along on rollers. If the mare rubbed at the door, cribbed, fiddled the latch with her lips... She could have slipped the bolt."

"Could have. I also studied the mechanism, and she would have had to slip the bolt, then somehow nudge the door aside from inside the stall. The rollers are oiled, but those doors are heavy. The grooms claim none of the horses have escaped before."

"We must have just missed each other. There's another issue."

The morning was growing warm, but having found Sebastian, I was reluctant to return to the house with him. I wasn't due in the nursery for at least an hour, and I wanted to know what he and Nathan Gillespie had discussed.

"How did the mare get *into* the stud paddock?" Sebastian said. "The fence is six feet high and sturdy as hell, lest the most valuable horse on the property go calling without permission. The grooms swear the gate was securely bolted when they found the mare where she ought not to have been."

"So we have mischief rather than a mishap. What does Mr. Gillespie make of the situation?"

The hermit's grotto came into view. The side of the structure facing the manor had been fashioned to look like the entrance to a cave set into the wooded hillside. Entering that cave led to a sort of summer cottage. The side facing away from the manor included a flagstone floor, padded wicker furniture, and opened onto a terrace with a pretty view of the river.

"Mr. Gillespie," Sebastian said, stopping some yards from the cave-entrance side of the grotto, "all but accused his former ward of salting the punch and turning the mare loose. In the same breath, he said he himself wasn't on hand when the punch was brought out, and the former military among the grooms might see putting the mare in with the stallion as a kind of joke."

"A joke that could cost somebody his job, Sebastian? Somebody knew the mare was in season, or they'd never have risked turning her out with a breeding stallion. That suggests guests were not involved."

"Gillespie was reluctant to accuse Nicholson, but we know what the children saw."

"We know what the children think they saw."

"*You* are reluctant to accuse Nicholson," Sebastian said, stepping closer. "As am I."

I was considering the possible uses a married couple might find for a secluded grotto when a faint trill of laughter drifted from the interior of the structure.

Drat the luck. "Did you see any sign of Miss Gillespie when you were in the stable, Sebastian? She claimed to have been visiting her mare."

"I saw neither bonnet nor hair bow."

"We didn't run across her either. Perhaps she threw herself at you to obscure the fact that she was trysting with somebody else." Enterprising of her, if that was the case.

"Somebody other than Nicholson." Sebastian tugged me back in the direction of the house. "We haven't been here twenty-four hours, and already, I wonder if we shouldn't leave for Ashmore."

At Ashmore, we had separate bedrooms, our own staff underfoot, and less than romantic memories.

"To leave now, over bad punch and a loose horse, would be rude." I did not consider that the rabbit's sortie rose to the level of mysterious. Pet bunnies were a law unto themselves, as I had reason to know. "Mrs. Gillespie befriended your sister, and thus we owe our hostess."

"I would not leave over bad punch and a loose horse, Violet. I would leave because there are schemes afoot I'd rather not see us dragged into, schemes that could turn dangerous."

My first thought was that Sebastian was exaggerating, but then I recalled Lord Jasper trying to turn the mere act of drinking from a mug into some sort of mating display, Miss Fontaine stroking Mr. Dinwiddie's coat in a most sensual manner, and Mrs. Gillespie's grudging addition of neighbors to an activity as mundane as cricket.

The potential for drama—from foolish wagers, to the young lady of the house being compromised, to deadly challenges on the field of honor—was real.

As was the potential for farce. "We stay for now," I said, "but we share our misgivings with Hugh and Ann, and you stick close to me, Sebastian."

His smile was patient. "While the prospect of sticking close to you has ever had strong appeal, I doubt anybody will try to put you in harm's way, Violet Marie."

"It's not my safety that concerns me, my lord. Miss Gillespie accosted *you*."

I thought he'd laugh at that riposte, for which I was prepared to deliver a sharp elbow to his ribs, but Sebastian did not laugh. He did not, in fact, say another word all the way back to the manor house.

⁓

We detoured into the library because I was intent on reviewing the maps of The Falls again. I wanted the comfort of a mental diagram of the property secure in my head, and I sought ideas for where a children's scavenger hunt might be safely undertaken.

The room itself was lovely, with a fireplace at each end and a third in the middle of the outside wall. Matching French doors on either side of that central hearth led to the terrace, and tall windows provided both light and window benches. The appointments were elegant and comfortable—save for the hunt scene over the mantel.

The pack in full cry. Reynard, fortunately, was outside the frame.

The high ceiling kept the room cool, and Sebastian and I appeared to have the place to ourselves.

"The park is too large for a scavenger hunt," I said, peering at the folio-sized pages of an atlas, "and too devoid of good hiding places." The Falls manor house was laid out to offer many lovely views of the river. The map also showed the folly built at the top of the cascade, which in its day had doubtless offered stunning vistas, including a lovely perspective on the house itself. The cliff had eroded, and the folly was now considered unsafe.

A pity, that.

"We're not doing the children's scavenger hunt inside," Sebastian replied, looking over my shoulder. "The house has too many excellent hiding places, and they are all too close together."

Steps sounded on the spiral staircase that led up to the mezzanine. "You're getting up a game of hide-and-seek?" Lord Jasper asked. "Haven't enjoyed that particular diversion in years, but the possibilities are interesting."

He wore the lightest of hunter green linen jackets, but was otherwise attired as he had been for cricket. A good-looking fellow, with limpid dark eyes to go with wavy sable hair and a loose-limbed, graceful form.

Lord Jasper made a particularly impressive contrast to young Viscount Cranston, who followed Lord Jasper down the steps. Cranston's collar was starched so outrageously high as to require a slight lift of his lordly chin—a pale, pointy feature—at all times. Whereas Bryon had worn dark locks elegantly curling over a high forehead, Cranston's blond tresses looked to have suffered the worse end of a brawl with curling tongs.

He pushed limp bangs from pale blue eyes and stumbled at the bottom steps.

Lord Jasper caught him in a near hug. "Steady on, there's a good fellow."

"Beg pardon." Cranston straightened himself and his waistcoat. "Most humbly beg pardon." His fair cheeks flamed, and he made another swipe at his hair.

"Spiral staircases are the very devil," I said, "and the metal ones are noisy. One wonders why so many libraries have them. How can one read with all that racket?"

"Perhaps the point," Sebastian said, "is that one cannot sneak about using a set of metal steps. Her ladyship and I sought to consult the maps in anticipation of a scavenger hunt for the children. We hope to entertain the infantry, not lose them, or not lose them for very long."

When had that project acquired a marquess among its managers?

"Assign an adult to each team of children," Lord Cranston said.

"My grandmother had the best scavenger hunts at Yuletide, and we always had one adult on each team. Grandpapa's team never won, but they did spend an inordinate amount of time searching the pantries. Aunt Chloe's team usually finished first, though Gran claimed they had the least frolic."

Lord Jasper's smile was pained.

"What a lovely idea," I replied. "Perhaps Lord Jasper would like to team up with the young ladies? And Dunkeld can take the boys' team."

"You mustn't pit the boys against the girls, my lady," Cranston said with the earnest helpfulness of a first former. "That makes for endless crowing on the part of the victors and revenge-pranks from the losers for the rest of the holiday. I have twenty-three first cousins —twenty-four as of last week—and I know of what I speak."

And all twenty-four of them, as well as their parents, in-laws, and household retainers, regarded this dandified sprig as the head of the family.

"We'll bear that in mind," I said. "Who would you nominate for a team captain, my lord?"

Cranston was so painfully young, not even of an age to have come down from university. Sebastian hadn't been much older when my father had sent him off to war.

"Why don't you volunteer, Cranston?" Lord Jasper asked. "Herding brats will be a change of pace from being herded by our charming hostess." He winked at Lord Cranston, bowed to me and Sebastian, and sauntered out the open French door, then paused on the terrace as if to provide us an opportunity to admire his form *de derrière* before ambling out of sight.

"I'd be happy to lead a team," Lord Cranston said as another blush suffused his countenance, "but the real strategist here is Greer Nicholson. His team would win, I assure you."

"How can you be certain?" Sebastian asked, when I wanted to get back to studying the maps.

"I'll give you an example," Cranston said, shoulders relaxing beneath their padding. "When Great-Uncle died, my poor mother was expected to step into the duties of a London hostess. Mama was no more suited to that role than I am suited to... Well, she didn't have a clue how to go on. Mrs. Gillespie told her the way of it: You invite Wellington to a dinner you say you're giving for Prinny and tell Prinny that Wellington is coming to dinner, and wouldn't it be lovely if Prinny could drop by too? They both come rather than offend the other, and your dinner is the talk of the Season."

Rather like inviting a marquess and his father-in-law the earl? "But that's Mrs. Gillespie's strategy, not Mr. Nicholson's."

Cranston shook his head. "Greer thought it up when he was younger than I am, and Mrs. G learned the trick from him. He used that approach with the boys at school. Claimed he was off for a beer that evening with one bully and invited the other, and so forth. He hadn't a title or older brothers and hadn't been all that well tutored, so he had to manage as best he could. Greer ran rings around Headmaster, to hear Lord Jasper tell it."

I suspected Greer had no inkling that he was the object of puerile hero worship.

"Is that why you accepted Mr. Gillespie's invitation?" Sebastian asked. "Because you consider Mr. Nicholson a friend?"

"Mama said I must not offend such a formidable hostess, and I knew I was simply to make up the numbers. Miss Dottie's lovely, of course, but she's not... Mama said I'd not be a target of the matchmakers, though I did want..." No blush this time, but a bashful lowering of lashes.

"You wanted to enhance your acquaintance with Mr. Greer?" I hazarded.

Cranston tugged at the edge of his lace cuffs, his fingers lingering as Annis's still did on the edging of her blanket when she fell asleep.

"We're all pockets to let," Cranston said miserably. "Lord Jasper, Dinwiddie, me... I can't speak for Fontaine or Sir Min, but the rest of us... Mrs. Gillespie invited us because she knew we'd accept the free food and drink—that's our recompense for making up the numbers—and we won't get airs regarding Miss Dottie. She's an heiress, you know, but we are hoping Nicholson might take pity on us."

Lord Cranston had lost me, which was saying something when I'd grown up deciphering the mumbling of four brothers and the mutterings of our father.

"You want to invest with Nicholson," Sebastian said, as if that conclusion was sitting in plain sight. "Failing that, you hope he'll toss some advice your way, or recall your situation when he's looking for titled partners to give some scheme cachet."

Cranston brushed a relieved glance in Sebastian's direction. "Nicholson's a good sort. Dinwiddie says if Nicholson had charm, he'd be the toast of the City. He doesn't have charm. Neither do I, though Dinwiddie could charm the knickers off... Beg pardon. Dinwiddie has family connections and the keys to Mayfair because of his grandmama the duchess. Nicholson, though, can turn tuppence into sovereigns, to hear Mama tell it."

"It helps," Sebastian said, "to be born with money. Turning a small fortune into a larger one is much easier than turning nothing into something."

His lordship left off twiddling his cuff. "Don't I know it, sir. It helps not to have twenty-four cousins. It helps to be dashing and witty. It helps if one's mama has a notion of economies. I left university..." He trailed off, looking abruptly older than his years. "Forgive me. One ought not to complain of a situation most would envy."

"One ought not to wager," Sebastian said, "if one has limited resources. Start there, and you won't regret it. Not on a horse race, not on a hand of cards. You can't help playing for penny stakes at Mrs. Gillespie's whist tournament, but if somebody starts suggesting foolish wagers, you excuse yourself to heed the call of nature, or pretend you need fresh air to clear your head."

"I can hold my... Oh. I see." His smile was angelic. "Makes perfect sense, and there's already talk of a horse race. The Frenchman—not Fontaine, the other one, St. Something—has a chestnut gelding that looks born to run. Great big beast with quarters on him like a..."

I wandered away while Sebastian was regaled with a panegyric to Charlemagne's hind end.

Impecunious bachelors were a fixture of polite society, and making up the numbers was one of their few useful endeavors. A whole cricket team of impecunious bachelors struck me as... scheming. Another means by which Tilda Gillespie would show Mr. Nicholson in a good light before Dottie could compare him to the available gentlemen in Mayfair.

The bachelors well knew what their purpose was and hoped to salvage some gain out of the situation. They sought to curry Greer Nicholson's favor, but would any of them have benefited by putting him in a bad light?

As I peered again at the detailed rendering of the Gillespie estate, I realized I'd asked the wrong question. Nicholson was well-heeled, had known Dottie for years, and had her mother's approval. Who among the bachelors would *not* benefit from seeing Nicholson put in a bad light?

CHAPTER TEN

Sebastian

"Violet came upon me when Miss Gillespie was..." I did not know how to describe the incident on the path that morning. Violet had instructed me to warn St. Sevier what was afoot, and thus as we assembled for the second night's buffet, I took a moment to...

Make a fool of myself?

"The young lady was making free with your person?" St. Sevier suggested softly. His gaze was on the ladies, who were across the terrace, chatting with Miss Fontaine and some other sweet young troublemaker.

"Miss Gillespie claimed she'd turned her ankle, but the symptoms included clutching at my shoulders, plastering herself against my chest, and chasing my chin with her lips. Violet was not amused, and neither was I."

"And you explained the situation to your marchioness?"

"As much of the situation as I know, which is precious damned little." Violet's group was joined by Sir Miniver, looking resplendent in evening attire. He was a widower and a few years older than the general run of the house party bachelors. He was also a father twice over and a neighbor to the Gillespies.

Then too, Lord Cranston had not classified Sir Min among the impecunious ornaments.

"What you know," St. Sevier said, nodding amiably to Monsieur Fontaine, "is that Miss Gillespie sought to be found in a close embrace with a married marquess, a situation that could ruin her."

St. Sevier smiled genially at Tilda Gillespie, who waggled her fingers at him as she breezed past on Lord Jasper's arm—or with Lord Jasper on *her* arm, from the looks of the situation. Nathan Gillespie stood at the bottom of the terrace steps in earnest discussion with the Bechtels, and a casual glance upward revealed children on the nursery balcony surveying the whole.

"You are mentally on reconnaissance," St. Sevier said as a footman offered us champagne from a tray. "We are not at war, Dunkeld."

We both accepted drinks, though I did not intend to imbibe much. If the evening went well, I would end it sharing a bed with my wife, and that prospect demanded a clear head.

"And yet," I replied, "we might be in enemy territory. Violet is upset by what she cannot explain, and a young lady attempting to ruin herself just as her come out is in the offing makes no sense to Violet."

"Because Violet is sensible, as is my Ann, though Violet was wandering about at will half the morning. I doubt your marchioness was supposed to find you with Miss Gillespie in your arms, but somebody was. This is good champagne. Goddard's vintage, I'd guess. The clarets are from Fournier's, suggesting Mrs. Gillespie has stocked her cellar with an eye for quality."

"St. Sevier, I am all but attacked in broad daylight, my wife comes upon me in a compromising situation, and you maunder on about the wine?"

St. Sevier raised his glass in Ann's direction. "To peace," he said, "and good French wines."

"To peace," I echoed, saluting Violet.

"Violet's movements were unpredictable," St. Sevier said, sipping such that his gaze never left his wife and managing not to look ridiculous for that bit of nonsense. "Your marchioness was not intended to know of your lapse with Miss Gillespie."

"I did not lapse. I was called upon to aid a damsel, and she ambushed me."

The young lady in question swanned up the steps on her father's arm. She wore a pale green evening dress cut daringly low, though modesty was preserved by a cream silk fichu.

No sign of a limp, and she had not been with her father two minutes earlier.

"You have no reputation for raking," St. Sevier said, "unlike some of those fellows. Dinwiddie is a favorite of the widows, Lord Jasper plays too deeply, and Sir Min is said to have gone through a difficult period after the death of his wife."

Upjohn had brought me much the same report, along with word that Lord Cranston's mother had a gambling problem, while the Thurmonts, despite being *merely gentry*, were on good terms with the whole shire and owned the adjacent property.

"How do you know these things?" I asked.

"Ann tells me. She collects intelligence from the maids, from Mrs. Bechtel, from the governesses, and so forth. Violet has done the same through the good offices of Miss Hewitt."

Violet had disappeared to the nursery at the end of the morning. She had then shared lunch with Lord Cranston and the fellow who'd bowled out Dinwiddie at cricket—a Thurmont of some stripe. Before I could extricate myself from Monsieur Fontaine's company at lunch —did I not miss Scotland?—Violet had taken herself off for a nap, without soliciting my escort.

I had the sense, gained from long experience with Violet's moods, that she was hurt and trying not to show it.

"I haven't been idle," I informed St. Sevier. "Under the guise of checking on Hannibal, I made another tour of the stable this afternoon. Those sliding stall doors were installed at significant expense last year."

"Mr. Gillespie takes great pride in his cattle." St. Sevier somehow turned a mere observation into a condemnation of hunt-mad Englishmen, blood sport, and equestrian ostentation.

"He does, and yet, that stable sits in the middle of the frequently damp English countryside. I tried the doors on all the stalls flanking Ariadne's."

"You call her Ariadne. Next, you will be introducing her to Hannibal."

This was St. Sevier's lumbering attempt at humor. "Her door rolls smoothly aside. The doors adjacent are all in need of an oiling. One of the grooms said Miss Gillespie made quite a scene a fortnight back about having to wrestle open the gates of hell to give her mare a treat, and Mr. Gillespie ordered the door oiled."

St. Sevier peered at me. "Somebody knew that. Somebody knew the mare could be quietly removed from the barn and just as quietly turned out with the stud."

"Or somebody observed that the stall door had been oiled, or Miss Gillespie saw to it that the stall door was oiled, and then *she* created a little drama on the first day of her mama's house party."

A drama that Mr. Gillespie laid at Greer Nicholson's feet, for no reason I could ascertain.

A gong sounded from within the house, our signal to line up for the buffet. St. Sevier finished his champagne and set his glass on the stone balustrade.

"And then Miss Gillespie creates another drama with you," he said, "or tries to. Who was the intended audience, if not Violet?"

"Nicholson, perhaps. He'd been sent in search of the young lady by Mrs. Gillespie, who is trying to make a match between Nicholson and Dorothy."

"But how could Miss Gillespie know he was searching for her, much less where to look? I do not like this intrigue and carrying-on,

Dunkeld. Ann says we must remain here for the duration because it is the first fashionable invitation we've received."

St. Sevier began walking toward the steps, which led into the garden where the buffet had been set up under a long white tent.

"Ann and I will enjoy dinner with the Fontaines this evening," St. Sevier went on, "and our foursome will speak impeccable English so that the other guests can remark on the appeal of the French accent, and never mind that the good denizens of The Falls to a person were eavesdropping on our conversation. Then we are to be subjected to the first round of the whist tournament, where we will be again separated from our own dear spouses and kept up far too late to conform our habits to good health."

I knew this gratuitous, testy mood for what it was, knew what careful surveillance of Madame St. Sevier portended, because I'd suffered the same torment for the entirety of Violet's pregnancy.

"St. Sevier, Ann is in great good health. She has a highly skilled physician devoted to her wellbeing. She delivered Fiona safely under awful conditions. You have to wait until she's ready to tell you."

Where a suave, if grouchy, Frenchman had been, a purely anxious husband now stood. "She does not want me to worry. I, who should by rights have no children, am apparently to be thrice blessed, but Ann will not say a word until the early dangers have passed. Does she think I cannot count? Does she think I pay no heed to her female miseries?"

He went off into French muttering, about how complicated the female mind was and how a loving husband hardly knew what to say or how to comport himself when faced with such complexities.

"St. Sevier."

He fell silent as we approached the end of the line of guests. "Do not presume to lecture me, Dunkeld. I am a man in torments."

"You are no longer a man sleeping in the damned dressing closet. Count your blessings."

I was treated to a painfully keen perusal, then a devilish grin and a punch on the arm, which I would not rub while St. Sevier was on hand to gloat.

"Just so, I will count my blessings and wish less fortunate men luck with their own troubles. Perhaps you should plead a headache and retire before the whist tournament?"

"Gentlemen do not plead headaches." Though the notion of dodging the whist tournament appealed strongly.

As it happened, I was partnered with Ann St. Sevier, a shrewd player who didn't take stupid risks. Violet had the great misfortune to be paired with Greer Nicholson.

As the hour approached midnight, yet more drama—of the potentially deadly variety—arose at the table where they played. Violet sat in the midst of the imbroglio, looking as if she was ready to start knocking together heads, and devil take the hindmost.

～

"The cards are marked," Sir Miniver Holmes said. "I take no joy from stating that fact, but neither can I tolerate cheating, no matter who the culprit might be. We are at The Falls to enjoy good company and pleasant diversions, not to be fleeced by some jackanape abusing the Gillespies' hospitality."

To his credit, he stopped there rather than spell out the rest of the accusation. He and Nathan Gillespie had opposed Violet and Greer Nicholson, and Sir Min's team had been losing badly. Their table now formed the center of a tableau, with the gentlemen on their feet and some of the ladies rising as well.

Violet remained seated, as befit her station, though the exaggerated serenity of her expression suggested the king's peace was in imminent peril.

"This is surely a misunderstanding," Mrs. Gillespie said, coming to her husband's side. "What say we simply end play for the evening at the previous hand, and I will have new decks for us to use for the next round."

"A perfectly sensible suggestion," Mrs. Bechtel said, taking her husband by the arm. "Servants are careless, the cards become less than pristine. One need not make high drama out of a coincidence."

She glowered at Sir Min, and it occurred to me that a frolic with Mrs. Bechtel might have figured prominently in the *difficult period* he'd suffered in mourning. Perhaps Tilda had been forced to invite them both for form's sake, and perhaps she'd engineered more mischief.

"Handle them yourself," Sir Miniver said, holding up a half-dozen cards. "Feel the edges. If you do not perceive attempts at marking, I will be most surprised."

Mr. Bechtel accepted the proffered cards. "Some wear," he said after a moment's examination. "We've been playing all evening, and other teams have played at this table." He offered the cards to his wife, who shook her head.

I expected Nathan Gillespie to echo our hostess's suggestion: Set aside the results of the hand in progress. Bring out new decks for the next evening of play—send a rider to London for them if necessary—and brush the whole sorry business under the nearest Axminster carpet.

Mr. Gillespie stood next to his wife, her hand wrapped over his arm. I realized in the next instant why he remained silent. He was our host. He was also Nathan's former guardian—*and the magistrate.* He was attempting to remain impartial.

While a bad situation could soon descend into dueling, scandal, and worse. "I would like to see the entire deck," I said. "Every card."

"Thank you." Violet rose and remained at the table. "A sensible suggestion. If the cards are merely worn, then the markings along the edges will have no pattern. They will be random nicks in no particular order. If the cards are marked so as to facilitate cheating, we will soon have evidence of same. For that matter, I'd like to see the rota of who sat at which table when."

"Oh, I've tossed that in the rubbish," Tilda said. "We were on the final games, and I had no more use..."

Ann St. Sevier was examining a piece of foolscap propped on the mantel. "Somebody made a spare copy, apparently," she said, handing Violet the list. "How fortunate."

"We need only focus on the last half-dozen games," Violet said. "Fresh decks were provided when we broke for snacks."

"This is all simply unnecessary." Tilda's good cheer had taken on a grating quality. "I insist that we remove to the library for a nightcap and put this unfortunate situation behind us. I know Sir Miniver would never bring unfounded accusations, but there must be some innocent explanation."

The party of interest, the party with the most at risk, finally spoke.

"Examine the cards," Greer Nicholson said, addressing himself to me. "Examine them thoroughly. Examine the second deck as well and all the decks at every table."

Mr. Bechtel cleared his throat. "But he's... Beg pardon, my lord, but your wife was sitting at the table in question."

Bechdel was, albeit politely, accusing the Marchioness of Dunkeld of cheating at cards. The man was either very brave or demented. Violet pretended to further examine the list of players and tables.

"Then you, Bechtel, will examine the cards with me," I said, "as will... My lady, might I have the name of another gentleman who was not seated at this table?"

"Cyrus Thurmont," Violet said. "Leo Fontaine, Thomas Thurmont..."

"Cyrus Thurmont will do." Of the universally popular Thurmonts. "The rest of you will please heed Mrs. Gillespie's suggestion and repair to the library for a nightcap or retire to your rooms. We will examine the cards, talk to the principals involved, and see the matter sorted."

Sir Miniver appeared unhappy at that direction, but he nodded to Bechtel and offered his escort to Mrs. Bechtel. Tilda looked as if she'd rather remain behind to flutter and hover. Nathan told her to see to her guests.

Not their guests, *her* guests.

"Sir Miniver means well," Gillespie said, returning to his seat. "He knows half the eligibles are pockets to let, and one of them probably thought to earn an illicit coin or two. Better to nip that behavior in the bud. I confess I simply hadn't noticed any irregularities. I'm not much of one for sitting about swilling port and wagering for pennies myself."

"If Sir Miniver meant to nip cheating in the bud," Violet retorted, "he'd do so by muttering in the men's retiring room about worn cards. In the alternative, he'd have quietly had a word with *his host*, who happened to be his partner, when nobody could overhear."

Greer Nicholson went to the sideboard and poured a tray of brandies. "We country fellows don't all claim as much tact as you might be accustomed to in more rarefied circles, my lady." He set a drink before Gillespie. "May I offer anybody else a brandy?"

Such gracious behavior suggested Nicholson was not concerned about being found out as a cheat—or that he was a very good cheat and a thespian besides.

Violet accepted a drink and took a ladylike sip. "Mr. Thurmont, perhaps you'd begin the examination of the cards. I believe Mr. Bechtel and his lordship have a few questions for me, and then I must see to matters in the nursery."

If nothing else, this house party was reminding me of the extent to which an infant impinged on a woman's freedom, even a very privileged woman who had abundant conscientious staff in the nursery.

"I wouldn't know where to start," Bechtel said. "The whole business is so unfortunate."

Thurmont circulated about the room, assembling each deck and placing them in the middle of their respective tables. "I thought we'd want to note which decks came from which table," he said. "In case we find more... *evidence of wear.*"

He was the fellow who'd bowled Dinwiddie out, and his appearance was that of the quintessential son of the gentry—straw-colored hair, tallish, and twinkling blue eyes. His gaze held intelligence, and clearly, he was not cowed to be in the presence of a peer.

"A good thought," Violet said, rising and setting her drink on the sideboard. "All I can tell you is, we cut for the deal using the deck in question, and Sir Min got the first deal. The deal rotated to me using the second deck, which I assure you has no unusual wear on the edges. Mr. Gillespie then took the deal in his turn, again using the supposedly marked deck. In the middle of that hand—our third—Sir Min made his announcement. We are playing for pennies, so Mr. Gillespie's comment about down-at-the-heel bachelors appears inapposite. The objective was to disrupt an evening of pleasant play, not to fleece anybody."

"More disruption," Greer said. "I daresay this is the most disrupted house party Tilda has ever given."

"And all the disruption," Gillespie said, "seems to hover about you, my boy. I don't care for this, but her ladyship makes an interesting point. Pennies and shillings aren't worth risking anybody's honor. No matter the condition of the cards, nobody lost a fortune to a cheat."

I was busy examining the suspect deck and had to agree with Sir Miniver in one respect: The deck was marked, cards subtly nicked along the edges, sometimes once, sometimes multiple times, such as a card sharp would mark a deck in anticipation of controlling the play.

"I have nothing to add to Lady Dunkeld's recitation," Greer said, taking a seat at the adjacent table. "Like mine host, idling about at a card table for hours holds little appeal for me, but one cannot be rude. Her ladyship is a skilled player, the cards favored us, and we were doubtless to continue advancing on the winners' side of the tournament. Sir Min is accounted an excellent shot and a hothead. The sum in question will not matter to him if he thinks he's been cheated."

"He hasn't parted with a penny," Violet snapped. "Nor will he until the final reckoning of sums owed more than a week hence. This whole business strikes me as another sorry prank, and of no moment save for the gossip it will engender. Unless anybody has further questions for me, I'm off to the nursery."

She rose, and if any fellow did have further questions, her manner gave him cause to keep his peace.

"I'll light you up," I said, taking a lamp from a sconce. "And, Gillespie, you and Nicholson might as well join the others in the gallery or repair to your beds. If you have questions for Sir Miniver, put them to him quietly and in private. Thurmont and Bechtel, have a look at the other decks, but leave them on their assigned tables. I'll return in a moment."

The habit of command remained from my days in the army. Mostly, I sought to share a bed with my wife and was motivated to diffuse the accusation aimed at Nicholson sooner rather than later.

Violet tarried by the door while I adjusted the wick on the lamp.

"What is it?" I asked, because she surveyed the gallery with a disgruntled expression that suggested puzzles and intrigues in want of resolution.

"Look at the tables," she said softly while Gillespie finished his drink, Thurmont and Bechtel started on theirs, and Nicholson poked at the fire.

Thurmont had pushed the chairs in as he'd made his way around the room, and thus the gallery was tidy, as if in anticipation of the next evening's play. In the middle of each table sat two neatly stacked decks.

This setup was tradition for whist. To save time, the dealer's partner shuffled one deck while the dealer passed out the cards of the deck in play. Protocol dictated a little ballet for cutting the cards and passing the deal between rounds, with every member of the foursome having a part in the dance.

"Two decks per table," I said. "Spare decks doubtless stacked in the sideboard."

"Look at the table where I was playing, Sebastian."

That table also had two decks, the one that had drawn Sir Miniver's fire and the second deck, waiting for its turn at play.

"They are the same," Violet said very softly. "The marked deck and the second deck have the same pattern on the back."

I steered her into the corridor rather than draw anybody's notice. "Bad form, to use two decks with the same pattern." Very bad form. One of the many dictates of whist protocol was that the two decks be easily distinguished so they would never be intermingled—inadvertently or otherwise.

"Tilda Gillespie would never be guilty of bad form," Violet retorted, starting for the stairs. "The two decks should always be of different design, and that rule was observed at every other table."

"You are suggesting that somebody substituted the marked deck at the last minute." I caught up with her on the landing. "That implies we are dealing with a purposeful cheater, but why? What's the point of relieving you or Sir Miniver of tuppence? I can see no reason why Nicholson would pull such a prank, not when he's already under suspicion for wrecking the punch and turning out the mare."

Violet paused at the top of the steps. "And possibly for the loose rabbit. Does he know he's under suspicion?"

"In the interest of fairness, somebody ought to have warned him, and he's been asked some pointed questions."

Violet resumed her progress more slowly, and it occurred to me that three or four hours hence, she would be trudging back up these stairs for the same purpose. Three or four different times tomorrow, she'd make the same trip, as she'd been making it daily for months.

How could she not be exhausted?

"You heard Lord Cranston extolling Nicholson's acumen with money," Violet said as we approached the nursery suite. "Nicholson is shrewd, clever, astute... lacks charm, but what matters charm when a man has a gift for turning a profit?"

"He's no barbarian. He brought a drink to Gillespie when that fellow was clearly rattled. He's solicitous toward Miss Gillespie, and he's tolerant toward Tilda."

"Precisely. He's not a fribble. I like that about him. If he were to cheat at cards, he'd use the correct pattern on the back of the deck. Tilda's decks have one of four standard patterns—red, blue, black, and green. Greer Nicholson would be sure to match the pattern of the deck he'd pinched. He wouldn't pinch one deck and substitute a marked deck of a different color. I should have noticed that the two decks were the same color and pattern. You will examine the marked deck very closely, Sebastian?"

"With a quizzing glass, if need be."

"You must do it tonight, sir, with a witness or two, and then bring the deck upstairs with you. You cannot allow Gillespie to put it in a safe, because everybody from Nicholson to Dorothy to the butler might have the combination."

"We will sleep with the deck beneath our pillows."

"You take my point." Violet kissed my cheek, lingeringly, and I had reason to hope her affection was not simply over a deck of cards. "I knew you would. I won't be long."

I caught her in an embrace. The hour was late and the corridor deserted, not that I cared if somebody found me hugging my wife.

"You will go straight to bed, Violet Marie. Don't even think of returning to the gallery or prowling the library. Suspicion has fallen on Nicholson, but if you attempt to meddle tonight, all eyes might turn on you."

"Let them," she said. "I weathered gossip enough when I was married to Freddie, and if it weren't for that bit about Sir Miniver's excellent aim, I'd—" She broke off abruptly and yawned. "Sorry. I'm out of the habit of socializing at such a late hour. I suspect both Hector and Ajax have fought duels. Men are so stupid. Some men."

I wanted nothing more than to remain with my wife. To tend to Maeve with her and burp the baby when Violet had finished with her.

"You are asleep on your feet, madam. Should I send Hewitt to you?"

"Lucy is doubtless keeping Upjohn company. I dismissed her

before supper. I'll have Bevins make a start on my hooks and appease modesty with a shawl when I return to our rooms."

She bussed my cheek again and disappeared into the nursery, taking my heart with her.

~

I returned to the gallery because Violet expected that of me. I found Cyrus Thurmont and Greer Nicholson sharing a drink before the fire, the picture of young masculine pulchritude in idleness.

"I'll give you this, Nicholson," I said, taking up the marked deck and seating myself at an unused table. "If you did cheat, you are awfully coolheaded about it."

Thurmont peered at me. "Is that an accusation, my lord? If so, I'd be happy to serve as Nicholson's second."

Nicholson ran a finger around the rim of his glass. "Cy, don't be a dunderhead. Dottie would skewer us both with her hatpins, and Tilda would finish the job long before the marquess took aim at me."

"I'd have to refuse the challenge," I said, examining the top card of the deck. "Might somebody bring me pencil and paper?"

"You'd refuse," Thurmont said, "because of your almighty title, or because you know Greer can shoot the flame off a candle at forty paces?"

No pistol was reliably that accurate, even in the hands of an expert. "Neither." I ran my fingers around the edge of the card, finding no markings at all. "Did you two substitute a clean deck?"

Nicholson rummaged in a sideboard and produced pencil and paper. "We did not, and while I am too sensible to issue a former soldier a challenge, Cy can be more impulsive, so you'd best have a good explanation for that question."

Thurmont came up on Nicholson's side. "His lordship has already said he disdains to defend his honor over pistols or swords, but I have three brothers and—"

Nicholson elbowed his friend in the ribs, the most human,

normal behavior I'd seen from him. "Stow it, Cy. Sir Min wasn't wrong. The cards are marked, and if his lordship can't get to the bottom of it, Nathan, as magistrate, might well feel compelled to... Nathan can't do anything, can he?"

"Correct," I said, making a note of my findings regarding the two of diamonds and going on to the second card. "Gambling for coin is illegal, and debts of honor such as one incurs at the card table are not enforceable by the law."

"Hence the term," Nicholson said, "'debts of honor.' You are looking for a pattern in the marks?"

Thurmont remained on his feet. "We still don't know why the marquess won't set foot on the field of honor."

I passed the two of diamonds to Nicholson. "No markings that I can determine. Of course, in a trick-taking game like whist, maybe the lowest cards need no marks, but I would still expect something to indicate the suit."

"Cy, fetch the man a quizzing glass," Nicholson said, fingering the card than passing it back to me. "You haven't asked me if I realized the cards were marked."

The seven of clubs had two nicks, on adjacent sides. "Did you?"

"Of course, but we were playing for pennies, and the other parties at the table included a neighbor of long standing, the closest thing I have to a father, and a marchioness known in the surrounds for her outspokenness. A marchioness whose husband was on hand— a former soldier—and whose titled papa is due to grace us with his presence in mere days. Which of them should I have accused, my lord?"

In a display of his legendary acumen, Nicholson had probably parsed those options before the first trick had been taken.

"You accuse Sir Min," Thurmont said, brandishing a quizzing glass from the depths of the sideboard. "I certainly would. He probably realized you were on to him, so he fired the first accusation."

"What would Sir Min's motive be?" I asked.

The young fellows exchanged a look as I noted the markings of the seven and moved along through the deck.

Nicholson spoke first. "Tilda had something of a fling with Sir Min shortly after he lost his wife. If I knew the details, I would keep mum about them, but I don't, so we need not expire of mortification. The fling, if it was an actual fling and not simply the platonic infatuation to which grieving romantic heroes are prone, ended when Mrs. Bechtel became Sir Min's next source of consolation."

And I had dragged Violet the length of the realm for a front-row seat at this farce? "Why invite a former amour and the woman who turned his head?" I asked, working my way through more cards.

"Because," Cyrus Thurmont said, folding himself into the chair opposite me, "people will talk." He'd raised his voice to a falsetto. "We must arrange our entire lives in response to the fact that people will talk. Why don't you duel?"

"Cy, cease yapping."

"I don't duel for at least four reasons. Verify my findings, Thurmont, while I appease the rudeness that passes for your curiosity. First, life is precious—my life, yours, Nicholson's, the goosegirl's — and despite a lot of talk to the contrary, blowing a man's brains out does not prove his guilt, innocence, good intentions, or bad form. Killing him in some dung-strewn pasture only proves greater luck for the victor, and at the cost of another man's life."

I paused to make more notes as Thurmont began a list of his own with my discards.

"Second, dueling is illegal. The law rightly views it as premeditated murder, and I have no wish to give the Lords a chance to make an example of me."

"You're a bloody marquess," Thurmont said. "They'd never let you hang."

"I am a *Scottish* marquess. I don't take stupid risks if I can help it, and giving a lot of English peers a chance to hang me would be foolish in the extreme."

"These marks aren't making sense. What's the third reason?"

"My wife would kill me, and I would deserve her wrath, while she has done nothing to deserve a second occasion of widowhood so early in life. Her ladyship would take umbrage at my foolishness not for her own sake—she is well equipped to soldier on through the worst terrain—but because we have daughters who deserve my love and protection as they take their places in the world."

"I like your marchioness," Nicholson said. "Means what she says, says what she means. I daresay she does not live her life in fear of gabbling neighbors. Tilda says you are a love match."

Nicholson was posing a question, and he was doing it with the tact he wasn't supposed to claim.

"We are very much a love match. I have adored that woman since before I was shaving, and had not the war intervened..."

"Belmaine was a handsome rotter," Nicholson said. "He was older than I, but Tilda knows everybody, and she kept her eye on Belmaine. He was acceptable company at a Venetian breakfast, but never on the guest list for one of her formal balls."

I was better than halfway through the deck, and still no pattern had emerged. So far, eight cards had borne no markings at all, and those ranged from the two of diamonds to the jack of spades.

"Don't speak ill of the dead, Greer," Thurmont muttered, making a notation. "I still say Sir Min caused this whole stir. He's trying to look formidable before the ladies."

I took up the queen of diamonds. "You don't sleep with a man's wife, accept his hospitality, and then make accusations of foul play under his roof. That could have resulted in Gillespie calling out Sir Min, and I can't imagine a juicier bit of gossip."

Nicholson was peering into the flames on the hearth, ignoring our study of the cards. "Nathan can't take exception to Tilda's flirts. He'd look a very great fool if he did and also a hypocrite."

Thurmont wiggled his eyebrows at me across the table. "Gillespie was quite the dashing blade in his day. One can hardly credit it to see him now. Maundering on about ha-has and crops, hounds trailing him into the house, his missus off to London as much as she's at home."

Nicholson swiveled his gaze to his friend. "His lordship might not call you out, Cy, but you are insulting a man to whom I owe much."

"You are the one who told me what a wide swath old Nate cut back in the day. If I'm ever fortunate enough to win the hand of a lady I esteem, I won't abandon her for the grouse moors *or* the flesh-pots of Mayfair. Tilda despaired of him, and even Dottie has let a few things slip about her dear old papa."

Ancient history would not solve the present mystery, and yet, I had questions. "How could you know what Nathan was like as a younger man, Nicholson? You weren't living at The Falls until you were several years into the schoolroom."

"My mother and Tilda were best friends, and I was my mother's confidant from a young age. Nathan became my guardian while Mama was still alive, and thus our families were close even before I came to The Falls. Dottie was the little sister I'd never had, and Tilda and Nathan were my godparents."

That recitation rang true. As a youth, I'd run tame through Derwent Hall, one of several lesser-included neighbor boys who'd been befriended by Lord Derwent's sons. At the time, I'd had no title, a strange accent, and a fascination for the only Deerfield daughter.

Felix Deerfield, in particular, had become a good friend, and we'd served together on the Peninsula. No legal means existed to add an orphaned child to a new family, but bonds formed nonetheless, and society respected those bonds.

I passed the last card across the table. "The marks are random, from what I can tell." I took up the quizzing glass and appropriated the portion of the deck Thurmont had examined. "I have dealt with crooked decks often enough, in the army, at university... The system has to be simple, because the dealer has only a moment to assess each card as he passes it out. The usual gambit is to mark the suit promi-nently if that's relevant and then high or low cards. Nearly a dozen cards have no mark at all."

Close inspection of the two of diamonds revealed no alteration of the design on the back, no pinpricks, no subtle blottings. The other cards I examined were similarly pristine.

"So the cat chewed this deck and this deck only?" Thurmont asked, setting his pencil down. "We exonerate Nicholson because whoever marked the deck was inept?"

Nicholson was back to gazing into the fire.

"Whoever marked the deck," I said, "knew what they were doing and was likely holding the randomness of the pattern in abeyance until accusations grew more heated. Any number of bachelors here would benefit from setting Nicholson up for criticism and then— much to everybody's relief—saving him from the gossips."

Nicholson broke his reverie to snort. "Because Dottie is protective of me and would look favorably upon my defense counsel? I can assure you, Dunkeld, most of these fellows are courting me far more... Oh."

"You're saying somebody wants Nicholson in their debt?" Thurmont murmured. "Odd way to earn a man's allegiance, by setting him up for scandal, then appearing to ride to the rescue. This is all getting too complicated for a mere country lad, and I have a tramp through woods ahead of me yet. I will depart, content with the fact of Greer's innocence. Gentlemen, I'm off to bay at the moon."

Nicholson rose and extended a hand to Thurmont. "Mind the path. See you tomorrow for more cricket. Please bowl Lord Jasper out, will you?"

"Consider it done." He jaunted off toward the French doors, but stopped before stepping onto the terrace. "Dunkeld, you said there were four reasons you would not take up arms against Greer. Dueling is stupid, the peerage might hang you, and her ladyship would dine upon your bones, but what's the fourth reason?"

I wanted to review the whole situation with Violet—after we'd all the pleasures proved—but Cyrus Thurmont was a friend of the family and, more to the point, a friend to Nicholson.

"Nicholson never had the deal," I said. "Sir Min, her ladyship, and Gillespie all took a turn dealing, and it's the dealer who benefits from handling marked cards. Of the four people at the table, Nicholson is the only one who *could not* yet have benefited from cheater's tactics."

I waited for Nicholson to add to my narrative, but he merely smiled.

"Ah," Thurmont said. "Innocent. I knew it. I will pass along your lordship's keen observation on the morrow, and by noon, Nicholson will again be the cynosure of all aspirations, at least to the extent that darling Dottie doesn't already hold that honor. Night, all."

He slipped into the darkness, destined—lucky fellow—to sleep in his own bed.

"A good egg," Nicholson said, "as you are, my lord, if I may presume to say so. I trust you will keep the marked deck in your custody?"

"I shall, and I will have a word with Sir Miniver and Gillespie first thing tomorrow. Do you have any recollection when the marked deck came into play?"

"What difference does it make? Play concludes at different tables at different times, and people were swanning about the room all evening. Anybody could have slipped the marked deck onto our table or had a footman see to it under the guise of discreetly replacing a worn deck."

He was right, and he was lying by omission. "In other words, the marked deck showed up when Gillespie took up the deal."

Nicholson collected glasses from around the room and set them on the sideboard. "Nathan resents that I've been able to handle my funds with greater success than he did. He wants me out from underfoot, I know that, but he would never risk putting a black mark beside my name or beside Tilda's hospitality. I would stake my life on his loyalty to family."

"Let's hope it never comes to that." I collected the marked deck and took my leave. Violet awaited me *in bed*, and what was the point of reminding Nicholson that Gillespie was no family to him at all in any legal sense?

CHAPTER ELEVEN

Violet

I heard the bedroom door open and pulled the blanket more closely around me, though the night was hardly chilly. The park stretched out below the balcony, bathed in moonlight and shadows.

"Violet?"

"Out here."

"I'll join you in a moment."

I'd loved Sebastian's voice since I'd first encountered him perched impossibly high in my favorite climbing tree. I'd loved the fellow himself since the next moment after that, when he'd challenged me to climb up—far higher than I'd dared go before—and enjoy the view with him.

End-of-evening sounds came from the bedroom. Clothing rustling, water splashing against porcelain. A cravat pin tossed into the vanity tray perhaps. Then Sebastian blocked the light coming through the French doors for a moment before taking a place at the porch railing. His arrival scented the night with a hint of cedar, and I loved that, too, to say nothing of the sentiments inspired by the sight of him silhouetted against the night sky.

Doomed sentiments, but sincere.

"Mr. Thurmont," he said, gaze on the shadowy park, "is taking the path where you found Miss Gillespie and me earlier today. Toddling on home. He's a good sort."

"I would have said Sir Min was a good sort, but announcing a marked deck like that was dunderheaded in the extreme."

Sebastian settled into the wicker chair beside my chaise. "If the objective was to make Nicholson look like a cheat, then Sir Min should have waited until Nicholson had the deal. You and Sir Min had each held that honor for a full round, and Gillespie was dealing when Sir Min made his accusations. The person at the table least likely to be cheating was Nicholson, and yet, Sir Min directed his ire at Nicholson."

"Give me your wrists," I said, sitting up enough to deal with Sebastian's sleeve buttons. "The cards were not marked when I handled them. I learned how to spot that sort of cheating before I put up my hair." I slipped the sleeve buttons into the pocket of my dressing gown.

"How did you learn to spot a cheat?"

"Mitchell was too grown up to play cards with Hector, Ajax, and Felix, so I became the fourth of necessity until you showed up. Stood me in good stead when I went off to school. Freddie educated me regarding more subtle tactics—palmed cards, dropped cards, silver teapots used as mirrors, signals between partners, the list is endless."

Sebastian extracted the dubious deck from his inside breast pocket and passed it to me. "I found marks on the sides, and only on the sides, and eleven cards had no marks at all. I could discern no pattern, and Cyrus Thurmont as well as Nicholson himself concur in that finding."

I handled the cards carefully in the near darkness and passed them back to my husband. "Nothing on the backs." For a man intent on consummating our vows, Sebastian was being blessedly patient.

He—and I—would have to be patient awhile longer.

"The cards were not marked when you handled them," he said. "When the deal passed to Nathan Gillespie, the cards were marked, and yet, Sir Min accused Nicholson of cheating."

The inconsistency Sebastian pointed out had one solution. "*Nathan* picked up the wrong deck. The two decks were the same, and he had a fifty-fifty chance of picking up the clean deck or the marked deck. Had he grabbed the clean deck, then Nicholson would have been left to deal with the marked deck. We need to have a very pointed discussion with Sir Min."

"Pointed and private. I did not want to confront either him or Gillespie without conferring with you first."

Between one breath and the next, I was hoisted from my chaise, blanket and all, and settled into Sebastian's lap.

"You, sir, have very odd notions of conferring."

He kissed me, a sweet, lazy, minty greeting between spouses. "Married notions. The whole business with the cards is puzzling. Gillespie has no reason to cheat and every reason to ignore the matter. The cards are marked, or most of them are, but any given pattern of nicks shows up on two or three different cards, and the nicks themselves follow no rubric. That says we aren't dealing with a true cheat, but rather, a prankster with exceedingly bad taste. Kiss me."

"Sebastian, you should know—"

He kissed me, and though I had been married to a rake and been the inamorata of a passionate and sophisticated Frenchman, Sebastian *knew things*—about kissing and about me—such that his advances were uniquely... stirring.

I indulged in a sumptuous exploration of my husband's person, which was naughty of me in the extreme. His dark, silky hair, the slightly bristly texture of his jaw, the magnificent breadth of his shoulders, and the delicate wonder of his lips.

While we yet kissed, he stood with me in his arms.

"Sebastian, put me down."

"Now why would I do that when I've been longing to hold you since you put up your hair?"

He had held me from time to time, relatively chaste, friendly embraces, most of them. "Put me down, in the first place because I said so, and it is my person you heave about with such manly ease. In the second, put me down this instant because there is something you should know before we share a bed."

"Your past is your business," he said, sinking back into the wicker chair and settling me across his lap. "My past, if it's of any interest to you, is unremarkable."

"The issue is not our individual histories." Why did the topic at hand have to be so awkward? I, Violet Marie Deerfield Belmaine MacHeath, now Marchioness of Dunkeld, was never at a loss for words, but the situation left me abruptly tongue-tied.

"You are upset because Dottie tried to compromise me on the path," Sebastian said. "Violet, I have explained that situation as best I understand it—"

I put a finger to his soft, plush, amazingly skilled lips, then whispered in his ear.

He drew back, expression unreadable by moonlight. "Your menses? Your bedamned menses plague ye now?" His embrace shifted, from cherishing as a lover cherishes, to enfolding me in an equally dear but more protective manner. He rested his cheek against my hair, and I might have felt him chuckle. "*Mo ghràdh-sa.* Only you."

I could not quite parse his murmuring—*my love something*—but the tenderness of his tone touched me inordinately. I'd felt twinges while nursing Maeve, but twinges and lactation were of a piece. Then I'd changed into my nightclothes and seen proof that my female biology was asserting itself at the worst possible moment.

"I can sleep in the dressing closet," I said. What few males I'd known well enough to acquaint with my bodily rhythms had distanced themselves from the whole subject of lunation.

St. Sevier had remained carefully affectionate, while waxing subtly clinical about the business. My brothers had made vulgar innuendos, and my father had simply left the room if such an indelicate topic ever found its way into a family conversation.

The old hypocrite. Freddie had slept elsewhere when the inconvenience was upon me, and he'd not been one for sleeping alone.

Sebastian, by contrast, had always shown sympathy for the considerable pain I endured every twenty-eight days. Even as a very young man, he'd offered me a medicinal tot from his flask, or a hug, or poem.

"You'll no' be sleeping in the damned dressing closet, Violet Marie, and after tonight, you won't be going to the nursery at all hours either."

That attempt at high-handedness woke me up. "Don't be daft. Maeve is too young to wean. She's taking some solid food, true, but—"

Sebastian hugged me to silence. "For God's sake, woman, will you never listen to me? If the baby stirs, Bevins will bring her to us. She will alert me, and you will remain abed if you please. When you and Maeve have finished, I will burp the child and return her to the nursery. I am that girl's father, and you need your rest."

He was not Maeve's father, except that a father was as a father did, and he proposed a very paternal scheme.

"We can try it," I said, subsiding against his chest. "What did you mean that your past was unremarkable?"

"Nothing," he said, tucking the blanket around me. "Go to sleep, *mo chridhe*."

"Nothing, Sebastian?"

A tired, husbandly sigh went out of him. I cuddled up, such that his heartbeat was a subtle tattoo beneath my cheek. The stars were a glorious display in the summer night sky, and despite whatever nonsense was brewing among the other guests, despite the jest nature was playing on me, I was deeply contented in my husband's embrace.

For me to be held, to be comforted and cosseted, eased some ache in my soul. I was all but asleep when my husband whispered against my ear.

"There has never been anybody for me but you, Violet. There never will be."

I feigned sleep, lest he discern that his honesty moved me to tears.

～

Sebastian had at some point in the night moved us to the bed, and in his arms—even on that lumpy mattress—I slept like a drunken sailor newly arrived to port. For once, I had not been needed in the nursery overnight, a miracle that had befallen me only twice before we'd left Scotland.

"God bless mashed peas and healthy babies," I muttered, shoving another pin into my hair. Sebastian had decamped earlier with a kiss to my cheek and a comment about looking in on Hannibal.

To my delight, I had married a good cuddler. A very good cuddler. I'd drifted up from dreams at least twice during the night to feel Sebastian's hand gliding gently over my lower back, easing an ache that usually grew worse through the first day of my misery.

A whisper had come to me in the darkness. "*Cadal, mo chridhe.*"

Sleep, my heart. And I had slept, wonderfully well. Instead of the cramping I anticipated, I awoke inordinately refreshed and with a fulsome supply for Maeve. As I added one last pin to my chignon, I surveyed my reflection in the mirror.

I look happy. I am married to a wonderful man, we are in good health, and a beautiful baby awaits me in the nursery.

That optimism was, of course, merely the result of a good night's sleep. After months of not enjoying same, uninterrupted slumber had me nearly giddy with good cheer. Maeve shared my mood and was soon greedily breaking her fast.

"Dare I hope last night was the start of a trend?" I mused as Bevins folded a stack of clean linens.

"All the excitement fair wore her little ladyship out," Bevins said. "I can try a few spoonfuls of porridge at night, if you like, my lady. She's managing the peas quite well, and you need your rest."

Maeve had reached the drowsy stage, so I put her to my shoulder and dealt with my bodice. "His lordship has another plan." I explained Sebastian's decree while Maeve smacked my shoulder and gurgled happily. "I told him I'm willing to try his scheme, but if you'd rather not travel the corridor in the middle of the night with a baby..."

"Won't be no trouble a'tall, my lady," Bevins said, passing me a cloth. "The marquess does dote on you, don't he? Most men have no earthly idea..."

She fell silent as Sir Miniver entered the nursery. He cut a red-haired, blue-eyed dash in his riding attire, and based on a faint horsy scent, he'd already gone for his morning gallop.

"My lady, good morning. My ladies, rather." He ran a gentle finger over Maeve's russet curls. "I trust we are in good spirits this morning?"

Maeve grinned at him, and when Maeve was happy, I was happy. "We are," I said. "Maeve is a wonderfully healthy baby, and we are fortunate in our nursery staff. Have you come looking for your boys?"

"I did, indeed. I promised they could watch some of the cricket match if they remained on good behavior. But they are boys, and Holmes boys, so I must allow them to run the length and breadth of the park and climb a few trees before expecting anything like good behavior."

He had a nice smile, blue eyes crinkling at the corners, a dimple forming in his left cheek.

Maeve chose then to delight herself with a stout little burp. This provoked her baby-laughter, and both Bevins and Sir Miniver smiled.

"Good digestion is a blessing," he said. "Miss, do you know where my hooligans have got off to?"

Bevins took Maeve from me. "Hide-and-seek, sir, last I heard. The older children have been playing it by the hour. The whole nursery floor is fair game, but you might start in the schoolroom. Prodigious lot of cupboards there. They know the attics are forbidden territory, which means you might find them on the attic steps."

"I'll help you look," I said, though the children had been at The Falls long enough to have found some excellent hiding places. "I also wanted to discuss last night's card game with you."

I brushed a hand over Maeve's little head, wishing I could linger with my daughter, though my discussion with Sir Miniver wanted discretion.

"We'll see you before lunch, my lady," Bevins said, waving bye-bye to me. "A peas and porridge banquet. Wish Mama farewell." She waved again, and Maeve swung her hand about in the general direction of Bevins's ear.

"Bye-bye," I said, waving to Maeve and feeling not at all like a fool. Sir Miniver, to my shock, joined in the general nonsense, but then, he was a father twice over, and a father with no partner in parenthood.

"I owe you an apology for last night," he said as soon as we'd gained the corridor. "I grow impatient with these frivolous young blades getting up to tricks for the sheer deviltry of it. They don't realize that in an instant, life can turn from frolic to tragedy. Marking a deck of cards when playing for pennies was somebody's idea of a diversion, and I ought to have kept my mouth shut."

Not long ago, he'd been a dashing blade himself, though he was a widower now. "It gets worse," I said. "Lord Dunkeld examined the marked deck closely, and many of the cards had no markings. Others had the same markings, and Dunkeld found no discernible pattern. The ten of clubs might have the same marks as the three of diamonds or no marks at all."

"Then somebody sought to make a fool of me," Sir Miniver said. "Easy enough to do."

Around a corner, a door slammed, and a tattoo of feet pounded down the corridor. Two children, I'd say, and having a grand time with their hide-and-seek.

"You do not strike me as a particularly foolish man," I said.

The smile came again, sadder. "I have been, from time to time. I am glad to have come upon you, though, my lady. Lord Ellersby claims you are deadly skilled at pall-mall. Will you agree to be on my team?"

Viscount Ellersby was my oldest brother, Mitchell, heir to the Derwent earldom, sensible to a fault, and devoted to his wife and daughters.

"How do you know my brother?"

"He was a year or two ahead of me at school. We've kept in touch. Do say you will be on my team."

In all modesty, I had to admit that I was good at pall-mall. I knew all the tricks and had a very accurate eye. How else was I to have kept pace with my siblings?

"When does this tournament start?"

"This afternoon, weather permitting. Mrs. Gillespie appointed six team captains, and it's up to us to recruit the rest of our quartet. Each team must have at least one lady."

Pattering feet thundered around the corner, then Annis and Fiona pelted past, flinging a, "You must not say you saw us!" over their shoulders before dodging into the schoolroom.

"Are there any lady captains?" I asked.

"I will gladly yield the honor if you desire it, but I understand the ladies will take the lead with the battledore tournament. The gents are in charge of bowls next week, and if there's a three-legged race, I plan to develop a sudden and serious megrim."

"So much competition," I murmured. "We will all go home exhausted."

"So many bachelors," Sir Miniver countered. "Exhaustion is one guarantee of good behavior, or so we were told in the army."

More proof of the military's clodpatedness. "I will be on your pall-mall team, and I suggest you recruit Madame St. Sevier as well. She can be very determined when set upon a goal."

Sir Miniver's response to that sally had to wait, because his sons emerged from what I took to be the stairway to the attics.

"Seen any girls?" the larger of the two asked. "We found the Bechtels, but they were whispering, so that was easy. We haven't found Fee and Annis."

"That way," Sir Miniver said, pointing in the opposite direction from the schoolroom. "I could swear I heard somebody galloping down that corridor not five minutes past."

"C'mon!" The larger boy grabbed his sibling by the arm, and they were off.

"Well, we did hear somebody in that corridor," Sir Miniver said when the boys had disappeared. "Besides what fun is hide-and-seek if one's quarry is in plain sight? I am off to find Madame and perhaps Cy Thurmont. He's a natural athlete and has plenty of siblings. Gives a fellow a head for strategy."

I let Sir Miniver have the last word, because my good mood had yet to abandon me—though why wouldn't a surfeit of siblings also give *a woman* a head for strategy? I was disinclined to swat flies while pretending to enjoy a cricket match, so I made my way to a public room I wanted to thoroughly explore: the portrait gallery.

The gallery received good light, though the paintings were all positioned such that none hung directly across from a window. The room had been thoroughly tidied, and last night's tournament might have taken place at some other manor house.

I nonetheless went to the nearest of the room's three sideboards and began systematically examining each cupboard and drawer. I was on the second sideboard, the one closest to the table where I'd last played, when a voice like a whipcrack had me straightening, a pack of cards in my hand.

"My lady," Tilda Gillespie said, "may I help you find something?"

∾

"Yes," I said, "you may. I am looking for answers."

"In the sideboard?" Tilda's manner hovered between indignant and curious. I outranked her by birth and to an even greater degree by marriage, and she was clearly hesitant to offend me.

I had found a trove of decks of cards and set them one by one on the top of the sideboard. "Yes, in the sideboard. If you have more marked decks, you want to know that sooner rather than later."

She closed the door and advanced into the room. "Greer sent a rider to London for fresh decks. We will set them on the table with seals unbroken when play resumes."

Two dozen decks of cards sat in stacks on the sideboard. "Let me guess, Nathan balked at the expense?" I pushed a stack of decks toward her. "You are looking for any irregularities along the back or the edges, the edges being the more usual site of tampering. Examine the pattern on the back for visual irregularities or pinpricks. When the suit of the card matters, an alteration that could be spotted from across the table would be helpful."

She took up the first deck. "Did Belmaine explain this to you? He was said to have a head for numbers and a memory for detail, and that explained his luck at the tables and in commerce."

Was that a subtle dig at a husband who had had associations *in trade*, or merely an idle observation?

"Freddie had both, and I grew up with a quartet of rascally brothers." In truth, only Ajax and Hector aspired to rascaldom. Felix was sweet, and Mitchell had ever been too serious and burdened by his prospective consequence as heir to the title.

"This one's clean," Mrs. Gillespie said, setting aside her first deck and taking up a second. "I envy you those brothers. I was an only child, as Dottie is. Nathan and I hoped for more children, of course, but that wasn't meant to be. I know Nathan was disappointed not to have a larger family, but he has never reproached me."

How good of him, when the lack of more progeny might well be laid at his booted feet. "I often wished I was an only child." My decks were also passing muster, though I had expected they would. "Then this soft-spoken Scottish boy moved into the neighboring estate, and my brothers befriended him. That was the best turn they ever did me."

Katie had confided that Felix had kept a close eye on Sebastian in Spain, and there was probably more to that tale, but I wasn't to know of it—yet. Enough nights cuddled in the darkness, and I might eventually hear Sebastian's side of the story.

"I've told everybody I know that you and the marquess are a love match."

"We are." Though an unconventional one. "I do not particularly care if Society takes us as such."

Tilda started on another stack of decks. "You should care. I'd known Nathan all my life, but he is nine years my senior. To me, he was always an adult and something of a mystery. My parents chose him because he was a known quantity, he came from a good family, and he'd agree to the terms of my settlements. I was pleased with the match, but I gather Nathan had to be talked into it."

She turned and gestured with her chin to a portrait of a dark-haired young man seated on an obliging boulder in a standard rural setting: verdant fields bordered by lush forests, a river ribboning into the distance, blue sky vaulting over the whole complete with puffy clouds and the loudly symbolic soaring eagle.

Gillespie's stance was a casual, cocky contrapposto, with his right hand on his hip and the left stroking the head of a magnificent black mastiff. His expression was confident and benign, as if he truly was lord of all he surveyed and expected to live out abundant years in that happy state.

"He was a handsome devil," I said, starting on my second stack. "Probably full of himself at that age."

"Nathan can still be full of himself. I suspect this will be the last house party he allows me, at least until I can get Dottie settled with Greer."

This again? "Why Greer? Why not Sir Miniver or Mr. Dinwiddie or Lord Jasper?"

"Sir Miniver is a lovely fellow, and a neighbor, but if you were Dottie, would you want to take on the raising of another woman's sons?"

And was that a slap at Annis? "For many, the fact that Sir Miniver has children in the nursery might increase his appeal. He seems to cherish those boys."

"He does, you are right, but Dottie is young and deserves to be more than a widower's consolation. Dinwiddie has been all but financially cut off by his family in hopes that he'll make something of himself, and here he is, swilling my champagne like any other idler. Lord Jasper is a fribble who will wager himself into the River Tick betting on whether the sky will clear by two of the clock. I haven't found a single marked card, my lady."

"I should hope not, but one wants to be sure. I gather Cranston is too young. What of Fontaine?"

"Cranston is also very much under his mother's thumb and has a family of biblical proportions, all of them pockets to let. Fontaine's sister is a notorious flirt, though Fontaine himself seems a decent sort."

A decent French sort, who would expect his wife to dwell in France, while Dottie could probably not contemplate setting foot outside the Home Counties.

"You have assembled a rogue's gallery, Mrs. Gillespie. Is this in aid of enhancing Greer's appeal?" Right down to including a notorious flirt over whom the rogues were doubtless to make fools of themselves under Dottie's discerning nose.

Though as to that, Miss Fontaine seemed perfectly well behaved to me.

"My lady, these fellows are saints compared to what Dottie will encounter in London. You had a come out, and your father is an earl. Imagine what Dottie faces, when she hails from mere gentry."

The gentry, in my experience, were only *mere* when they chose to be. Many of them had greater wealth than the neighboring peer and lineages that went back to antiquity, of which they were vociferously proud. They typically chose candidates for the House of Commons, were no less involved in local elections, and many held the parish living as well.

To hear the average squire tell it, the gentry were the backbone of the nation, the bedrock of her commerce, and the guardians of her morals—all while turning rural house parties into bacchanals and frittering away generations of wealth at the race meets.

Merciful powers, my thoughts could have been plucked from my father's head.

"Dottie is an heiress," I said, taking up my last stack. "Surely that will weigh in favor of a successful Season?"

"Dottie is an heiress, but the solicitors have given me a discreet peek at what Nathan proposes as her settlements. If she's to trade on her fortune, she'd best wed a patient man."

"You make me worry for my daughters."

"Well, you should, my lady. If anything were to happen to the marquess, the title would pass to some cousin, and there you'd be, a young widow with only girls in your nursery."

As the conversation progressed, I gained a sense of why Tilda Gillespie was such a gracious hostess, why she cultivated both literary and social luminaries: She believed their reflected light was her best hope of avoiding the shadows herself.

That she had such a low estimate of her own worth might be attributable to her upbringing or to her marriage to full-of-himself Nathan, but polite society also preferred its women meek and biddable. Given that reality, Tilda was either shrewd or pathetic, perhaps both.

Her situation gave me more reason to love my husband. Sebastian had married me knowing that another man's son might inherit the Dunkeld title. That had meant nothing to him, compared to the ostracism and scandal the child and I would face had I remained unmarried when I gave birth.

"Should anything happen to Dunkeld," I said, "the girls will want for nothing, save his loving presence in their lives."

This was so in part because Freddie had left me well set up and in part because Sebastian had insisted on making arrangements for both children. I knew not what discussions he'd had with St. Sevier regarding Maeve, but the matter of Maeve's security had been resolved to their mutual satisfaction.

I did not know Tilda Gillespie well, but in the course of this conversation, she had dropped the air of a gracious, confident hostess and become a fretful mother. I presumed on her honesty with my next question.

"Do you suspect The Falls is in difficulties?" I asked, returning my decks to their place in the sideboard cupboard. "Is that part of Greer Nicholson's appeal—he's financially secure?"

She passed me her decks. "I'm not saying Greer is Love's Young Dream. He's too sensible, but he and Dottie are fond of each other. They will rub along without high-flown expectations. If you've never been poor, my lady, you have no idea how terrifying that state of affairs can be."

Her gaze went to the portrait of her husband as a young man. "Nathan no longer even attends the race meets. He hasn't bought a new hunter in more than a year. Dottie's settlements are modest. What I had to go through to gain his assent to this house party... He wanted budgets and ledgers, right down to the last bottle of port. Something is afoot, and when I ask..."

"He tells you not to worry your pretty head?" I offered Freddie's memory a grudging nod of thanks. He had educated me regarding finances to a shocking degree. Money had been a game to him, one he'd expounded on enthusiastically and played with exquisite skill. He'd explained everything from the working of the Exchange to the role of the tattle sheets in sinking and making fortunes.

"Nathan dismisses my inquiries. Are we satisfied that the cards have not been tampered with?"

"We are. The marked deck was a prank, apparently." I explained the particulars to her as we abandoned the sideboard to stroll past the portraits.

"Pranks are Lord Jasper's specialty," Tilda said. "I suspect him of tampering with Dottie's mare. He'd find it hilarious, poetic, and daring to turn a young lady's mare out with the stallion, and some of the other young men are just foolish enough to wager on the success of his mischief."

Did Lord Jasper also fear invisibility? As a marquess's spare, he well might.

We paused before the portrait Tilda had pointed out earlier. Upon closer examination, the rendering of Young Nathan Gillespie had caught something in his gaze besides confident privilege. Viewed from immediately below, his expression suggested an emptiness, a lackingness.

Handsome, fit, and confident of his place, but... incomplete. Restless and aimless. Not yet a man, for all he had attained a man's years.

"Who painted this?"

"My mother. She was very talented. I did this one." Tilda gestured to the next painting, which depicted a pale young woman and a small boy. This little fellow, too, had an air of confidence, but for such a small person, he gazed out on the world with enormous seriousness.

"Greer Nicholson?" I asked, searching the boy's painted features for a likeness to the man.

"And his mother. Clarice doted on Greer. He was a posthumous child, a miracle, really, considering how unwell his father was toward the end. When I painted this, Clarice was already fading, though she tried to hide her illness from us and from Greer. He knew, though. Children do."

"While you only suspect that finances trouble your husband?" That would explain all the competitions. A game of battledore cost only the use of equipment that had probably been gathering dust in the attics for years. Venetian breakfasts, fêtes champêtres, ridottos, country dances, regattas, and such were much more involved and put a much greater burden on the staff.

But then again, Tilda was competing with a stable full of hunters and an armory full of fowling pieces. Perhaps the myriad competitions simply reflected her embattled marriage. We would not, after all, disband the house party without at least one lavish ball.

"Perhaps Mr. Gillespie is practicing economies in anticipation of next year's London expenses," I said, studying the serious boy and his wan mother. He reminded me of somebody, about the eyes, though his mama's influence was evident around the chin.

Wellington, perhaps? A particular recent Sir Thomas Lawrence portrait of Wellington in scarlet military regalia, arms crossed, expression reserved and resolute without quite crossing into hauteur.

Tilda ran her finger along the bottom of the portrait and came away with faint evidence of dust.

"Nathan needn't worry that I will bankrupt us in London," she said. "Funds were set aside in my settlements for the presentation to Society of my female children. My mother wanted to ensure that her legacy as a hostess lived on, and that meant providing her granddaughters' entrée, such as one gains during a successful Season. I honestly don't know what troubles Nathan lately. Perhaps he suffers the ill humor of a man who has prided himself on his masculine appeal for his entire life, and now he beholds gray hair, wrinkles, and more of same in his future."

"Don't we all, if we're lucky?"

"Try explaining that to a fellow who cut a dash in his youth and is now dependent on his wife's dwindling fortunes. No sons, rents falling, the throne occupied by a profligate buffoon. Peace bringing with it as many problems as the war created... Nathan reads the newspapers and despairs."

This discussion clarified for me the gravamen of Greer's appeal as a match for Dottie. He would provide her—*and her parents*—security, true enough. He would also never cut a dash, as that phrase alluded to stupid wagers, irresponsible reproduction, chronic inebriation, and muttonheaded pranks. He might bore Dottie to tears, but he'd never mystify her with his moods or provoke her to plot house parties as a sort of domestic revenge.

And yet, for all that, I liked Greer Nicholson. He was an adult, perhaps to a greater degree than his guardian had ever been.

"Does Dottie esteem Mr. Nicholson?" I asked, looking for some hint of softness in the little boy's countenance, some humor, some... joy. Though he'd never known his papa, and his mother had been dying even as this portrait had been painted.

"Dottie and Greer will suit," Tilda said, taking a handkerchief from a pocket and wiping at her fingertip. "They have had the benefit of long, close association, and neither will expect the other to fulfill romantic fancies."

I thought of Sebastian whispering to me in the night, of his hands applying a firm, gentle pressure to my secret aches.

"I know you want only the best for your daughter, Mrs. Gillespie, but I have had the experience of marrying the suitable match my father chose for me, and then more recently, wedding a man of unrelenting honor who also reads me poetry, rubs my back, and cuddles with me by moonlight."

Tilda's smile was sad as we moved on to the next portrait. "You are newly wed to the marquess. I thought myself in love with Nathan for the first two years of our marriage."

And she clearly missed that sense of wonder and possibility, still, after all these years.

"Dunkeld and I are already parents, and we've traveled the length of the realm together. I know love changes, but I also know Dunkeld. I wish for your Dottie the same respect and affection I feel toward my husband."

"You sound like your mother, my lady. She was devoted to her earl, though I know Derwent drove her to distraction on any number of occasions. I can assure you, with your father on hand, these pranks will cease. Derwent is no snob, but neither does he suffer foolishness, especially from young men. Another legacy of your rascally brothers, I presume."

She patted my arm and swanned off, leaving me to ponder an unnerving thought: The look on young Greer Nicholson's face said *he* did not suffer fools, even at a tender age. Could the stirring of resemblance I saw in his likeness be because that boy put me in mind of my own father?

CHAPTER TWELVE

Sebastian

"Ann says we will not attend another house party for quite some time," St. Sevier observed, "not even if the Regent himself is host."

Charlemagne and Hannibal ambled along a shady bridle path. Birds sang early-morning arias in the hedges and all around us, the countryside ripened toward harvest. I had left Violet slumbering in the lumpy bed without me, as I had for the past five mornings.

St. Sevier's wife and mine were in apparent accord. "Violet opines that if Wellington's officers were largely bachelors, it's no wonder defeating the Corsican took years."

"Perhaps the Corsican's military genius had something to do with that." St. Sevier drew Charlemagne to a halt and gestured with a gloved hand down a side path. "*Bon Dieu.*"

That last was added at a near whisper.

At this early hour, Miss Dorothy Gillespie was in a passionate embrace with a gentleman whose face was mercifully obscured by her bonnet. The couple was perhaps a dozen yards away and so absorbed in their enthusiasms—and so loud was the nearby waterfall —that St. Sevier and I passed by unnoticed.

"That young lady had best be careful," St. Sevier said as we crested the hill and beheld the cascade in all its plunging glory. "She attempted to make free with my person not three days ago. Ann found the situation hilarious, but I have made it a point not to idle about in solitude since."

We rode on past the remains of the folly, an open-sided octagonal building perched on the edge of the precipice. In years past, the folly had doubtless offered a safe enough place to view the magnificent scenery below, but the cliff face was eroding apace. One good storm and the whole structure could well vanish into the pool far below.

I steered Hannibal along the narrow path that hugged the trees. "Too many pranks have been played at this house party, and too many tempers could easily flare into foolishness over a lady's accusations."

"And here I thought my Gallic charm gave me irresistible appeal. Miss Gillespie said she'd turned her ankle. Being a physician, of course, I—"

"Fell for the ploy even faster than I did. Did Ann come upon you?"

"Nobody came upon us. When I realized the young lady had the same designs upon my person she previously aimed at you, I caught her up like a wayward ewe and carried her to a bench. I had deposited her thereupon and informed her I would fetch her proper aid when Mr. Nicholson and the Thurmonts arrived on the scene. The young lady conveyed to me that I was to exercise discretion, as if I needed that admonition."

"Where was this?"

"The conservatory. I passed through on my way to the cutting garden."

"Leaving bouquets on Ann's pillow?"

"I'm certainly not leaving them on anybody else's. And no, this is not a gesture I ever offered Violet. We had yet to reach the phase where dignity must give way to—"

"I would not have asked."

"One perceived as much, but you must know that Ann is..."

"Your first love and your last. One perceives as much, for God's perishing sake. Your solicitude toward your wife is a lesson to every callow swain on the premises." We descended from the wooded path to a hard-packed trail along the river. A third of a mile on, a cluster of half-timbered buildings gathered around a gray granite church with a gleaming steeple. "Shall we race?"

"*Non.* Your Hannibal is recovering from the tummy ache. My Charlemagne would allow him to win, out of respect for the elderly and concern for the tender sensibilities of the recently infirm. Then I would have to find some other obliging fellow to humiliate on horseback to restore Charlemagne's good spirits. Much wagering would result, and we have enough drama at this gathering as it is."

"You do not want to make an arrival in the village all windblown and sweaty in defeat."

"*Tu es an idiot, mon ami.*"

St. Sevier had used familiar rather than polite address and called me his friend, which pleased me inordinately. He'd also sunk his weight into his heels and gathered up his reins.

Hannibal—who had enjoyed blessed good health for the past week—was ready to demonstrate some speed. Because I did not want to overtax my horse, and for that reason *only,* we thundered onto the village green in a dead heat.

"You see how polite my Charlemagne is," St. Sevier panted, whacking his horse's sweaty neck. "He challenges, but he does not offer insult to the aged. Such a good boy."

For form's sake, I offered the requisite reply. "Another furlong and you would have been eating our dust."

"Oh, perhaps, then you would have collapsed into the grass beside your good beast, because the shadows beneath your eyes say you are getting less sleep than I am. My excellent capabilities as a physician would be necessary to revive you."

We walked a turn around the green to let the horses blow—also to enjoy the exhilaration of a good gallop.

"Shall we revive ourselves with a mug of ale instead?" The modest inn was apparently open for business. A half-grown girl in a wrinkled apron gave pots of heartsease on the inn's porch a drink, then dashed the rest of the bucket down the steps and commenced scrubbing.

The steady ring of a hammer on metal sounded from the smithy's forge, and a towheaded boy grazed a piebald donkey on the green.

"Ale will suffice," St. Sevier said as we dismounted and loosened girths. "Why do you suppose Miss Gillespie is accosting strange men in lonely locations?"

"Lonely, but not lonely enough. I've passed through the conservatory myself. The battledore nets are set up on that side of the house, so the conservatory sees plenty of traffic. Miss Gillespie came upon me on a path that leads to the Thurmont estate. One assumes servants and neighbors would both feel free to use it."

"Why court ruin?" St. Sevier posed that question while offering Charlemagne a drink from the communal trough. "You and I have wives to whom we are devoted. We could not appease convention by marrying the young lady if scandal ensued. Ann has played chess with Miss Gillespie and says she has her mother's streak of guile."

"Violet concurs and further opines that young ladies need guile if they are to contend with Mayfair Society."

The horses made a noisy business of slaking their thirst, and then Hannibal got a look in his eye that meant he was considering pawing about in the trough and making a great mess.

"Enough," I said, tugging the reins. "We can't have you getting another bellyache." I led my horse to the inn's shaded hitching rack and wrapped the reins around the rail, an unnecessary precaution. Hannibal would stand until Judgment Day if commanded to do so.

St. Sevier was observing the same precaution when the donkey brayed a salutation to the horses. The boy waved to us, and his motion drew my eye to the side of the smithy nearest the river.

A heavily pregnant young woman stood close to a man, though the deep shadows of early morning obscured his features. Because a shaft of sunlight struck his boots, I took him for a village lad or yeoman. His footwear was sturdy and reasonably clean, but going a bit frayed on the long seams up the back of the calf.

A day for trysts, apparently. I hoped for the expectant mother's sake that she was trysting with her spouse, but something about the pair's posture suggested an argument more than an interlude.

"Come," St. Sevier said quietly. "My thirst for ale grows compelling." He, too, had doubtless seen the couple and noted the woman's condition.

"Was it awful?" I asked, though my brain had not informed my mouth that such a question was in the offing. "Knowing Violet was expecting?"

"At first, yes," St. Sevier said. "Joyous, too, though I was torn between my renewed love for Ann and my worry for Violet. Then I saw that you and Violet were resolving matters between you, and that you and she were not... hostile to me."

"And here I've always thought the French were a clever lot."

"I saw as well," St. Sevier went on, starting for the inn, "that Ann was not hostile to anybody, including my handsome self or my former amour. My worry abated to something I could manage, and then Maeve was safely born. I am too grateful for the arrival of a healthy child to be anything but pleased. For Violet, for myself, for all of us."

"You can say it, you know. To me, to Violet, and doubtless to Ann, you can say it: Maeve is your daughter. She's my daughter too." Just as Annis was Violet's daughter. "Someday we will figure out how to convey the truth to our Maeve."

Ann, abetted by Violet, had set us on this course, which was the only sensible path. As one who'd been a homesick boy longing for his family, I thought that affording Maeve a few extra relatives was a fine plan.

St. Sevier and I climbed the glistening steps of the inn, and he brushed a glance around the green, no doubt taking in the couple still secreted in the shadows of the livery.

"I never did thank you, Dunkeld, for the name."

"Which name?"

"Maeve *Fleur* Caledonia MacHeath. Such a grand appellation for such a tiny person."

"Mostly Scottish, with a nod to the flowers in Violet's honor." A French nod, as Violet herself had pointed out with some satisfaction. "I wasn't about to name any child of mine after an English queen."

He put a hand on the door. "My mother was called Fleur, after the fleur-de-lis. Perhaps Ann told you?"

I had asked her for suggestions, and she'd immediately put forth Fleur. St. Sevier's other grannie had gone through life burdened by the name Alphonsine.

"One needn't belabor coincidences." I used the boot scrape out of habit, though my footwear was free of mud. "You are paying, by the way. I failed to bring any coin." I had, of course, brought a few coppers in my pocket, but what did that matter when French national pride was on display?

"I am paying, and we will drink to the health of the ladies and to your good fortune."

I did not like the sound of that last part. "Which part of my good fortune?"

"The part about your father-in-law will join the house party later today. Surely you rejoice to contemplate such a development, and I know Violet will be delighted as well."

"Bollocks and bedamned." I shoved the pride of France through the doorway and rejoiced overmuch to have made him stumble—and laugh.

∾

The first time I had come across Violet—Lady Violet Deerfield at the time—crying, she had been alone in the Derwent Hall stable, weeping into the mane of her stalwart mare. To see my dauntless companion, debate partner, source of greatest frustration, and the inspiration of my youthful dreams in distress had nigh parted me from my wits.

Another female might have lied to me, making a delicate reference to a megrim or a spat with her governess. Violet had baldly announced that her damned menses were paining her *again* and that she ached from her eyeballs to the arches of her feet. She further railed that the only way to escape the pain was to conceive a brat—a temporary solution bringing with it unbelievable risk and bother—or to grow as old as Methuselah's mother.

She had whirled from her mare into my arms and given me my first experience physically comforting a female in distress, and not just any female—my very own Lady Violet.

I had known even in my youth that she would never be mine in any socially acknowledged sense, but she had been mine to love, vex, challenge, and admire. I had been nothing more than a cantankerous Scottish marquess's insurance policy against escheat. When my titled uncle had married a much younger woman, I had lost even that status.

The past five nights had gratified some need I'd carried for years to be Violet's comfort and confidant. She was a champion cuddler, tucking herself close and arranging me however she pleased. I was not a marble saint—proximity to a luscious and beloved woman had the predictable effect—but that effect was muted by concern for Violet and respect for what she endured.

"How was your ride?" she asked, rising from the vanity and kissing my cheek.

Someday I might take such kisses for granted—someday half a century hence. "You were right." I caught Violet in an embrace, needing to have her in my arms. "St. Sevier worries for Ann, who is trying not to burden him with needless anxieties. Too much tender regard, not enough honesty. Might I look forward to a ride with you tomorrow morning?"

I had no idea how long The Indisposition lasted, but Violet was an accomplished and enthusiastic horsewoman.

"I haven't ridden since..." She took the pin from my cravat and started on the knot. "Since I galloped off to stop St. Sevier from being bound over for the assizes. A quiet hack after my morning visit to the nursery would be enjoyable."

The house party had given us a chance to become domestically intimate, rather than erotically intimate. Violet valeted me, I brushed out her hair. She tugged off my boots, I dealt with her hooks. I treasured our growing familiarity and suspected Violet did too.

"Tell me of the village," she said, unrolling my shaving kit as I stripped down to my breeches. "Prosperous, struggling, or something in between?"

"Prosperous, I'd say. No neglected drains, the roofs all in good repair. The inn serves a good summer ale at a reasonable price. The livery was tidy and the horses in good weight. We must commend Gillespie for seeing to the village, however much he might be a trial to his wife."

Violet moved the vanity stool so she could watch me shave. She'd done the same on several other occasions, and I found her interest in even so small a thing as my morning ritual encouraging.

"Nathan Gillespie should get little credit," she said, "according to Miss Fontaine, who heard it from Cyrus Thurmont. Greer Nicholson is more or less the unpaid steward of the estate. He has modernized the agriculture and animal husbandry, looked after the tenant housing, and articled some of the village boys to tradesmen closer to London, with the understanding that they'll come back to The Falls when they've learned their craft."

I lathered up my face and began the peculiar expressions necessitated when a man sought to wield a blade against his whiskers.

"How do we know Nicholson isn't simply carrying out Gillespie's orders?"

"Because they have great rows over the whole business, apparently. Gillespie holds forth about economies being necessary in difficult times, and respect for worthy traditions always having served The Falls well. Nicholson fires back, citing pamphlets, yields per acre, and progress. My father has the same arguments with Mitchell, though Mitchell would never gratify Papa by shouting."

"Perhaps your brother should gratify himself by shouting. Derwent's due to arrive later today, lest we forget."

Violet's gaze met mine in the mirror over the washstand. "One tries not to dwell on inevitable disappointments. You must promise me you will never wear a shirt when you shave."

"I'm careful. Shaving soap doesn't stain."

"I like to watch your back, watch the muscles ripple and bunch, and you stand with your feet slightly apart and braced. That stance is manly."

I wanted to kiss her for that, except my face was still half lathered, and I was all but undressed. "You may watch me shave, bathe, and dress whenever you wish. Please recall that we will plead a teething child if Derwent becomes bothersome."

Violet rose to drape a towel over my shoulder and lingered in the vicinity long enough to smooth a hand down my back and over my fundament.

"Papa will behave," she said, returning to her stool. "The bigger the audience, the more he's the gracious patriarch and the less he's Lord Vexatious Pomposity. Ajax dubbed him thus. Besides, he and the Gillespies are apparently as thick as thieves. Papa will know most of the guests, the neighbors, and the servants. They will all flatter him, and he will radiate gracious goodwill like a lighthouse sending beams of illumination out to sea."

"You dread his company."

Violet's smile was wan. "It's worse than that. I am a mama now. I might develop sympathies for the old reprobate such as one parent feels for another. My siblings and I came in very rapid succession, and then Mama went to her reward much too early. Derwent did the best he could, I suppose."

I finished shaving and washed the last of the lather from my cheeks. "Next, you will be telling me he meant well." Violet and I did not often discuss Derwent's meddling. When as a young man I had approached the earl about permission to court his daughter, he'd laughed in my face and offered me a choice: accept an officer's commission at his expense, or be banished from Derwent Hall forevermore.

And for that, I did not judge him. By any measure save one, I would have been a poor match for an English earl's daughter. What earned Derwent my unending ire was his confident assurances that Violet would never entertain my suit and that I was a mere amusement to her.

At the time, I hadn't had the wisdom or the confidence to doubt his lies, and he'd known that.

He'd offered Violet no explanation at all for my departure, I hadn't realized she'd needed an explanation, and thus Violet and I had become strangers. Thinking I'd abandoned her, she'd dutifully accepted Freddie Belmaine's proposal, and a happily *never* after had followed.

"Derwent might tell you he meant well," Violet said, rising. "You won't hear me defend him on those grounds. Must you put on a shirt?"

"You look so hopeful." And she looked so kissable, though I did not dare indulge. "Do I conclude your indisposition has passed?"

"For the present. Ann says there's no telling when it will come around again, given that I'm still nursing a child day and night." Violet leaned into me, wrapping her arms around my waist. "I might be persuaded to nap at any point today. I'm that worn out by all the battledore and gossip."

From beyond the open French doors, a shout went up, then a round of applause. "I am not making love to you for the first time while we are serenaded by that... that riot."

Violet eased away. "If we wait for a perfect moment, Sebastian, we will never consummate our vows. The bed is lumpy, we are tired, the other guests are getting up to nonsense, and Miss Gillespie is apparently courting scandal, while her mother is trying to matchmake before the young lady is officially out. If we wait for moonlight and roses..."

She sank onto the chest at the foot of the bed. I took the place beside her and possessed myself of her hand.

"Perhaps you should put that shirt on after all," she said. "Your restraint is equal to the occasion, but for myself..."

"You want to get our initial lovemaking over with?"

"No... yes. Maybe."

I waited, dreading what I might hear, but determined that Violet's honesty would be respected.

"I dreamed of you for years, Sebastian. I thought you had left me for the glory of war, and then I realized half my vexation with Freddie was because he wasn't you. He had no interest in books. He was uncomfortable with silence. His affections always led to the same unsatisfying destination, and worst of all..."

She leaned into me.

"Worst of all?"

"He never *listened* to me, unless it was to decide how to placate my latest fit of exasperation with him. I tell myself we simply did not suit."

"But you fear the greater lack was on your side of the balance sheet? It absolutely was not, and, Violet, my dearest, you need to know something."

"If you have a mistress, I will adjust Sebastian. I won't like it, but I will... You married me out of gallantry, and while we are fond, very fond, of each other, I cannot expect... You said we would not have a white marriage, and I grasped that an heir of the body is desirable, but..."

I waited, and Violet muttered something against my shoulder.

"I beg my lady's pardon?"

"I will hate you and your mistress, both, but then, how can you not hate St. Sevier?"

A valid question. "I did try. Felix wrote to me. Told me you were not emerging from mourning, that some malaise afflicted you. The family consensus was to leave you in peace, because that's what your father and brothers had always done when they couldn't be bothered to take an interest in your situation. Leaving you in peace wasn't—in the opinion of your youngest brother—having the desired result. Felix stopped short of summoning me to London, but the plea was evident in his words."

"You did not come."

"I *could not* come, not immediately. Annis was vastly unsettled. The previous marquess had left the castle in bad straits, the finances were a mare's nest. All of that might not have kept me away, but I believed that you had rejected my suit without even bothering to deliver the you-do-me-a-great-honor speech."

Violet laced her fingers more tightly with mine. "Had you come to London, I might well have turned you away in truth, Sebastian. I refused most visitors, and I thought... Well, you know what I thought."

"You did not refuse to see Hugh St. Sevier. Somehow, he charmed, prescribed, and doctored his way past your defenses and your melancholy. By the time I could travel south, he was your escort of choice, and you were no longer a ghost in your own home. *I owe him*, and I will always owe him, because he guarded your spirit when I could not and did not. Now he must trust me to guard you and his daughter, and he and I are at peace."

My wife and I were not quite at peace, but I had great hopes for our immediate future. "There's something else you should know, Violet."

She sat up straight. "You will not shock me, Sebastian. Say on."

I kissed her knuckles. I was shocking myself with these disclosures, but Violet deserved nothing less than the truth.

"When it comes to consummating the vows, *mo chridhe*, your experience vastly eclipses my own."

Violet's brows drew down. "But you were..."

"A university student, then a soldier, then a peer, and yes, all three statuses are renowned for profligacy. I tried my hand at debauchery—I was a very angry fellow when I reached Portugal—but mostly succeeded in giving myself a series of megrims. I come to you, not exactly untried, but far from..."

She regarded me most solemnly. "Far from jaded?"

Violet's word choice was a diplomatic courtesy. "I come to you determined to acquit myself well," I said. "Very well. I would rather wait out the battledore tournament and the cricket match than have our first memory be a disappointment to you."

"Oh, Sebastian." Violet straddled my lap and looped her arms around my neck. "You could not, on your worst day, ever disappoint me. As long as we are honest with each other and allow no one to come between us..."

The rest of her thought was lost in a spree of such delectable kissing that I wished I'd left off my breeches as well as my shirt. By the time Violet allowed me a pause to gather my wits, I was prepared to ignore cricket teams, stray military bands, and news of a French invasion.

I could not, however, ignore raised voices just outside our parlor door.

"Everlasting powers," Violet muttered, climbing off my lap and heading for the parlor. "Somebody is in a ferocious temper. Best put on a shirt, my lord—for now."

~

By the time I'd donned a shirt and waistcoat, the combatants were apologizing for disturbing Violet's morning. Greer Nicholson, looking for once less than composed, was nearly effusive, while Nathan Gillespie's contrition was more grudging.

"And apologies to you as well, my lord," Nicholson said, bowing. "I should have reserved my discussions with our host for a more private location."

Before Gillespie could mutter his version of same, Violet offered her gracious-lady smile in all directions. "What seems to be the difficulty?"

Men who had been bellowing angrily two minutes before were now united in silence. They clearly underestimated Violet's skills with upset males.

"Come now, gentlemen," she said, "our families have known each other for ages. His lordship and I are aware that unfortunate accusations have been tossed in several directions in recent days. We want to help, and I'm sure my father would feel the same way."

Mention of the Earl of Derwent deflated Gillespie's ire to sullen resentfulness. "Her ladyship asked for an explanation, young man."

Nicholson sent Gillespie an exasperated look. "I merely inquired of mine host why, if he was dealing marked cards, he didn't simply ask for a new deck and spare me yet another cloud of suspicion. *He* was dealing, but *I* was accused. I realize Sir Miniver holds me in low esteem because I was dissuaded from going for a soldier at age fifteen as he did. I nonetheless did not deserve his accusations, and the man who has been like a father to me remained silent in the face of that insult."

I caught Violet's eye and motioned with my chin toward our parlor door.

"Come along," she said as I held the door for her. "This topic requires a resolution, and you need privacy to find that."

Neither man wanted to heed her, but I treated them both to my best Highland glower, and they filed in as ordered.

"I must confess," Violet said, "that Mr. Nicholson raises an issue about which the marquess and I have been curious. He has been placed under clouds of suspicion—for the loose horse and the ruined punch, that I know of—and then we have an open accusation of cheating at cards when he could not have been."

"Precisely," Nicholson said. "We were on the second trick, and there's Sir Min in high dudgeon, while Nathan impersonates a sphinx. At least Tilda tried to diffuse the situation."

"I am the magistrate," Gillespie countered, pacing before the hearth. "What was I to say? 'Leave the boy alone'? You're not a boy, and you clearly aren't thinking. I have told you and told you that this lot of bounders and cads Tilda has recruited will scheme to put you in a bad light. They haven't your privileges. They haven't your means. They will deliver as many elbows to your figurative ribs as are necessary to knock you out of the race."

Nicholson sank into the armchair by the empty hearth. "*What race?* I am not racing anybody. I am trying to make up the numbers as politely as possible, though Tilda knows I have all the social grace of a water buffalo. I am firmly in trade when I'm not tending my acres. These other fellows have titles, wealthy families, wealthy families *with* titles... What perishing race?"

Violet answered him when Gillespie appeared unwilling to. "Tilda seeks a match between you and Dottie."

Nicholson's features shuttered. He might have been one of those Roman busts with blank, unsighted eyes for all the emotion in his expression.

"Dottie's not out yet," he said. "Nobody should be matchmaking or offering for her or scheming in either direction, and this entire discussion has wandered off the topic. You allowed my good name to be questioned, Nathan, and you have done nothing to repair that damage."

"I can *do* nothing," Gillespie said, taking a rude stance at the French doors, his back to the room. "If I attempt to meddle, it will look only the worse for you. Tilda doesn't understand that. The best thing you can do is be called away to pressing business in Town. How many times must I state that before you accept it as the truth?"

I could see Violet's mental mill wheel turning furiously, while I had the same questions Nicholson did: If Gillespie, the magistrate, had pointed out that Greer could not have benefited from the marked

deck, but that he, Gillespie, as the dealer, should have been accused...
Sir Miniver's little scene would have been dismissed as a prank.

More easily dismissed.

"Did you realize the cards were marked, Mr. Gillespie?" Violet
put the question gently. "The round had barely begun, and I confess
I was focused on strategy rather than on how worn a well-used deck
might have become."

Gillespie turned and regarded Violet as if he hadn't seen her
previously. "You are very much your father's daughter, my lady, and I
mean that as a compliment. No, I had not realized I was dealing in
scandal. One doesn't normally finger the edge of a card when dealing.
That takes skills I lack. There I was, wishing the evening to perdition,
wishing the whole gathering to perdition, though Tilda does set great
store by her socializing, and the next thing I know, Sir Min is on his
feet, eyes shooting fire and some speech from the third act of a Drury
Lane farce coming out of his handsome mouth."

Gillespie took the second wing chair, though neither man should
have been sitting while Violet remained on her feet. She remedied
their oversight by perching on the sofa and patting the place
beside her.

I did as she asked, enjoying the extent to which she had the situation in hand.

"Mr. Nicholson,"—she turned earnest blue eyes on him—"have
you considered absenting yourself from the gathering?"

Nicholson rubbed a hand across his brow. "I've promised Tilda
I'll stick it out, and I do not go back on my word. She says tucking tail
would only exacerbate the gossip, just as Nathan claims *a few quiet
words in my defense* would have made the situation worse. Dottie has
asked me not to abandon her, and as it happens, I agree with Tilda. I
know I *did not* ruin the punch, and I *did not* turn the mare loose, and
I *did not* cheat at cards, and thus I am that much more determined to
stay the course."

Gillespie rose. "Then I have nothing more to say. I've given you
the benefit of my advice: Leave before the next accusation is one I

cannot in good conscience ignore. Derwent is a magistrate, and if I felt I had to recuse myself from the situation due to conflicted interests, he will be on hand to see justice done. For your own sake, be careful, Greer. Be very, very careful."

He nodded to Violet and stalked out, leaving us with a bewildered and upset young fellow.

"I love that man," Nicholson said, remaining in his armchair. "Nathan put me on my first pony, let me name the puppies in spring, and saw that I had only kindly tutors. But I am no longer a boy, and he plainly resents me. I take an interest in the land. I don't consider myself above the neighbors or the tenants. I've had funds invested on 'Change since I was in leading strings, and I have a good head for numbers. I can't help any of that, but he…"

"My father claims I was a changeling," Violet said. "Derwent asserted with great confidence that the fairies stole his true daughter and left a contrary, ungovernable pisky in her place."

That comment added another item to the long list of blunders for which Derwent should be made to pay.

"Gillespie is losing his only daughter," I said. "Losing his only offspring to adulthood, marriage, and Society. He isn't ready for that, isn't ready for irrefutable proof of his own mortality. I suspect no parent is, but Dottie has grown up while Gillespie was debating whether to put the winter pasture in mangel-wurzels or turnips."

"Half each," Nicholson said, rising. "The heifers give more milk when fed the mangel-wurzel, and it makes a decent beer. People prefer turnips, and the greens are said to be especially good nutrition for the ladies. But it wasn't the winter crops that distracted him."

Violet got to her feet without my assistance. "What preoccupied him?"

I rose as well, wondering if Gillespie had been preoccupied by a *who* rather than a *what*. He and Tilda were apparently not a love match, and the money had come from her side of the bargain. Did Gillespie nurse old resentments over long-lost love?

"The grouse moors called to him," Nicholson said. "The hunt

field. For a time, he took up yachting. He likes doing the parlor sessions—likes playing the wealthy squire—but he's happiest engaged in sporting pursuits. I never meant to take on the management of The Falls, but Nathan was gone so much, and then Tilda would drag him up to Town in the spring... Somebody had to tell the stewards when to plant and when to take off the hay, and to be honest..."

Violet laid a hand on his sleeve. "To be honest, you are better at running this place than he is? Is that why his solution to all your difficulties is for you to simply pike off?"

"*He* has piked off," Nicholson said slowly, as if realizing this for the first time. "When Nathan and Tilda get to rowing incessantly, when Tilda and Dottie are on the outs, when Tilda's cousins come to sponge at the holidays, Nathan is least in sight. He has his own funds, but the truth is, Tilda could live independently if she chose to, and Nathan knows that. He, by contrast, could not support this property on his own resources."

"Strategic retreat is an old and much respected tactic," I said. "But that's not what bothers you most, is it?"

"Nathan's retreats bother Tilda exceedingly," Nicholson muttered. "But we're used to them by now, just as he knows better than to interfere with her social calendar. What bothers me is that if *I* did not pull all these pranks, then who did? And why isn't Nathan— the magistrate, our host, Dottie's papa, and Tilda's husband—getting to the bottom of them? Dottie is preparing for her come out, and any mischief done at this house party will follow her up to Town. That worries Tilda, and thus it ought to worry Nathan."

What a logical fellow he was, but was he an honest logical fellow? He was under clouds of suspicion for reasons.

"His lordship and I," Violet said, "will keep a sharp eye out for any more mischief. With the Earl of Derwent on hand, perhaps whichever Lancelot is getting up to tricks will rethink his strategy."

"Another week," Nicholson said, hand on the door latch. "For another week, for Dottie's and Tilda's sake, I can endure."

On that melodramatic note, he bowed to Violet and departed.

"Families," Violet said, sinking onto the sofa. "Such histrionics. Would it have been asking too much for Nathan to apologize for his silence? I understand his reasoning—the louder the defense, the greater the inference of guilt—but he did nothing, and he said nothing in mitigation of Sir Miniver's accusations. Not one word even in private for a young man who has been like a son to him."

"Perhaps another interview with Sir Min is in order."

Violet worried a nail, an anxious habit she'd had since childhood. "We will have to inform Papa of the goings-on. Whoever seeks to put Greer Nicholson in a bad light might see Derwent's arrival as an opportunity to disgrace Greer before an august party. Papa also knows these people, and he might have some useful insights."

"You are willing to seek Derwent's opinion?"

She left the sofa and curled in my lap, a delightful, if preoccupied, armful. "Ruined punch is wasteful and mean, and we did see—or the children saw—somebody answering to Greer's description tampering with the contents of the punchbowl. The mare getting loose is a higher order of wrongdoing. If she catches, she could die delivering the foal, and she'll certainly be out of action for a time as valuable riding stock."

"Which amounts to property damage, of a sort. I agree. And allegations of cheating at cards could have escalated to pistols or swords. Which begs the question..."

"What's next?" Violet said, snuggling closer. "A week to go, as Greer said, but what's next?"

CHAPTER THIRTEEN

Violet

My father, the rock upon which my childhood had been built, the original source of all my personal consequence, the Deerfield patriarch, and the author of my greatest frustrations, was aging.

On previous occasions, I had noted that Papa was more gray, or that lines around his mouth that used to signify fatigue had grown permanent. My observations had been casual, but now... I was a parent, and that had indeed shifted my perspective.

Papa was still spry, still charming when he chose to be, but I noticed in the hours following his arrival that his hearing was not as keen, and his clothing didn't fit him quite as perfectly as it ought. A button was a bit snug over his belly, a seam at the shoulders a trifle loose. Over another buffet meal, he flirted outrageously with the ladies, and that flirtation had become... harmless, perhaps even a bit silly.

Not quite pathetic. Papa would never be pathetic, I hoped.

"So I missed all the excitement?" he asked, handing his empty plate to a footman. He and I had taken our meal while sharing a bench on the terrace. We were making a public display of cordiality, but I was also simply spending time with a parent who might be taken from me sooner than I'd expected.

Sebastian had greeted Papa with lordly geniality, then gone off to do the pretty with Miss Fontaine.

"You missed the worst of the pranks," I said, "but you were spared five days of cricket too. Be thankful for that. You never saw such a lot of strutting and preening in your life, and that includes when Hector and Ajax first came down from university."

The children had been caught up in the pranking too: The Holmes boys had confessed to playing a combination scavenger hunt and hide and seek in the parental apartments. One boy would hide an object—a book sitting on a bedside table, for example—and the other would be challenged to find it. In the case of my mother's diary, the first boy had hidden my treasure, a supper gong had sounded, and the search had been abandoned.

By the time the young rapscallions could discreetly return to the scene of their foolishness, Sebastian had come to my rescue. The boys had confessed their puzzlement to Bevins—how had the book returned itself to its proper location?—who'd passed the details on to me. By agreement with the children, there would be no more such games outside the nursery, on pain of bread, water, and copious bible verses.

"Young men," Papa said, nodding at Sir Min across the terrace. "Wretched fools suffering a permanent case of the horn colic and trying to drink it into submission. I was a young man just last week, you know."

"Feeling old, Papa?" The evening was pretty as only rural summer evenings could be. A slight breeze stirred the air, bringing with it the scent of scythed grass. From the park came the late-day chorus of birdsong, and the setting sun sent fairy-tale beams through the stately oaks edging the formal parterres.

I would miss my father. Someday not too distant, I would miss him. Annis would have a few memories of him, Maeve even fewer, and I would tell them stories about the old earl, as my mother had told me stories of grandparents I could barely recall.

"I am feeling ancient, if you must know. My baby girl has become a mother, and she's wed to some Highland barbarian. I console myself with the fact that the barbarian owns an estate in the civilized environs of the Home Counties. All that notwithstanding, Perthshire is damned far way, Violet, and nobody has a more exaggerated capacity for venerating home turf than the Scots."

Perhaps because so many of them had been driven from it. "You will always be welcome at the castle, Papa, and Sebastian is the most civilized of men."

"He's devoted to you. I'll give him that. Always has been. Is he treating you well, Violet?"

Clearly, my father needed to hear an affirmative answer, but he would have relished an opportunity to take Sebastian to task as well.

"I esteem my husband *wildly*, and my regard is returned in full measure." Unless the gods were unspeakably perverse, we would that very night engage in the most intimate expression of wild, mutual regard.

"You're happy, then?"

"Often tired, but yes, I'm happy."

My father, a glib and sociable man, remained silent, and for a time, we simply sat side by side, watching shadows overtake the fading sunbeams. Had the occasion not been public, with other guests milling about the terrace and laughing and talking, I suspect Papa might have nodded off for a postprandial nap.

My husband approached, and Papa came subtly alert.

"Derwent." Sebastian had apparently extricated himself from Miss Fontaine's company. He acknowledged Papa with a nod. Because Sebastian held the higher rank, Papa really ought to have risen and offered Sebastian a bow.

Instead, Sebastian took the place beside me on the bench. "I have fallen into the clutches of the press-gang, Violet. My apologies in advance."

Well, damn. I'd been counting on an early night. "Which press-gang is it this time?"

"Darts night in the village. Guests against the locals. Derwent, will you join us?"

"For darts in the village? You know, I'd honestly enjoy that, but I've reached the point in my day where the spirit is willing, but the flesh is intransigently opposed. Then too, I don't see as well as I used to, and my pride urges a demurral. My money is on the locals, though, particularly if the Thurmont boys side with them. Tilda has assembled an ostentation of fribbling peacocks where a regiment of eligibles ought to be. The Thurmont lads are worth the lot of them put together, though Sir Miniver isn't a bad sort. Any bets going as to engagement announcements at the final ball?"

"Dottie isn't even out yet," I said as repressively as I could in polite surrounds. "Don't encourage ill-bred behavior among the bachelors, Papa, or I will deal with you severely."

"So like your mother," he said with an odd wistfulness. "Nathan would consent to seeing his daughter engaged before her first Season. Reduces the expenses considerably and gives the young lady a confident foundation upon which to meet all the tabbies and gossips. Though the bachelor pickings here are curiously slim, which suggests Tilda is up to something."

Papa was purely fishing. He likely knew exactly what scheme Tilda had put in motion, but he sought to know if we were aware of her machinations.

"Tilda seeks a match between Greer and Dottie," I said. "She tacitly solicited my aid in bringing that objective about."

Papa sat up, an old hound catching a whiff of intrigue. "And you abetted her folly?"

"Why do you call it folly?" Sebastian asked. "Nicholson is of good character, of age, solvent, has all his teeth, and is already all but running The Falls. If even royal cousins can marry, why not a match between Dottie and her father's former ward?"

"I've nothing against the fellow," Papa replied. "I've known him since he was in short coats and Dottie since birth. But Greer, for all his many virtues, is a plodder, and Dottie is... more like her mother. She thrives on being adored."

Neither Sebastian nor I asked just how ardently Papa might have adored our hostess in years past.

"Gillespie hates these house parties," Papa said. "Poor fellow is happiest tramping his acres with a fowling piece and a hound or two. We're alike in that regard."

Five years ago, even two years ago, I might have snorted at that assertion. Nobody had done the Town whirl as enthusiastically as Papa. Nobody had more committee connections in the Lords, or a keener sense for how to finesse matters with the Commons.

But there was that wistful note again, the tone of a man admitting truths long ignored. "While Sebastian maintains order in the darts team ranks, you and I will pay a call on the nursery, Papa. The girls were very impressed with your grays and are hoping you will grace the infantry with a visit."

The part about the handsome matched grays was true. I suspect Papa's presence in the nursery would be more a matter of curiosity than anything else. Small children baffled him, which usually came across to the child as annoyance.

"You offer me a graceful exit," he said, rising somewhat stiffly, "and I will accept it, even though it means subjecting myself to juvenile company. Dunkeld, acquit yourself well. The honor of the family regiment and all that... Mind you don't drink too much of the ale. The local publican makes a smooth brew that kicks like a street brawler come the next morning. I speak from wretched experience."

While Papa took his leave of our hostess, Sebastian escorted me to the foot of the terrace steps.

"Nathan put about the notion of fielding a darts team," Sebastian said, "but this lot will do more drinking than anything else."

"You are concerned?"

"Talk around the port last night grew... awkward. Somebody alluded to crooked decks, and the moment became uncomfortable."

"Which somebody?"

"Cranston, I believe. He couldn't possibly have meant anything by it, but the room grew quiet until St. Sevier asked for an explanation of some detail of the cricket rules. Nicholson left the room soon afterward. I have every confidence that when St. Sevier and I decamped, speculation started up again."

"Somebody is stirring the pot. We suspected they would."

Sebastian stood close enough to me that we might have been exchanging sweet nothings—except that we were not.

"I might be out quite late, Violet. St. Sevier will come along, and I had hoped Derwent might lend his calming influence, but he's leaving the governess's job to me."

I slipped an arm around Sebastian's waist and leaned into him. "I have plans for you, my lord. Wildly passionate plans." I was still adjusting to the idea that Sebastian's past included little in the way of romping.

The notion was touching, but put a burden on me to be knowledgeable, to acquit myself well. Whatever else my previous lovers had expected of me, sexual confidence had not been on the list.

Sebastian bussed my cheek. "Your plans are but a shadow of my own, my lady, but you'd best not wait up for me."

"I hate those words. I suppose I can dream of you for one more night." I kissed his cheek, a reciprocal wifely peck to any observers, though my disappointment was immense.

"If you two are through canoodling," Papa said, "then I must make my obeisance in the nursery. Mind the ale, Dunkeld, and caution our favorite Frenchman to do the same. Violet, if I am not mistaken, the lookouts will have seen us finish our meal. Let's get their report, shall we?"

I glanced upward to see Annis, Fiona, and four other children peering down from the nursery's balcony.

"You used to do the same," Papa said. "As did I, in my wicked youth." He nodded to Sebastian, and thus I resigned myself to another night of restless dreams—and only dreams—on the lumpy damned bed.

∾

I rounded a bend in the forest path and saw yet another uphill stretch ahead. "Tilda finally schedules a picnic, and all I want to do is curl up in a hammock with a good book." That wasn't *all* I wanted to do. Sebastian had returned quite late the previous night, and I'd awoken an hour before dawn to find him dead to the world beside me.

I had just decided that the delicious moment had come to seduce my husband just as Bevins had tapped on the bedroom door. I'd followed Bevins back to the nursery rather than risk disturbing my spouse. When I'd finally returned from dealing with a fussy and voracious baby, seduction had no longer topped my agenda.

Tonight, then—provided I could remain awake.

"I could carry you," Sebastian said, taking my hand as we started up the next section of the hill. "If it's any consolation, St. Sevier likely had no sleep at all. He was called away to a birth that was going badly. Never have I seen a man more enthusiastically abandon a darts tournament, and in the pouring rain too."

The path rose in a series of switchbacks to the highest elevation on the property, not far from the top of the cascade. Most of the party had chosen to take the longer, gentler way around, but I had wanted a respite from the other guests. I hadn't figured on a steep and slippery trail.

"Is there no midwife in this neighborhood?" I asked.

"The midwife asked for his assistance. A first-time mother in difficulties. He wasn't at breakfast, not that one would ask for details over the porridge."

"I assume everyone behaved at the tournament?"

"If you're invited to choose sides for the rematch, stick with the Thurmonts. They are damned skilled and well liked. The ale disappeared apace, and the innuendos were starting when St. Sevier was called away. The notion that a village woman might not live to see the dawn subdued those who would have stirred the scandal pot. The Thurmonts left shortly thereafter, and that ended the competition. Behold, a bench. Take pity on me, *mo chridhe*, and say we can tarry a moment to admire the view."

"We can tarry half the afternoon, though I suspect for the downhill journey, the ladies will eschew the pony carts and demand handsome escorts."

We settled on the weathered seat, which looked out over a canopy of treetops to the countryside below. The view was dramatic for southern England, and the falls thundering in the distance to our right made it more so.

"I like our vista in Perthshire better," I said. "The land hasn't been tamed, and the light is more intense."

Sebastian wrapped an arm around my shoulders, and I leaned into him, the moment taking on an unexpected sweetness.

"A week from now," he said, "we will be at Ashmore, and we can sleep until noon, picnic three times a day, and spend entire nights in the same hammock if we please to. How did Derwent's tour of the nursery go?"

"The girls were not particularly impressed, but the boys were happy to explain their toy soldier victories and pall-mall defeats to him. I realized that Papa simply doesn't know what to do with a little girl. Doesn't know how to converse with one, what to ask her. All he said to Annis was, 'Aren't you a pretty little thing?' when she'd wanted to show him the map she'd drawn of the park."

"I've seen that map, and it's damned accurate, but then, the nursery overlooks the back of the property, so she has nearly the perspective of a balloonist."

"You are not to mention the word 'balloonist' in the hearing of the children, Sebastian."

He closed his eyes and tipped his face up to the midday sun. "Napoleon's official balloonist was a woman. Less weight to get aloft probably made the job easier."

"Are you going to sleep, my lord? The children might well already be on the hilltop, and we must not leave Bevins to manage them all on her own."

For this one event, Tilda had decided to include the older children. They would come with the nursery staff, of course, but I intended that Annis would eat with us. She was our daughter, and the sooner polite society accommodated that reality, the better for them.

"You are sad," Sebastian said, without opening his eyes. "Is it Derwent?"

"How can you know what I'm feeling?"

"Something in your voice, in your silences, in the way you look at this glorious prospect and think of Perthshire. I do, too, but I'm still glad we came south."

I was reminded of the Sebastian I'd known long ago, a quiet, noticing youth with a kind heart. I could tell that boy anything and trust that he would not judge me for foolish opinions or tender sentiments.

"Papa is slowing down, losing vitality. He raised me. He should have known enough to ask Annis if she preferred dogs or cats. Asked her if she had a favorite storybook or fable. He did not make the effort. Promise me that when we are old, we will make the effort to see our grandchildren as the wonderful little people they are."

"I promise," Sebastian said, opening those magnificent blue eyes and regarding me solemnly. "I promise, and I love you."

We tarried on the bench, indulging in passionate kisses, and then bided yet longer, recovering from our expressions of marital zeal. The last of our hike had us passing the decrepit folly, which when approached from below, looked to be anchored to the cliffside by little more than scraggily tree roots. From the top of the hill, the little building might look sound enough, but I saw the crumbling foundation as a metaphor for the relentless power of time to topple all edifices.

We were among the last to arrive at the summit, and that suited me well. The picnic was another entertainment to be endured, though the surrounds were pleasant.

The picnic grounds side of the hill overlooked the park and the manor house, with its gardens and outbuildings. An impressive view, and that was likely Tilda's intent. The guests would leave knowing exactly how much Miss Dorothy Gillespie stood to inherit from her mother.

The falls descended nearby from the other, wilder side of the hill, and many a stroll would doubtless be taken through the trees to admire that view as well. They would see the dilapidated folly, but even that sight added a romantic touch to the vista.

After some searching and a quantity of small-talking, we found our assigned blanket and basket, and I thought to go in search of Annis. Fiona was sitting between her parents six yards off and holding forth volubly in French. Papa stood in conversation with Sir Miniver and Nathan Gillespie, while the bachelors gathered around Miss Gillespie, Miss Fontaine, and the other young ladies.

The Holmes and Bechtel children were playing tag, but I did not see Annis.

Bevins crossed from the line of pony carts with undue haste. "My lady, I cannot find wee Annis. She and Fiona came along with me in the pony cart, and she wanted to show the old... the *earl* her map, but he wasn't interested."

"Perhaps she needed to visit the bushes."

Sebastian had caught my eye and abandoned the blanket to join us. "What's amiss?"

"Annis is amiss," I said. "Papa ignored her again, and she's done a bunk."

Bevins glanced around at the other guests. "Beg pardon, ma'am, but the earl didn't ignore her. He scolded her for being a bother, told her children should be seen and not heard and seen only rarely, and told her to take herself off before he turned her over his knee."

Sebastian seemed to grow six inches taller beside me. "He threatened *our daughter* with a spanking? Because she wanted to show him a map he'd been too rude to look at last evening?"

Bevins sent Derwent a look that boded ill for self-important earls. "Miss Annis doesn't cry, my lord, not in broad daylight. That old... milord had her chin quivering. She's probably taken herself back to the house."

The pony track swept down the gentler side of the hill in a wide, gradually descending curve, and Annis was not trudging along that path.

"Is something wrong?" St. Sevier had strolled over from the blankets, Ann at his side, Fiona holding her father's hand.

"Aye," Sebastian said. "Derwent vented his spleen at an undeserving Annis, and now the child is off licking her wounds we know not where."

Fiona took to studying her toes.

I knelt before her. "If you were Annis and your feelings were hurt, where would you go?"

"I'd go to my mama or my papa or my pony, but Annis hasn't got a pony here."

I rose. "Would she pay a call on Hannibal?"

"How would she find her way to the stable?" Sebastian asked.

She would find her way, as I always had, by dead reckoning. The stable was partly obscured by trees, but Annis, having studied the property, would know in which general direction it lay. We were debating who should be dispatched to search where and whether to alert the company when Greer Nicholson emerged at a jog from a path through the trees.

"My lady, Dunkeld," he panted. "The girl Annis is in the folly, and the structure is not sound. I did not dare add my weight to hers, and the height and view of the falls below has unnerved her. She's not safe, but I thought you would have better luck coaxing her to solid ground than I did."

Sebastian swore in Gaelic, while St. Sevier's profanity flowed in French.

I took off for the path leading through the trees.

～

The folly might once have sat back from the edge of the precipice by several yards, but time and weather had eroded the lip of the cliff to a dangerous extent.

Annis stood at the farthest edge of the structure, clinging to one of the supports, her gaze fixed on the trees rather than on the water roaring over the falls. Her complexion was as white as the churning depths at the bottom of the cascade. A wooden sign affixed to the steps of the folly proclaimed: No Admittance.

"Child," Sebastian called, "come away from there. Your meal awaits."

"I can't."

I saw Annis form the words more than I heard them. The water thundered relentlessly on as St. Sevier, Ann, and Fiona joined Nicholson, Sebastian, and me ten feet back from the edge.

"C'mon, Annis," Fiona said. "Please. We're playing tag."

Annis looked to me, and I saw a little girl who'd realized too late that she was in very great danger.

"Please do come," I said, dropping Sebastian's hand and waggling my fingers at Annis. "The folly was built too close to the edge of the falls and has grown rickety over the years. The blighted thing should be knocked over the side, but first you must get yourself out of there."

Annis was breathing shallowly and clinging to the pillar. She shut her eyes and shook her head. "I can't move. The waterfall is too far down, and I looked, and now my heart is going to burst, and I c-can't move."

Sebastian moved from my side, but I caught him by the wrist. "I'll get her. I know what it is to be stuck and scared. Let me go."

"Violet, no. If anything should happen, Maeve will need you."

"Nothing will happen, provided we don't waste the day arguing."

Nathan Gillespie emerged from the break in the trees, my father, Sir Miniver, and the Thurmont brothers with him.

"Keep back," Sebastian yelled, "and don't move about."

"Somebody needs to get the child out of there," Gillespie said. "With last night's rain, the folly could topple at any moment."

My father at least had the sense to keep his mouth shut rather than offer further statements of the obvious.

"Please," I said to Sebastian. "I weigh far less than you do—like Napoleon's balloonist."

Right in front of the gawking onlookers, he caught me in a hug, kissed me on the mouth, then stepped back.

"St. Sevier," he called, "Nicholson, Thurmont, we will form a human rope, and her ladyship will retrieve the girl. Annis, be brave another minute, and your mother will fetch you."

Nicholson got a grip on a stout oak a good five yards back from the steps of the folly, the Thurmonts formed the next two links in the chain, then St. Sevier, and last, Sebastian, who kept a grip on my hand.

"Annis," I said, pausing on the steps of the folly, "the view straight down would frighten anybody. Don't think about it. Look at me and think about Bella. She has traveled all the way from Spain and down from Scotland with you, and she's waiting for you back in the nursery. Would you like me to find some new buttons for her eyes?"

Annis shot a glance at me over her shoulder as I gained the top of the steps. "She wouldn't be my Bella with new eyes. Mrs. Yancy wanted to throw her into the fire. Mrs. Yancy said Bella had fleas."

"Mrs. Yancy was an idiot." I pretended to a briskness I did not feel. "We are well rid of her. Now let's get you free of this place. Can you take my hand?"

Sebastian, with one foot on the steps and the other on solid ground, held my left hand. I extended my right as far as I could reach, but Annis would have to make up the rest of the distance.

"I am telling my hand to move, but it won't listen." The child's voice quavered, and my heart was slamming against my ribs beat by beat.

"Let's make the exercise simpler. With one hand, you will keep hold of that post, as tight as you please, but the hand nearest to me will take a small rest from clinging to the post. Just let that hand rest, Annis."

More people were edging along the woods. The Fontaines, Lord Jasper, Lord Cranston. I saw on their faces the horror roiling in my own belly. A stiff breeze riffled through the foliage, and I wanted to scream.

Annis, though, had eased one hand away from the post. "I did it."

"Give that hand a good shake," I said, demonstrating with my own trembling appendage. "Get the blood moving, then hold that hand out to me. Just raise your arm in my direction... That's my girl."

Annis found the courage to comply with my directions, and I soon had a firm hold of her hand. "Mama, please don't let go of me."

"Never. Not ever, not if we have to stay here chatting until Yuletide, though that could get a bit chilly."

"Violet..." Sebastian's voice held a note of warning, and I realized that clouds were moving in. More wind, more rain, more danger, but not just yet.

I secured my grip on Sebastian and my grip on Annis. "You've done the hard part," I said to her. "You have a hold of me now, so you're safe. Just tell your other hand to let go, child. Mama and Papa are here. The bad moment is past. You've been very brave, and now we can go have lunch."

A peal of thunder reverberated in the distance, and I gave Annis's hand a little tug. "Come, my girl, or we'll get a soaking."

She still had a firm grip of the post, and how well I knew the terror that paralyzed her. "I got stuck once," I said. "I was swimming, and my foot became wedged in some branches. I thought I was going to die, just inches from the air I desperately needed, and I could not make my mind focus on how to get my foot free. I did not die, though."

"You went swimming?"

"Never alone. Even I knew not to indulge in that much folly. Your Papa was with me, and he realized I was in difficulties. He had the brawn to shift the branches, and so he got me free. I had to swim away on my own strength, though. Let go of the post, Annis MacHeath."

"Can you count to three? Bevins counts to three."

I heard one of the men mutter about the whole rubbishing shire counting to three.

"Of course. In French, Gaelic, or English?"

That earned me a ghost of a grin. "English."

"Very well. One... two... three..." I gave another little tug, and Annis let the post slip from her grip. We were out of the folly in the next instant, with Sebastian scooping Annis onto his hip and keeping his hold of my hand.

A cheer went up from the spectators while Sebastian, Annis, and I hugged as a family threesome.

"Was I really, truly brave?" Annis murmured, her nose mashed against Sebastian's shoulder as he moved us farther away from the precipice.

"You were wonderful," I said, blinking back tears. "I am very proud of you."

"What does the sign mean?" Annis said, lifting her head to gaze at the wooden board on the steps. "I can't read English as well as I read Spanish."

Sebastian set her on her feet. "It says 'No Admittance,' which means stay out, don't go there."

Annis peered up at him. "If it's dangerous, why not just say 'danger'?"

"If it's dangerous," Greer Nicholson muttered as the onlookers began to drift back to the picnic grounds, "why not knock the blasted thing down? Perhaps that's one argument Nathan and I won't have to have again."

Nathan was retreating with Sir Miniver, while Papa waited

where the path emerged from the trees. He was looking very stern, very much the earl.

Well, to blazes with him. I was a marchioness, and more to the point, Annis had called me *Mama*.

I marched over to my father. "I understand you owe Annis an apology, my lord."

"I'd say the boot rather goes on the other foot, missy."

I counted to three in French and Gaelic. "Do not ever again refer to me as 'missy.' I am a grown woman, my husband's consequence exceeds your own, and your rudeness and threats hurt Annis's feelings and frightened her. You have bungled badly, Papa, and if you ever want to see my children, if you want them to have any familiarity with you at all, you will apologize to my daughter."

Annis was watching this discussion, as was Fiona. Ann and St. Sevier looked amused, while Sebastian's eyes danced.

"'Pologize," Fiona said, shaking a finger at Derwent. "You have to say sorry, or *pas de pudding pour vous*. Annis just wanted to show you her map, and *vous étiez méchant*."

"You *were* nasty, Papa. Fiona is right. The marquess and I do not permit violence toward our children. If we expect them to be mannerly and considerate, then manners and kindness must be shown to them."

"Violet, you are being—"

"Reasonable," Sebastian said. "Logical. A good mother. Best get it over with, Derwent."

Papa looked genuinely bewildered while another rumble of thunder sounded off to my left.

"Oh, very well." He drew himself up. "Miss Annis—"

"*Lady* Annis," I said, and Ann St. Sevier blew me a kiss. "My daughter is Lady Annis. Your granddaughter is Lady Annis." This was rank presumption on my part. Yes, a marquess's daughters were addressed as lady, but that courtesy was usually reserved for legitimate, biological offspring only.

A few yards off, Greer Nicholson and the Thurmonts had left off gesturing at the folly and pointing to the rocks below—planning a spot of demolition, no doubt—to watch a peer of the realm offer his apology to a small child.

"Lady Annis," Papa said, bowing. "I most humbly apologize for my tone and for my rudeness. It won't happen again, I can assure you."

Annis held out her hand, but she offered no words of absolution, and I was never more proud of that child. Papa bowed over her hand and then strode off into the woods.

Nicholson watched the ferns waving in the rising breeze. "I wish Tilda and Nathan had seen that. The Earl of Derwent apologizing to a young girl should be of greater interest to the gossips than loose horses and wrecked punch."

"I saw it," Sebastian said, "and the St. Seviers did too. That's witnesses enough. Shall we return to the picnic baskets, or wait here to get a soaking?"

"Best rejoin the madding crowd," I said, "and now that you mention picnic baskets, I realize I am famished."

The gentlemen took up the charming topic of explosives, while Ann and I shepherded the girls back to Bevins, who caught Annis up in a tight hug and whispered something to her in Gaelic. Annis was soon helping to pack up what had been unpacked less than an hour earlier.

"Her next governess will have to be a good teacher of Gaelic," I said, "and the Spanish might have to go by the wayside in favor of French."

"Annis already knows the Erse," Ann said. "Not perfectly, but with very little accent."

"*I* do not know the Erse, and believe me, spending the rest of my life in quiet study, far from house parties, at homes, musicales, and other abominations has very strong appeal."

"We have only a few more days to go before we can return to our respective homes and you can embark on your life of quiet study."

"While you do what?"

Ann's gaze went to her husband, and she grinned at me. "Need you ask?"

We enjoyed a mutual smirk and helped ourselves to the picnic baskets while jouncing back down the hill in the pony carts. The menfolk chose to walk, and I sent up a silent prayer that Ann's wish would come true—no more drama, no more excitement, no more pranks.

Alas, my prayer was not to be answered.

CHAPTER FOURTEEN

Sebastian

The bachelors had decided to make an event out of demolishing the folly, and the ladies—Violet included—had decided to leave them to it. Explosives that could further destabilize the clifftop were deemed unwise, so the business was to be carried out by main force. The elements obliged with a fine, sunny morning, which struck me as a personal insult to my mood.

Given the intensity of my frustrations, I could have whacked the whole thing down with my own efforts.

"You swing that sledgehammer with a papa's vengeance," St. Sevier said, passing me a mug of ale. "The younger fellows are impressed."

I downed half the pint and wiped my mouth on my wrist, my shirt having come off half an hour ago. "Maeve is teething."

St. Sevier made a sympathetic face. "So the mama is up and down all night, and maybe the papa too?"

"Of course the papa too. I cannot wait to be quit of this damned gathering."

St. Sevier took a delicate sip of his drink. "Ann says the same, but I would prefer that we find out who the prankster is before we disband."

His impassive gaze and careful tone said he had a reason for that preference. When St. Sevier kept pertinent facts to himself, he was usually wearing the hat of a physician honoring confidences.

"You heard something at that lying-in, didn't you? Something disquieting about the situation at The Falls."

Our elevation gave us a lovely view of gently swaying treetops, rolling fields, pastures dotted with livestock, and the river winding peacefully through the whole patchwork. A few stands of trees provided darker contrast, and to the west, the village sat snug and cozy around its green.

This was an Englishman's paradise, but immediately before us sat the pile of rubble that had been the folly, a cautionary heap of stone and weathered timber.

"The lady I attended after the darts tournament has arrived to motherhood without benefit of matrimony," St. Sevier said. "The women keeping her company made remarks that implied—"

A yelp went up from the young men gathered around the tap at the back of a dray.

Cranston was holding his mug away from his body while his sleeve dripped ale into the grass. "Careful there, if you please. My valet has enough work to do as it is."

Sir Miniver had shoved Greer Nicholson in the chest, and Greer —coat off, cuffs rolled back—looked ready to return the insult.

"Here come the elders," St. Sevier muttered as Nathan Gillespie and the Earl of Derwent stalked over from the shade of the trees.

"Pansy Miller had a good reputation until you trifled with her," Sir Miniver spat at Greer. "My housekeeper is the girl's aunt, and Mrs. Treadle is not in the habit of propounding falsehoods."

"I am telling you," Greer shot back, "I haven't trifled with anybody. In the first place, I know better, and in the second, I haven't the time."

"A woman can generally be trusted to identify the man who disports with her." Sir Miniver gave Greer a disgusted look. "Miss Miller's aunt attended her lying-in, as did her mother. Ask St. Sevier —he was there too. He heard her name you as the father of the first bastard born in this village in living memory."

I scanned the faces of the spectators, looking for any expressions of glee or satisfaction from the other bachelors. They instead appeared uniformly horrified, though whether they recoiled from Nicholson's alleged lack of honor or from the notion that he'd been unjustly accused, I could not tell.

"Why isn't Derwent intervening?" I muttered.

"Not his place?" St. Sevier suggested quietly.

"Since when has that stopped him from meddling?"

"*Vraiment*. I suppose it's up to you, *my lord*, to intervene, hmm?" He took my mug from my hand. "*Noblesse oblige* and so forth."

My title did not obligate me to intervene, but Violet would expect it of me. She was a stickler for justice, and that was a fine quality in any person, much less a wife.

"Sir Miniver," I said, "you have once again created a spectacle where none was required. A lady in extremis might say all manner of things. If Miss Miller has strayed with a fellow of lowly station, she'd choose to implicate not the true father, but a man of means and honor. That unfortunate fellow's choices as a gentleman would be to call the lady a liar or to pay for the raising of another's offspring. In any case, this is the wrong place to discuss such a matter."

"Damn right it isn't," young Cranston said. "Bandying a lady's name and all that, even if she ain't quite a lady... or not a lady anymore. Have a care for my young ears, Sir Miniver." He set his empty mug on the wagon bed and strode off toward the pile of rubble.

"The lad has a point," Lord Jasper said. "I might not have the highest opinion of Nicholson in light of recent developments, but nobody likes to see another man's linen hung out to dry in the town square."

"We have a wagon to load," Dinwiddie said, finishing his ale. "I vow I've never seen so much nonsense at one social gathering, and given some of my usual haunts, that is saying a lot." He joined Cranston at the remains of the folly and began loading the salvageable building stone onto the nearest wagon. Fontaine joined him, as did the other bachelors, save for the Thurmonts, who remained at Nicholson's side.

St. Sevier, still holding our mugs, came up on my left. "As a physician, I will keep anything said to me by a patient private. Miss Miller's family, of course, will be inclined to support her allegations, for obvious reasons."

Her family might well have put her up to making those allegations. "Nicholson and Gillespie, I suggest you find someplace private to discuss this between yourselves. Somebody needs to fashion a muzzle for Sir Miniver."

Sir Miniver stalked off without replying.

"We will discuss this now," Nathan Gillespie said, while Derwent maintained a watchful silence. "This is the last straw, Greer. I have given you the benefit of the doubt over and over, but if this is how you intend to behave, when the international capital of vice is but a day's ride away, then your welcome at The Falls has come to an end. As much as it pains me to say it, your choices are to marry the Miller girl or take a permanent leave of this property."

That was Derwent's cue as a friend of the family, senior statesman, and inveterate meddler to wade into the affray with *now let's not be hasty* and admonitions about *words said in anger*.

Derwent watched Sir Miniver's retreating form and said nothing.

Nicholson turned down his cuffs and busied himself inserting sleeve buttons. "If I am the father of Pansy Miller's child, then I will of course offer her marriage, but I am not her paramour, and I can prove it. St. Sevier, Dunkeld, if you would join Gillespie and me in his study at two of the clock, I would appreciate it. Cy and Tom, I'd like you to join us as witnesses."

Cyrus gave a terse nod. Tom snatched his jacket from the side of the wagon and tossed Cyrus his.

"Damned lot of nonsense," Cyrus said, shrugging into his coat. "This is the last time I agree to make up the numbers at any house party."

"Seconded and passed," Tom muttered. "We'll see ourselves to the manor." They collected their horses and were soon ambling down the pony track toward The Falls, Nicholson with them.

Nathan Gillespie had aged in the less than two weeks I'd been a guest in his home. He looked not so much angry now as he did exhausted, and yet, he'd not lifted a single rock nor swung the sledge-hammer even once.

Nor did he have any teething babies.

"I'd best alert Tilda to this latest drama," he said. "She won't stand for Greer philandering among decent village girls, and I confess I'm somewhat baffled by it as well. Derwent, you'll oversee matters here for me?"

"Of course, though they are young men, and they will talk. Tilda might be more worried about the gossip than about Greer being banished from The Falls."

In that, I suspected Derwent was wrong. Tilda could not be more devoted to Greer if he was her own son, and she'd chosen him as the ideal match for Dottie.

"I will require Madame's presence at this parlor session," St. Sevier said. "She was with me when I attended Miss Miller, and she needs to know what's afoot."

"Violet will be present as well," I said. "The ladies will keep us on our good behavior."

Derwent voiced what Gillespie was doubtless thinking. "Is that necessary, Dunkeld? Bad enough that Sir Miniver has appointed himself the town crier among the gents, but must we drag the ladies into it?"

"You made the point yourself, sir: There will be talk. Violet is the guest best placed to ensure the talk does not redound to Tilda's or

Miss Gillespie's discredit. Moreover, the village women are already well aware of the situation, and they will ensure the staff at The Falls is well informed."

To turn Derwent's own logic against him wasn't as satisfying as it ought to have been. The plain truth was that I wanted Violet on hand because she had a positive genius for solving social riddles. Accusing a man of ruining a neighbor's daughter went far beyond laying pranks at Nicholson's feet, and even beyond accusations of cheating at cards.

Violet was the best hope we had of getting to the truth before tempers flared and Greer Nicholson lost what little family he had.

～

"I have been thinking," Violet murmured as our jury of the whole assembled not in Nathan Gillespie's study, which was deemed too small, but rather, in the sprawling portrait gallery. Footmen placed three tea trays on the sideboard, then withdrew.

"You should have been napping," I replied just as quietly. "St. Sevier claims teething can go on for another two years." And he'd been damned cheerful conveying that information.

"There are respites," Violet replied. "Bevins promises me teething is like gout, with the occasional flare-up and long periods without symptoms. Bevins knows of what she speaks."

My darling wife was so tired and so resolute. Ann and St. Sevier appeared a bit battle-weary, too, as they chose a sofa against the inside wall.

"Why isn't Derwent here?" I asked. "Is he waiting to make a grand entrance?"

Violet chose a pair of reading chairs opposite the St. Seviers' perch. "He is a magistrate, Sebastian. If somebody admits to a crime, Papa would have to deal with it. If Nathan, as the king's man locally, hears of a crime and fails to deal with it, Papa would have to take note of that too. That wasn't what I was thinking about."

"Enlighten me."

Tilda was fluttering about the tea trays. Nathan stood by a window, expression grim. Greer and the Thurmont brothers were by another window, and while the Thurmonts were looking for once serious, Greer was the picture of calm.

"What is the goal of this house party?" Violet asked.

I humored her. "To entertain friends, to socialize, to..."

Violet waved a hand toward the laden sideboard. "Why go to all this expense? Why burden the staff? Why impose on the neighbors?"

"Because that's what Tilda Gillespie does best. She's a hostess, a fixture in Society both locally and in Town. She's..." I considered the gracious Mrs. Clothilda Gillespie. She struck me as an exhausted and anxious woman with whom age was catching up.

"She is *a mother*," Violet said. "With one chick to see safely into Society, one minion to carry on the legacy of her mama's hospitality and charm. Tilda is a mother who has formed a plan to ensure Dottie's success."

"Greer Nicholson is Tilda's solution," I said. "Or his pots of money and loyalty to The Falls are. This house party is the first step for Dottie and Greer on their path to the altar."

"Precisely."

Sir Miniver arrived in the company of a substantial woman, perhaps thirty years of age, dressed in a modest blue frock decorated with white embroidery on the hem and collar. She peered about the room as if trying not to gawk, then nodded to Ann and St. Sevier and was greeted by Tilda.

"The witness for the prosecution has arrived," I said as Nathan had a few words with the lady.

"We will have no prosecution," Violet muttered. "Or rather, we have had prosecution enough, considering that the point of the gathering was to put Dottie and Mr. Nicholson in a good light."

"Greer has been shown up in a very bad light. Nathan is convinced that the other bachelors are responsible, though that doesn't explain why Sir Miniver has been the loudest to toss accusations around."

A portrait of a young mother and her dark-haired, solemn little boy hung near where the St. Seviers sat. I recognized neither party, though something about the boy looked familiar.

Violet studied this portrait as if it held royal secrets by the dozen.

"Nathan has the right of it," she said. "Somebody wants to make Greer look so bad that he cannot possibly offer for Dottie, but I've asked myself: Why do that? None of the other bachelors appears to be panting after Dottie, or ready to marry, for that matter. Cranston is too young, Dinwiddie cannot support a wife, Lord Jasper lacks the maturity to appreciate a spouse, Sir Miniver needs a mother for his children, not somebody closer to their ages than his, and Dottie would never agree to dwell in France with Fontaine."

Violet spoke as if she'd mentally covered that ground previously and thoroughly.

"But clearly, somebody wants to knock Greer out of the running." Nathan's theory, more or less, was logical enough, but it hardly explained the situation with Pansy Miller. The Society fribbles cluttering up Tilda's guest wing would have had no occasion to meet the fair Pansy, much less talk her into naming Greer as the father of her child.

Sir Miniver, by contrast... Did *Sir Miniver* hope to marry Dottie?

"Please stop Nathan from conferring with the housekeeper," Violet said. "Sir Miniver is hovering over their conversation as if she's his star pupil."

I had my orders, so I rose and held up a hand. "Shall we be about the business of the day? The requisite parties are assembled, and I'm sure we'd all like to get this discussion behind us. Perhaps, Gillespie, you'd be good enough to introduce the lady and offer her a seat?"

If Nathan objected to my taking on the role of stage director, he had the grace to hide his displeasure.

"Mrs. Joan Treadle, ladies and gentlemen, housekeeper to Sir Miniver." He handed Mrs. Treadle into a wing chair, while Greer took a reading chair. Cyrus and Tom Thurmont remained on their feet on either side of Greer's chair. They had tidied up but had not changed out of their riding attire, and they managed to look formidable for a pair of good-natured local lads.

"Mrs. Treadle," I said, "thank you for joining us. Sir Miniver claims that your niece, Miss Pansy Miller, has named Greer Nicholson as the father of her newborn, is that so?"

"Aye, my lord. Pansy didn't tell us anything about the father the whole time she was carrying. Said he was a good sort, but not placed so as to offer for her. We never took that to mean Mr. Nicholson was at fault, but last night... The pains were bad, sir. We did not know if poor Pansy would live. If the child survived, he deserved to know who his father was."

"So Pansy named Greer Nicholson and no other as the father of her child?"

"Aye, my lord." Mrs. Treadle gazed directly at Greer. "I'm sorry, but she did say that, and the fevers might still carry her off. That tiny child is innocent, and his father should provide for him. I recall what it is to be young, and I know Mr. Nicholson to be a decent sort, but Pansy was brought up decent too. The situation should be put right."

Cyrus Thurmont's hands were balled into fists, while Tom, the younger brother, had fixed his gaze on the chandelier six yards down the gallery.

"Does anybody have any questions for Mrs. Treadle?" I asked.

"Not a question," Ann said, "but a clarification. Pansy did not volunteer Mr. Nicholson's name, did she? You and her mother asked her if the father could be Greer. You asked her repeatedly, and she finally said yes after you had flung that name—and no other—at her over and over."

"I had my suspicions," Mrs. Treadle said, sitting up straighter. "I saw Pansy walking out with a gent, not a village lad, a gent. Her ma did, too, and we put forth the logical name."

"I'm the only randy fellow in the shire?" Greer asked nobody in particular. "The only man capable of irresponsible behavior?"

Tilda Gillespie, having found an appropriately majestic wingchair in which to settle, stared hard at him. "Mind your tongue,

Greer Nicholson. You are *not* capable of irresponsible behavior. I have raised you from boy to man, and if any young fellow hereabouts would refrain from visiting a fatherless existence on a child, it is you. I don't say Pansy is dishonest, but she has a baby to consider. Greer is honorable enough to support even a child who is not his. That is the logic of the matter."

"Supporting the child will not restore our Pansy's good name," Mrs. Treadle shot back. "She's borne a bastard when she could have trapped yon fine fellow into marriage. She risked her life bringin' that baby into the world, and I'll see the truth aired on her behalf."

"Mrs. Treadle's word," Nathan said from his place by the window, "is that Pansy named Greer as the father, and though that confession took some prompting, as Mrs. St. Sevier says, Greer remains the only party accused. That is the operative fact."

"The operative fact," Greer said, rising, "is that most ladies will carry a baby for thirty-eight weeks. Forgive me for stating so ungenteel a reality, but I care for the land and beasts and have occasion to recall such matters. It's high summer now, and I was not on hand last autumn until nearly Yuletide. I traveled first to Paris and then to Bordeaux, before coming home for the holidays. Dottie did not want to endure the company of the Christmas cousins without my support. I cannot be the father of Pansy's child."

"He's a seven-months babe," Mrs. Treadle retorted. "Pansy said so herself just this morning."

St. Sevier cocked his head—merely that—and Mrs. Treadle abruptly found the tea tray fascinating.

"Monsieur, have you something to say?" Violet asked.

A silent conversation took place between my wife and her former paramour, and Violet apparently got the better of the encounter, because St. Sevier smiled slightly.

"I am an experienced physician with a particular interest in parturition. Madame St. Sevier has attended many a lying-in as well. Miss Miller did not give birth to a seven-months child. Her son is a great strapping fellow as newborns go, which is part of the reason she was in such difficulties. I can say with confidence that Miss Miller's baby is among the largest newborns I have ever beheld—ten pounds or nearly so—and he *cannot* be a seven-months child. He cannot be an eight-months child. He is full term at least, my word on that as an expert in the field."

"The lad is right good size," Mrs. Treadle said, somewhat apologetically. "Monsieur is right about that, but then, Pansy is no elf."

I had not thought that Greer Nicholson would go trysting in the village shadows where any could chance upon him in the company of his gravid paramour, but some fellow had been in close conversation with Pansy at the smithy not two days past.

Under the guise of helping myself to the offerings on the sideboard, I inspected Sir Miniver's boots. His footwear—this pair, at least—was quite spruce. No cracks or frayed seams. I took a plate of cakes to Violet, who accepted them with a faintly puzzled smile.

"If I am exonerated," Greer said, "might we disband this inquisition? I am very sorry Pansy is in difficulties, and I will happily settle a sum on her for the child, but the little—enormous, but little—fellow is no relation to me."

"Pansy named you," Nathan said repressively.

Tilda scowled at her husband. "And we know why any village girl would do such a thing. If nobody has any other pointless accusations to fling at Greer, I must see to the arrangement of tonight's centerpieces."

"A moment more of your time," Violet said gently. "Shall we excuse Mrs. Treadle? The rest of the conversation does not concern her."

"I'll go," she said, rising, "and gladly. Did you mean that, Mr. Nicholson? About a sum for the baby?"

"Of course. My own mother was left to raise me without benefit of a husband, so to speak, and that was hard enough with a legitimate son and plenty of means. My best wishes for Miss Miller's good health, and I will call on Mr. Miller later this week to settle details."

"I'll see Mrs. Treadle out," Sir Miniver said, "and I take it my presence is no longer required either."

Violet chose a buttery tea cake from the selection on her plate. "You would be in error, Sir Miniver. If you'd see Mrs. Treadle out and return here, we would appreciate it."

Not a ducal *we* or a royal *we*. A Violet *we*, speaking for the interests of truth and justice generally.

"I'll see myself out," Mrs. Treadle said, all but scampering from the room. The door had barely closed behind her before Nathan Gillespie was speaking.

"You just admitted your guilt," he said, advancing on Greer. "You took on the raising of that child because you lack the sense to keep your mouth shut. For the past two weeks, every prancing lordling and strutting peacock on the property has sought a reason to sully your reputation in Society's eyes. You have given them the fodder they need to render you an embarrassment to us all. You'd best return to France, sir, and this time for an extended stay."

"Nathan, really," Tilda said, getting to her feet. "What is wrong with you? If Society ostracized every bachelor supporting a by-blow in the countryside, then Mayfair would be a very dreary place indeed."

Husband and wife glowered at each other while Violet finished her tea cake. The silence in the room was broken by a thumping of feet overhead. The children engaged in more hide-and-seek.

"By all means," Nathan said, making a shooing motion with his hand, "be about your menus or centerpieces or whatnot. Don't let us keep you."

Violet dusted her hands and rose. "Mr. Gillespie, rudeness to one's spouse in public is never good form. One might say it's worse even than discreet infidelity."

The lioness was ready to pounce. If Gillespie knew what was good for him, he'd sit down quietly and stay as still as possible.

"Your ladyship." Greer Nicholson met Violet before she could advance on our host. "I assure you Nathan meant no disrespect. The situation would vex anybody."

Violet regarded him with what I could see was pity. "Mr. Nicholson, you are the victim here. You need not fly to Mr. Gillespie's defense. He meant well."

"What?" Tilda sent the single word across the room like a hurled dagger. "I'll not hear my husband maligned under his own roof."

"But it's not his roof," Violet said, "is it? This house belongs to you, Tilda, in as much as you are the beneficiary of a generous trust that includes The Falls. Dottie will inherit the lot of it, while Nathan is more or less a kept man. I suspect gambling debts, or the realization that his own parents would leave him poorly fixed, inspired Nathan to propose to you."

"It wasn't like that," Gillespie said. "I esteem my wife, and I always have, but you are right that I was an intemperate and impecunious young man. I saw in Tilda a chance to come right, to settle down and be done with a young man's foolish ways."

"Lady Dunkeld," Greer said, "I don't believe we need to air old linen. Not now."

"Yes," Violet said with ominous gentleness, "we do. You know, don't you, Mr. Nicholson?"

Tilda was looking at Nathan, a world of bewilderment in her eyes, while Nathan's gaze was on the portrait of Greer and his late mother.

Violet held her peace, though she was apparently far from finished.

Greer seemed to sense that he was in the presence of an unstoppable force and yielded on a sigh. "I've known since I was a boy," he said. "I was my mother's confidant, and in her last hours, she decided I was better off knowing the truth at even a young age, but she wasn't sure Gillespie himself was aware of the facts."

"What are you talking about?" Tilda moaned softly. "I don't know what you are talking about, and I must see to my... my centerpieces."

"I asked myself," Violet said as if our hostess hadn't spoken, "what's wrong with a match between Dottie and Greer? They are in charity with one another, they'd be quite well set up, The Falls would be in good hands. The match would be more sensible than romantic, but somebody was adamantly, determinedly opposed to allowing Greer to court Dottie."

She spoke with the measured cadences of the skilled orator, though I suspected Greer at least wanted to clap a hand over her mouth. I'd drop him on the spot if he made the attempt, which he seemed to perceive.

"But not all matches that appear sensible on the surface measure up to that standard," Violet went on. "What reason for keeping Dottie and Greer apart is sufficiently compelling that the marriage absolutely cannot and must not take place?"

"Greer won't beat her," Tilda said. "He's not a drunk. He doesn't gamble. He is in every way..." She went silent as Nathan collapsed onto a vacant sofa.

"The law forbids some marriages," Violet said. "Nominally, the lady must consent in all cases. She must be of age, and there must be no fraud by either party, but these considerations are not at issue."

"Just say it," Nathan muttered. "Say it and, for God's sake, be done with it."

Violet aimed her words at Gillespie. "The issue is consanguinity, isn't it? Greer and Dottie are half-siblings. Tilda's best friend found consolation in the arms of Tilda's husband, and Greer is the result."

Tilda sank onto the cushions beside Nathan. She looked as if she was working at a very difficult translation, but the words simply made no sense.

"If I hadn't been born," Greer said quietly, "Mama would have been destitute. Papa's will was the usual setup, with the estate going to his issue, and Mama's dower portion was expected to support her during her widowhood. The dower portion was mostly tenanted properties, and as we all know, rents have fallen precipitously in recent decades. Her lands were not well managed. If Mama could manage to produce a child, though, the picture for her in widowhood would be very different."

"And you, Nathan, obliged her?" Tilda asked.

He nodded. "You and I had no children, my dear. I didn't think there was any chance her scheme would bear fruit as it were, but then along came Greer. I regarded it as my penance to have a son whom I could not acknowledge. Then Clarice fell ill, and we were the only possible guardians to whom she would entrust the boy. My penance took on new and heartbreaking dimensions."

Tilda stared at her hands, the hands of a lady. Smooth, pale, pretty... She very likely wanted to wrap those hands around Nathan's neck, but her inherent dignity prevented that.

"I can see a resemblance," she said, "about the mouth. Greer, you've known all along?"

He nodded. "I wasn't sure Nathan knew. He could have reasoned that Mama was only hedging her bets as Papa's condition grew worse, but Mama was quite clear on the subject of my paternity: I am Nathan Gillespie's son. I cannot marry Dottie, and she wouldn't have me even if we were not half-siblings."

Tilda looked at the elegant gold watch pinned to her bodice, then at the clock on the mantel. She did not look at her spouse.

"I should be outraged. I suppose that will come later, and I will tear my centerpieces to shreds and develop a megrim. I've never had a megrim in my life. A first time for everything, I suppose."

"Consider yourself fortunate that no megrims have yet visited you," Violet said, returning to her wing chair, "because we have more to discuss, don't we, Sir Miniver?"

CHAPTER FIFTEEN

Violet

"This was all Nathan's idea," he said, running a hand through russet locks and pacing before the hearth. "Nathan convinced me that if I could knock Greer out of the running for Dottie's hand, I might have a chance."

Sir Miniver directed his reply at me, perhaps thinking a lady would be a more charitable judge than the gentlemen in the room. Clearly, the gallant knight deemed retreat to be the wisest strategy.

"Not much convincing needed." Nathan snorted. "You were keen to abet my scheme, my good fellow. Let's be quite clear about that."

Sebastian paused in the demolition of my plate of cakes—the plate of cakes he'd brought me himself—to aim a question at Sir Miniver.

"Nathan put you up to accusing Greer of cheating at cards?"

"Of course, and then Nathan bungled the whole business by picking up the wrong deck. I went to great lengths—great and risky lengths—to ensure the unmarked deck sat closest to mine host, and when it was his turn to deal, which deck does he pick up? The one he ought to have left for Greer to deal. What was I to do?"

"Keep your ruddy mouth shut and wait for further instructions," Nathan snapped. "But no, you had to go charging headlong into enemy fire, leaving me to deal with the mess."

"If you'd used your head in the first place," Sir Miniver retorted, "then I wouldn't have been forced to decide between—"

"Enough posturing," I snapped. "The result of this mutual fool-ishness is that an innocent man was suspected of dishonorable behav-ior. Given the nature of the guests, Greer could have been called out and murdered."

"It would never have come to that," Nathan said. "I'm the magis-trate, and only the greatest fools would think to duel on my very property."

The Falls was not his property and would never be his. "You are right, of course, Mr. Gillespie. The great fools would nip across the river and duel on common land or pop over to the Thurmonts' side of the woods and politely blow each other's brains out there."

Greer stared into the gaping maw of the cold hearth. "You would have seen me challenged, Nathan? Seen a pistol aimed at my heart?"

"You are my son!" Nathan thundered, surging to his feet. "I would have seen you hauled forcibly onto a Channel packet before I'd let anybody aim a gun at you. I know you to be sensible, and a sensible man would never accept a challenge over an insupportable allegation of cheating at cards."

Otherwise sensible men, from His Grace of Wellington to my own brothers, would never think of refusing such a challenge.

Sir Miniver stared at Nathan. "You bungled that business with the cards on purpose?"

Nathan nodded once. "Thought better of the original scheme, and I was right. The way I handled it, the evidence against Greer was too flimsy, and the whole business became nothing more than grist for talk."

Tilda sank her head into her hands. "I don't know you. I do not know who you are, and I'm fairly certain I would dislike you if I did."

Nathan put a hand on her arm. She flinched away from his touch. Perhaps somebody would be getting on that Channel packet, but it wouldn't be Greer.

"Best make a clean breast of it, Mr. Gillespie," I said. "Explain to us about the punch and the mare and the baby, and the rabbit, too, if that drama falls on your head."

Nathan ambled away from his wife and perched on a padded bench beneath the portrait of Greer and his mother.

"The rabbit was simply doing as he so often does, but the mare was easy. Dottie had made a fuss about the squeaky hinges on the beast's stall door, and I've been wanting to breed that horse for two years. Dottie and Tilda wouldn't hear of it, but truly, for going about Town, my daughter needs a more elegant mount, not an aging hack. I took the mare calling in the middle of the night. Nobody saw me. The grooms are run off their feet at Tilda's gatherings and all too happy to seek their beds at day's end. Dunkeld was focused on his ailing gelding, and that was that."

"And I gather Sir Miniver abetted you in once again pointing the finger at Greer?" I wanted guilt apportioned accurately. If Sir Miniver truly aspired to offer for Dottie, Tilda needed to know the full extent of his culpability.

"Sir Miniver and I might have mentioned how much time Greer spends in the stable, how loyal the staff is to him, and so forth."

"And then you campaigned to have Greer leave the gathering. What of the punch?"

"A last-minute inspiration. The boot-boy is always tagging after the footmen. Passing the lad a flask and telling him to discreetly add it to the punch just before the bowl was brought up from the kitchen was simple enough."

Greer exchanged a look with the Thurmonts. "The flask contained vinegar?" he asked.

"Apple cider vinegar, which even a dull palate would find an unpleasant addition to the recipe."

Tilda raised her head. "You are a fool."

"I am a father trying to protect my children from the worst possible mistake."

"*You* made the mistake," Tilda shot back. "You sought to protect your lying, philandering self. You might have simply told me the truth."

"We'll get to that," I said, because we would. Sebastian was apparently resigned to a more prolonged discussion, because he prowled to the sideboard once more and fixed two plates, bringing one to me. We had both been up most of the night, dealing with a fussy Maeve in shifts.

Then Sebastian had spent the morning in hard, physical labor while I had dozed and thought, and walked and thought, and visited Maeve and thought some more.

"I tried to salvage the punch," Greer said, sending a sidewise glance at his father. "I thought maybe with enough sugar... but I made it worse." He half winced and half smiled. "The stuff was roaringly awful."

"And that," Tilda said, "was the first impression our guests formed of my hospitality. I would never live down that punch, save for the greater foolishness that followed. The foolishness that has continued to follow."

"Which takes us to the matter of Pansy Miller," I said. "Was paternity of her child another accusation that was meant to go nowhere, Mr. Gillespie?"

On his lonely bench off to the side, Nathan looked like a schoolboy awaiting Headmaster's discipline.

"That accusation was meant to send Greer galloping for London, or send him for a repairing lease on his own estate in Sussex. I honestly hadn't considered that business with thirty-eight weeks. Partur-whatever-you-call-it isn't my lookout. I wanted Greer anywhere but where Dottie was. I have no idea who strayed with Miss Miller, and she did not want to implicate Greer. When her mother explained to her that Greer would weather the expense easily, and a child has to eat, the young lady apparently saw the wisdom of a little dissembling."

The memory of Maeve's birth would never leave me, the pain and hope and terror of it, the hours of suffering and the months of healing thereafter.

"You set Pansy's own mother and aunt to badgering her on what might well have been her deathbed," I said. "You manipulated a desperate young woman who'd never done you an ill turn, and all because you could not risk Tilda learning the truth."

"He risked me facing a bullet," Greer said, his characteristic dispassion acquiring a chilling edge. "Set me up to be labeled a cad and a bounder. He turned Dottie's first major social event into a farce and trespassed on all the hard work Tilda has done to build her standing in Society. He did this not because he feared for Tilda's regard, but because he feared she'd cut him off."

Tilda looked at Nathan as if he'd materialized from a cloud of brimstone, courtesy of the fiend himself. "Nathan? Is that what all this is about? My dratted *money*?"

"Of course not."

Greer arched an eyebrow. The Thurmonts both crossed their arms.

"The money," Nathan said huffily, "was not my first considera-tion. Dottie and Greer are my children, and you were determined that they should wed. Have the solicitors cut me off—I deserve at least that—but please know that I never wanted to hurt you. Clarice was desperate. You were happy with your social whirl. I thought no harm would be done, and..."

And *what*? What could possibly excuse or even mitigate Nathan's infidelity?

"And," Sebastian said, "Clarice *needed you*, desperately, while Tilda managed quite well without you."

My heart broke for my husband, because a man did not gain such an insight without having been made to feel utterly without value himself.

Nathan's throat worked, and he stared hard at the blank patch of wall across from his bench. "Precisely. I hoped matters would improve when we were blessed with Dottie, but Tilda saw a daughter as heiress to the title of Gillespie Hostess, not as a reason to rebuild the ruin our marriage had become."

"So you went hunt mad," Sebastian said. "Took up yachting, went shooting by the month, left the running of The Falls to Greer, and generally used any excuse to avoid the wife who had no need for you. For her part, Tilda told the solicitors to indulge your whims without limit in hopes that you'd appreciate her generosity, or at least notice her a little. All would have been well—miserable, but well—had not Tilda decided to make a match between Dottie and Greer."

"My wife enjoys a great sense of determination," Nathan said, pushing to his feet. "Always has. Shall I start packing now, Tilda, or wait until the guests have left?"

"I take my leave as well," Sir Miniver said. "I hope I would have made Dottie a good husband, but it's clear her affections are elsewhere engaged. You may all rely on my discretion regarding what's been said here, and I hope I can rely on yours." He bowed and departed, and nobody offered him so much as a muttered farewell.

Tilda, though, had yet to answer her husband's question, and that was fortunate, because I had more to say before she offered him his congé.

~

"Please fix Tilda a cup of tea," I said to Nathan. "Our hostess is in need of fortification." For my part, I was in need of sleep and in need of some privacy with my husband, but matters at The Falls were not yet sorted to my satisfaction.

Nathan complied with my direction. Tilda accepted the cup and saucer, took a sip, and set the tea aside. Better than dashing it in his face, and I took heart from her self-restraint.

"What strikes me," I said, "is that Nathan's actions have been, at bottom, well intended. My guess is, if he had it to do over again, he'd make very different choices."

I could feel every gentleman in the room willing Nathan to catch the bone of dignity I'd tossed him. I, too, wanted to see Tilda's husband redeem himself to the extent that he could.

"I would make very different choices," he said, sinking back onto his bench. "I was an idiot and then made a bad situation worse."

Tilda took up her tea again, but did not drink. "Clarice was charming. She could have imposed on any other obliging fellow, but she knew that our marriage was... less than devoted at that point. She probably thought I would not mind."

"Do you?" I asked, when every other person in the room likely wished I'd keep my mouth shut. Sebastian was smiling at his sandwich, though, and Ann and St. Sevier looked interested rather than appalled. "Do you mind that more than twenty years ago, your husband betrayed your vows with your best friend and the result is that fine gentleman by the hearth?"

Tilda Gillespie was a shrewd woman who'd endured much in the course of her marriage. Another lady might have sputtered with indignation, while she looked thoughtful.

"Clarice is dead," she said, "and in a sense, the man she disported with is dead too. When Dottie was born, Nathan did change. I begrudged him not one moment on the grouse moors or chasing after Reynard, because he'd stopped chasing skirts. I could hold my head up in Town, knowing that Nathan hadn't slipped into the garden with a lady who'd been my whist partner an hour before."

Nathan winced and had the sense to hold his peace.

Greer, though, regarded his father with a sort of bewildered disgust. "You'll let him off with a smack on the knuckles? He marries you for your money, cavorts with your best friend, tries to wreck this gathering and see me banished in disgrace, and you'll simply shrug and go back to your centerpieces?"

Sebastian took up a place lounging on the arm of my chair. Not quite the hug I longed for, but a comfort to have him near.

"That's one option," I said, "or you can pretend nothing has changed and repair to your neutral corners in Mayfair and on the grouse moors, provided somebody puzzles out how to convey the truth to Dottie."

"Must we?" Nathan muttered. "I'll go quietly, I promise. I'll fade into obscurity or take up an interest in New World butterflies, but must we continue to discuss this... this... situation?"

"Nobody can stop you," I said, "if you decide to chase butterflies instead of foxes or skirts, but then who will give Dottie away on her wedding day? The brother she hasn't been told about? Will this family allow an old mistake, compounded by more recent misguided behavior, to sunder all ties of affection?"

"What affection?" Nathan murmured. "I'm hardly here as it is, except when Tilda needs me to stand about as her personal Squire Lumpkin."

Nathan's self-pity was contemptible, though his words admitted of true pain. Nobody had needed him, and I knew how that felt. I knew how Tilda had felt as a young wife with a straying husband and an empty nursery. I knew how Dottie felt, being dragged off to make a come out she wasn't interested in.

I did not know how Greer—the victim of Nathan's most recent shenanigans—felt.

"As it is, Gillespie," Sebastian said, "you regularly banish yourself. Speaking as somebody who was sent far from home at a young age and forced to live with no family at hand, I cannot grasp your motives. I was so lonely, it nearly killed me, nearly choked my spirit with despair and longing. I would not wish that on anybody."

Sebastian's words were directed at Nathan, but they'd been intended for Greer. As a boy, he'd found a welcome at The Falls when he might have been shuffled off to public school year after year.

"Listen to his lordship," St. Sevier said, rising and drawing Ann to her feet. "I, too, was sent far from home at a young age, far from what few loved ones still survived in France. One can understand righteous fury and hurt feelings. One can even grasp that betrayed trust is a heavy sorrow. Hearts, though, do not want to stay broken. Hearts want to love and heal rather than sulk and seethe. I say this as a physician and as a man who for years had no family. Better to have imperfect love than perfectly justified rage."

Ann leaned into him, then took his arm and accepted his escort from the room.

"My brothers exasperate me without limit," I said, needing to take my turn as a witness for the defense of the Gillespie family. "My father saw me married to a flaming bounder, lied to Dunkeld about where my affections lay, and neglected me shamefully when I fell into the grip of a mourning malaise. I nearly hated him for a time. I have realized, though, that family is not intended to be perfect. Family is for teaching us how to love and be loved. Imperfections, our own and others', are a part of those lessons."

Cyrus Thurmont ambled over to the sideboard and heaped a plate with sandwiches. "What has this to do with Nathan being a regular ponce, and Greer getting stuck with managing The Falls, and Tilda wanting to get Dottie launched when Dottie don't want to be launched?"

"She's saying," Greer muttered, "they are *all* saying that we ought to muddle through rather than keep making the same mistakes—pretending, putting on appearances, making believe next year will be better when it won't."

"You ought to forgive each other and yourselves if and when you honestly can," I said. "You, Greer, forgive yourself for trying to outshine the father who never acknowledged you. Tilda and Nathan must be forgiven for allowing their marriage to languish, though heaven knows my first marriage could not languish fast enough to suit me. We make mistakes, but we can also choose to grow past them."

Tilda rose without the aid of any gentleman. "I am so angry. I am so toweringly, incandescently angry. I have been made a fool of, over and over, by my own husband. Then I think I have the perfect marital solution devised for Dottie, so that she will not know the pity and ridicule I've faced..."

"Nobody will make a fool of Dottie," Cyrus Thurmont said. "She's too sensible, too smart, and witty, and she knows her own worth."

Ah, so that's how the wind blew. "Sir Miniver said Dottie's affections had already been claimed by another. Would that other be you, Mr. Thurmont?"

He took great care choosing among the tea cakes. "I esteem Dottie. Always have."

"She was trying to make you jealous, wasn't she?" A wild guess that nonetheless explained her behavior. "Casting herself into the arms of men who would neither tattle nor offer to marry her, and she did so where you were likely to come across her."

"Greer ruined that scheme," Cyrus said. "Kept a close eye on our Dottie, had a stern word with her. Tilda's determination hasn't a patch on Dottie's, but I've told Dot it won't do. I have no prospects other than stepping into Papa's shoes when he sticks his spoon in the wall. Even then, there will be little enough to go around on that sad and—one hopes—distant day. But we are a loving and mostly happy family now, and I would not trade my station for Greer's if it meant giving up my family."

Thomas Thurmont joined his brother at the sideboard. "The Thurmonts are great company when it's time to make up the numbers, but we know not to get airs above our station. Don't take all the ham, Cy. A loyal younger brother must keep up his strength."

Tilda eyed the teapot, and I hoped she'd pitch it against the wall. "I want to do murder, and you fellows are fretting over who gets the last slices of ham."

"I want to do murder too, Mrs. G," Cyrus said, "but that won't

make me a suitable husband for Dottie, will it? Tom has his frustrations. Greer owns an estate—his boyhood home—that he hasn't even
seen for months. Pansy Miller—if she survives—is now the mother of
a bastard boy. You are out of patience with Nathan, while I…"

Tilda regarded him crossly. "You want to marry my Dottie."

"Our Dottie," Nathan said, looking up from his bench. "The girl
is our daughter, Tilda."

Tilda's posture presaged hurled epithets and flaming verbal
arrows. "Dottie deserves a Season. She deserves to waltz at Almack's,
have her presentation at court, do the carriage parade, and the whole
bit. *She is my only child*, and I'll not see her shackled to the impecunious son of an impecunious squire, no matter how charming or
besotted he is at the moment."

"She can have the whole Town do," I said, silently apologizing to
Dottie, "but she's known to be an heiress, as you were. Wouldn't you
rather she make a love match instead of being married for her
money?"

"I did not marry Tilda simply for her money," Nathan said,
leaving his bench. "She was a stunner, the brightest luminary in the
firmament, and she still is. Not an arrogant bone in her body, and she
wasn't silly either. The perfect example of charm and intelligence in
the same woman. You dashed wastrels will leave the last of the ham
for the ladies."

Tom Thurmont set the loaded ham fork back on the platter.
"We're not wastrels," he said. "We're gentry and poor, which is a
different matter entirely. You *were* a wastrel, sir, and when you could
have been managing The Falls, you were yachting, of all the
rubbishing nonsense."

Nathan looked as if he wanted to return fire, but Tilda stepped
between the two men, took the ham fork, and put the entire contents
on an empty plate.

"Cyrus, do I take it you seek to court Dottie?" she asked.

"I would consider paying court to Dottie an honor, ma'am. The
greatest honor of my life."

"I'll dower Dottie if you don't, Tilda," Greer said. "One of us should be happy, and my vote is Dottie, because if Dot's not happy, the peace of the realm is at risk. Besides, Cy is a good fellow, and Dot's made up her mind."

"Best we yield graciously," Nathan said, plucking a profiterole from a tray. "The girl will have her inheritance sooner or later. Nothing we can do about that."

"Yield graciously," I said, "but not immediately. Tilda is right that Dottie should take her place in Society and see something of the world before making any marital decisions. I suspect The Falls will be in want of a full-time steward in the near future, and that is a gentleman's occupation. If a year from now, Dottie is still receptive to Cyrus's charms, and Cyrus has acquitted himself well learning to manage The Falls, then marriage might come under discussion."

"No engagement?" Cyrus said. "Not for a year?"

Tom elbowed him in the ribs. "You'll be engaged, just not as soon as you'd hoped to be."

Sebastian rose from the arm of my chair. "Whereas Thomas," he said, "will be married. The sooner the better. By special license, if Pansy will have him."

Thomas looked horrified, then embarrassed, then as determined as Dottie and Tilda put together. "She didn't want to ruin my chances, said nobody holds a woods colt against a village girl. She expected me to lounge about Town being handsome and charming enough to snag some die-away heiress, but I told Pansy that won't happen. Then a few weeks ago, her ma started in on her about some cork-brained notion or other... I thought Nathan would be the butt of their scheme, because I saw Mrs. Miller conversing with him a time or two. I had no idea... no blasted idea, but I am as fine a shot as any man in this shire and beyond frustrated with recent developments."

Fortunately, nobody offered to serve as his second—or as Nathan's.

"There's enough frustration washing about this room to refloat Noah's ark," Tilda muttered, "but if you fathered that child, you really ought to marry Miss Miller, and you can't do that if Nathan puts a bullet through your heart."

"I tell you," Tom said through clenched teeth, "Pansy won't have me."

"I'll have you," Greer said. "The Falls will need a steward, and my man in Sussex is also getting on. If Pansy realizes you've found a post in Sussex, she might be more amenable to throwing in with you. Fresh start and all that. You'd have a year or two to tag around as understeward, while I..."

"While you," I said, "will tend assiduously to your investments."

Greer looked puzzled. "I always tend to my investments. The investments are one of few responsibilities I truly enjoy."

"What Lady Dunkeld means," Sebastian said, putting more profiteroles on a plate, "is that the bachelors who've witnessed this whole unfolding drama must somehow be kept quiet. You have something they want—business acumen—and they have something this family needs—discretion. If you let it be known that only the most trustworthy gentlemen are taken into your financial confidence, then Dottie's first Season might not be accompanied by more gossip than the Congress of Vienna."

"That's brilliant," Cyrus said. "That's quite brilliant. Of course, if Dot were already engaged, then the fortune hunters wouldn't pester her either. What young lady would want—"

Greer smacked him on the back of the head. "Every young lady deserves to have a pack of handsome lackwits panting at her heels for at least a short time. I nominate you to join me when I explain to Dottie that I'm her brother."

"She's long suspected," Cyrus said, popping a tea cake into his mouth. "Said you are too great a pest not to be related somehow. These are good cakes."

Tilda and Nathan stared at him. Greer took him by the arm. "We're off to find Dottie and confirm her suspicions. When this blasted house party is over..."

"You will have much to discuss with your family," I said, rising and slipping my hand into Sebastian's. "While I am off to enjoy a nice long nap."

Sebastian kissed my fingers and escorted me and our plate of profiteroles to our apartment. I did justice to the sweets, but alas, we both fell asleep on the lumpy penance and did not rise until Bevins summoned me for my late-afternoon appointment in the nursery.

EPILOGUE

Violet

The longest house party in English history was finally coming to a close, as most house parties did, with a celebratory grand ball. Dottie was the belle of the evening, and while she did dance every dance but for the waltzes, I noticed that her partners were also frequently in earnest discussion with Greer Nicholson.

The penultimate dance was to be a ländler, as close to the waltz as Dottie was allowed to come, and I was pleased to see that Nathan was standing up with Tilda. In the several days since he'd been confronted in the gallery, Nathan's demeanor had undergone subtle shifts.

"He's no longer her Squire Lumpkin, is he?" Sebastian said, passing me his glass of champagne.

I sipped—only sipped—and passed it back. "She's not the entirely self-sufficient Society hostess with no use for her own husband. I wonder what, precisely, they've been saying to each other."

My darling smiled down at me, and though I was far from objective, I did believe I had beheld no more fetching sight than my Highland laddie in his formal kilted finery. Sebastian tucked a curl behind my ear and bent close.

"He said, I need you, I love you, I desire you."

"And she said, I need you more, I love you more, I desire you more. Someday soon, I'll know how to say it in Gaelic."

We goggled at each other with mutual besottedness, though we had decided not to consummate our vows on the lumpy abomination. We would wait until we were home at Ashmore—less than twenty-four hours hence. We would spend much of our future on that estate, and I hoped we'd conceive siblings for Maeve and Annis at Ashmore too.

"I'm stealing your husband." Ann St. Sevier had come up on Sebastian's right and wrapped her hand around his arm. "He's the only fellow in a kilt here, and as the only Scotswoman, I deserve the honor."

Sebastian set his glass of champagne on the nearest bench and bowed. "The honor is entirely mine, Madame. Violet, you will save your waltz for me."

"All my waltzes." I blew him a kiss, feeling more lighthearted and at peace than I had in ages. The road to this moment had been long and at times daunting, but I was married to the love of my life, and at The Falls, we'd come through some sort of trial together. The Gillespies had not known how to be a family, but Sebastian and I had been able to show them.

"My lady." St. Sevier bowed formally. "I see that a beautiful adventuress has made off with your husband. Might you console us both with the honor of this dance?"

Hugh looked so handsome in formal attire and so much himself in the little touches—the lace edging his cravat, the polished amber glinting at his cuffs, and the slightly too-long chestnut hair brushing his collar.

"The honor, dear sir, is entirely mine." I curtseyed, and he led me out. We had danced on several occasions, though never a ländler. The patterns were intricate, romantic, and yet also dignified. I'd learned to appreciate the ländler and the dancing master who'd insisted I become adept at the steps.

I'd learned to appreciate St. Sevier, too, and to my credit, I'd had the courage to let him appreciate me as well.

"Was the baby really all that large?" I asked.

He grinned. "A Hercules among babies, though I hope the poor fellow avoids that name. Both parents are quite robust specimens, but the true difficulty for the mother lay in the disproportion between the pelvic opening—"

I pretended to stumble. St. Sevier could prose on about medical arcana all night. "St. Sevier, are you ever glad we did not marry?"

His smile shifted, and I suspected he was watching Ann over my shoulder. "I don't think of our past like that. I am certain we would have been abundantly happy and quite well suited, but with Ann... She's to have a baby, Violet. My baby, one I get to keep and see every day and spoil and... I hope that confession does not pain you, because my joy is limitless."

The dance separated us for a few beats, and then we came back together, our hands clasped overhead.

"When you see me whisper to Sebastian about how bright Annis is and how happy she's become racketing about with Fiona, and Sebastian uses the moment to touch my shoulder, does that pain you?"

We promenaded a small circle, both hands clasped.

"Not pain," St. Sevier said. "My heart sighs a little, to see you so very happy, but the sigh is sweet. We can live only one life at a time, and one grows sentimental at a late hour after a good glass or three of brandy, but one does not regret."

How delicately—and courageously—he wielded honest words.

"You put it well. One does not regret. Will you take Ann to France before the baby comes? You and she never really had a wedding journey."

"I want to. I want to show her so much of my homeland, but harvest approaches, and this house party has been..."

"Your last for quite some," I said. "Ours, too, if the Deity is merciful. Send Fiona to us and take Ann traveling for a few weeks once the harvest is under way. Fiona can help me with my Gaelic and Annis with her French. She can get a taste of a younger sibling's effect on the nursery by spending more time around Maeve."

"You are generous and kind, my lady."

"I know what lies ahead once the baby arrives. Go traveling with Ann now, and enjoy yourselves."

A determined light came into his eyes, and when Ann claimed him for the good-night waltz, and Sebastian claimed me, I suspected Madame would be informed of upcoming travel plans.

Sebastian escorted me onto the dance floor, and we waltzed a little extravagantly for a settled married couple. My husband led with grace and daring, and the steps became a joy. I could feel the other dancers watching us, even as a few candles guttered, and the quartet went into a slower reprise of the melody.

"My joy is limitless," I said, echoing St. Sevier's words.

"This time tomorrow, your pleasure will be limitless too, my lady."

"As will yours."

He spun me under his arm and caught me in a closer embrace than propriety allowed, then stole a kiss.

We finished the dance without further displays of marital ebullience, though it was a near thing indeed.

Through the leave-taking in the morning, the journey to Ashmore, and the flutter of activity required to welcome the lord and lady home, Sebastian and I remained commendably decorous.

We even managed a picnic supper with Annis and Maeve, much to the amusement of the staff.

When darkness finally, finally fell, though, I made a protracted visit to the nursery and instructed Bevins that for the next four hours, I was not to be disturbed for anything less than an angelic chorus announcing the end of days.

Bevins opined that with the excitement of travel, Maeve was likely to sleep very, very well, and I was not to worry.

I did not worry, not about the baby and not about embarking on intimacies with my husband. Sebastian had been right when he'd predicted that in his arms, my joy and my pleasure would both be limitless, while I had been wrong.

There is a sight I regularly behold more fetching than my Highland laddie in all his kilted splendor: that same splendid laddie wearing nothing but a loving and determined smile!

TO MY DEAR READERS

I had such fun writing this series, but even I was ready for Violet and Sebastian to add a happily ever after to their sleuthing. We might well hear more from these characters, though I'm also starting a new historical mystery series later this year. Lord Julian Caldicott survived Waterloo and years of battling across Spain, but solving Mayfair's most vexing mysteries might be his undoing...

Before we get to his lordship's whodunits, I have another *Mischief in Mayfair* romance on the way. **Miss Devoted** comes out Feb. 21, 2023 on the retail sites (Feb. 7 on my **web store**), and features Mr. Michael Delancey, whom we met in book two, **Miss Delightful** (Dorcas and Alasdhair's story). Michael is a churchman hiding dangerous secrets and Mrs. Psyche Fremont is a widow who dreams of gaining artistic acclaim. So what's our hero doing all nakey-nakey on page one? Excerpt below...

I hope to follow up Michael and Psyche's story with a happily ever after later this year for Trevor, Marquess of Tavistock, who has been kicking his handsome heels in France for far too long. He claims he's learning how to make champagne, but I wonder what he's *really* been up to.

After that it's more *Mischief in Mayfair*, and more happily ever afters.

And I wish you, as always...

Happy reading!
Grace Burrowes

Read for an excerpt from **Miss Devoted**!

MISS DEVOTED—EXCERPT

Chapter One

To be naked in a room full of intently staring strangers had become a sort of relief. Michael Delancey—vicar's son, ordained priest, and rising star at Lambeth Palace—shrugged out of his dressing gown and let his mind go quiet.

The drawing instructor made a few remarks about the difficulty of accurately rendering hands and feet, and the need to pay attention to the smallest shadows—beneath the chin, below the ankle bone—and then Michael was posed, semi-recumbent on a chaise, one foot on the floor, one arm flung back over his head.

The posture was restful, though after twenty minutes, Michael's arm began to tingle. The only sounds in the room were the soft scratch of charcoal or pencil against paper, the occasional cough, or one page being set aside so another could be begun.

Berthold, a fussy old Frenchman with a meticulous eye for detail, murmured critical comments to this or that student, and time drifted along in a peaceful trickle of moments.

"And now, *mes prodiges*, we draw more than the fingers and the toes," Monsieur Berthold said. "We have noted before the regularities of our model's features, the nobility of the brow, the fine angle of the chin, the lovely musculature, and the perfect symmetry of the dark brows. This man is quite attractive." Monsieur's remarks, while flattering, might have been describing a marble effigy, so dispassionate was his praise. "Now I pose him thus..."

Berthold demonstrated for Michael a sitting posture, one elbow braced on a thigh, gaze on the floor.

"Now, the handsome face is hidden. Draw this man so that without seeing his eyes, without knowing the set of his mouth, or the angle of his nose, he conveys merriment. He is about to spring up and give a shout of joy, to laugh with great glee."

Michael, staring at his feet—scrupulously clean, second toe longer than the great toe—could not see the consternation in the room, but he could feel it in the silence that greeted Monsieur's challenge. Berthold had a whole speech about the difference between an artist and a draftsman. The draftsman rendered accurate likenesses and could make a fine living doing so.

May the good God bless and keep and draftsman.

The artist put truth on the page, the whole truth. The visual truth, the emotional truth, the moral truth. All a bit high flown when the audience was a room full of young men many of whom were more adept at draining a bottle than drawing that same bottle sitting on a sunny windowsill.

One lone stick of charcoal began scratching away. High up, farthest from the center of the room. That would be young Mr. Henderson, who preferred the longer perspective. Slight, blond, barely emerging from adolescence. Henderson never said much, but when he did pose a question to Monsieur, the answer came without the usual garnish of sarcasm and criticism.

Henderson had talent and didn't feel compelled to bruit that about. Lord Dermot Anthony, by contrast, had sizeable talent and an even bigger mouth. Always in the front row, close enough that Michael could smell the sour aroma of debauchery blended with expensive shaving soap wafting from the lordly person.

Everybody professed to like Lord Dermot, and even Monsieur offered him the occasional encouraging remark. Lord Dermot's mama, the marchioness of Stanbridge, was a noted patroness of the arts.

As the minutes crept by, Michael mentally steeled himself for his next obligation, dinner with his sister and her doting husband. Dorcas had chosen well, and she set a fine table. Alasdhair MacKay, Michael's brother-by-marriage, was a fine fellow with a sly sense of humor and a fondness for smooth whisky.

The drudgery though, of being polite and mannerly toward some pretty widow or spinster in training for three or four hours... The hope in the lady's eyes, the determination in Dorcas's, and the sympathy in MacKay's...

The session came to an end, and Bertold passed Michael his robe. "Our thanks, as usual. We will see you again on Tuesday, sir."

Michael donned the dressing gown and belted it loosely, then took himself to the changing room. Clothes maketh not the man, but rather, the masquerade. A priest wore sober attire, though he need not be shabby.

Michael enjoyed fine clothes. Perhaps if he showed up at Dorcas's with a stain on his cravat and a smear of charcoal on his cuff... But no. Dissembling for personal gain would not do.

He was making his way through the academy's grand foyer, wondering if he had time for a quick stop on Circle Lane before he was due for dinner. Just fifteen minutes, not really a visit, more of a sighting. He was too intent on his plans to watch where he was going, and thus he and Henderson collided right in the doorway.

"Beg pardon," Henderson muttered, tugging down his hat brim. "Entirely my fault. Do go on."

"My apologies," Michael said, bowing. "I was pre-occupied. After you."

Henderson bustled through the door and jogged down the steps, soon disappearing among the pedestrians thronging the walkway. Michael stood on the terrace, reviewing what he'd just learned.

Henderson, who preferred to sit in the studio's most shadowed corners, who rarely spoke at all, and who never joined with the other students in the general jockeying for status, was distinguished by more than talent and eccentricity.

Henderson had the unmistakable bodily endowments of a well-formed woman.

Order your copy of ***Miss Devoted!***

Made in the USA
Las Vegas, NV
29 December 2022

64382918R00154